GIVING IN

STONEVIEW STORIES BOOK ONE

LOLA KING

Copyright © 2021 by Lola King
All rights reserved. No part of this publication may be reproduced, stored or transmitted in any form or by any means, electronic, mechanical, photocopying, recording, scanning, or otherwise without written permission from the publisher. It is illegal to copy this book, post it to a website, or distribute it by any other means without permission.
This novel is entirely a work of fiction. The names, characters and incidents portrayed in it are the work of the author's imagination. Any resemblance to actual persons, living or dead, events or localities is entirely coincidental.
All songs, song titles and lyrics contained in this book are the property of the respective songwriters and copyright holders.
The author acknowledges the trademark status and trademark owners of various products referenced in this word of fiction. The publication/use of these trademarks is not authorized, associated with, or sponsored by the trademark owners.
Special Cover edition
Cover art by Wild Love Designs

To anyone who has ever given in, taken that leap of faith or dived into the unknown. I hope it was as wonderful as you dreamt it would be.

It is impossible to love and to be wise
    Francis Bacon

TRIGGER WARNING

This book is a dark bully romance and contains dubcon sexual scenes, bullying scenes, age difference and other scenes that some readers may find triggering. Jake is not a hero and some characters in this series are unredeemable. If this is something you are not comfortable with, please do not go any further.

If you are a fan of alpha assholes full of flaws and if you are a fan of love so wrong that it feels right, then this book is for you.

This book ends in a cliff-hanger! Jake and Jamie's story is far from over.

Enjoy!
Lots of love,
Lola ♥

PLAYLIST

Barcelona - Brother Leo
New Americana - Halsey
Find What You're Looking For - Olivia O'Brien
Perfectly Wrong - Shawn Mendes
Swim - Chase Atlantic
Darkside - grandson
Nails - Call Me Karizma
Call It What You Want - Taylor Swift
Trainwreck - BANKS
Bad Drugs - King Kavalier, ChrisLee
Casanova - Allie X
Hotter Than Hell - Due Lipa
Passion and Pain Taste the Same When I'm Weak - Tove Lo
Are U gonna tell her? - Have Lo, ZAAC
Señorita - Kurt Hugo Schneider, Marilyn Bailey

Daddy Issues - The Neighbourhood
B*ad This* - Machine Gun Kelly, Camila Cabello
Still Don't Know My Name - Labrinth
Dancing WIth out Hands Ties - Taylor Swift
War of Hearts - Ruelle

PROLOGUE
JAMIE

Barcelona – Brother Leo

October, Halloween Ball Night ...

Nathan. Jake. Nathan. Jake. Nathan. Jake.

My heart beats to the rhythm of my raging thoughts.

I let Jake lead me away from the dancefloor and into the hallway. His hand on the back of my neck is tight and possessive. The control that emanates from him is unsettling.

There are a few things I now know about him.

Jake never needs to say a word for anyone to know what he's like. He simply dominates. There is no other option, no mercy, no compassion. Jake takes no prisoners, what he wants, he gets.

There are a few things I now know about myself.

I'm not as good as I thought I was. I'm not the innocent girl my friends and family think I am.

Jake ruined that for me. He ruined me.

In the best way possible.

I'm not sure what we are. I'm not sure what we are doing. I'm not sure where this is going. But I know for sure I should have never accepted to go to the ball with him. It was a mistake.

One amongst many others.

I take a shallow breath as Jake meanders his way through the school until we're in the cafeteria. No one is going to find us here.

It's him and me now.

Nathan. Jake. Nathan. Jake. Nathan. Jake.

Oh, Nathan. No one can make me feel as safe as Nathan does. He's my anchor, he's my prince charming. He saves me from the nightmares, from the bad guys, from the trauma I endured in my life. He protects me like no one ever has.

I don't have time to wonder what I'm doing here. As soon as the door closes, Jake pushes me against the wall and grabs my long dress.

I'm completely out of breath. My mind isn't clear. It's been fogged up by Jake's powerful scent, his burning skin, his soft hair.

His sinful beauty.

Sinful. That's what Jake is… The devil hidden behind an angelic face. No one could have expected what was hiding behind the golden-boy act. I sure didn't.

Jake is the epitome of darkness. The kind you're happy to drown into. The kind that calls your name and you fall into without an ounce of regret. Before I can think of what's going on, my panties are off and in his back pocket.

Prologue

On his knees in front of me, he puts one of my legs on his shoulders.

My head hits the wall behind me, and a flash of my darkest desires takes over.

Jake grabs both my thighs tightly in his strong hands and squeezes. His hot mouth is on my wet pussy the next second.

I let him take over me like a starving man. His tongue is fire inside me, burning pleasure all the way to my core. He laps and nibbles until the leg I'm standing on gives up.

He doesn't let me fall though. He grabs my hips as I unhook my leg from his shoulder. In one push he has me lying down against a table. His mouth is on mine, his tongue driving me insane. I can taste myself on him.

"You taste like heaven, Angel, you know that?"

I can barely nod an answer. One of his hands has now slipped under my dress, my naked pussy welcoming him home.

"I want to ruin you, Jamie. Say you want it too."

I moan an answer as a finger slips in. I don't even know what I meant to say.

"Always so wet for me, Angel." He bites my lower lip, making me shriek.

"If you beg really good, I'll make you mine." Another finger. Another moan.

"Jake," I mewl. "I need you."

His thumb strokes my clit so slowly I cry in a mix of pleasure and longing.

"I want to hear you beg, Angel."

"Please..."

"Please what?"

I tremble under his dark voice. His other hand is on my jaw the next second.

"Eyes on me. Now."

I hadn't even realized my eyes had closed. I open them, meeting the ocean that is his gaze. His fingers curl in me and I whimper in pleasure.

"Your moans make me want to hurt you, Jamie. I want to hear your cries. I want you to plead for mercy."

"Make me," I reply, my voice barely a whisper.

The predatory glint that shines in his eyes makes me shiver. I want him. God, I want him so bad.

The sound of his belt unbuckling is music to my ears. I feel on a cloud of lust, in a storm of sexual desire.

The tip of his hard cock slides between my wet lips. He bends down, biting my nipple through my dress, licking and gnawing, making me squirm in craving.

"I'm going to make you mine, Angel. And once I do, I'll never let you go. I'll be there, always, keeping you close."

His hands grab the hem of my dress, pulling, tearing across my chest. It rips. My beautiful dress Nathan bought me for the ball.

Nathan.

Wake the fuck up, Jamie. Nathan!

"Wait. Jake. Stop."

I snap out of my vision of pleasure. Jake is still on his knees, right in front of me, eying my naked pussy, a few inches away from it.

I put a trembling hand on his shoulder.

He needs to know that I'm honest this time. This is real, he *has* to stop.

1

JAMIE

New Americana – Halsey

Two months earlier ...

I don't realize that the bus enters Stoneview. I've spent the last fifteen minutes trying to follow the text argument the girl in front of me is having with her boyfriend. I am one hundred percent out of line since I don't know who she is, but my curiosity is almost an illness. If I could control it, I would, but I can't. Mom loves repeating the story that my first steps were to walk over to our living room window to follow a heated conversation one of our neighbors was having with the mailman. I don't do it to gossip, I do it because I find everyone's life so interesting, especially compared to mine. I feel like everyone could be the main character of a film or a good book.

When I finally notice that we're parking, I'm the first one ready to hop off the bus. Thinking again, I'm probably the only one getting off in Stoneview.

"Alright, let me park young lady." I hear the driver. I can't reply, I'm just too excited to see my mom.

Spending the summer at Harvard Summer school was exciting, especially since the city paid for it, but I'm buzzing to be at home again, eat my mom's cooking, and just be with her and my best friend in general. The doors open and I jump out, my backpack hitting against my back in the process.

I take a deep breath, simply happy to be back in Stoneview, Maryland. The air is not as hot and heavy as when I left seven weeks ago. I spot my mom right away and run into her arms. She grabs me tight as I push on my toes so my head rests on her shoulder.

"I missed you so much," she says, her face in my hair.

"I missed you too." My voice is overwhelmed by the happiness of smelling her strong perfume and feeling her soft skin. For a second I'm five again and she's cuddling me after kissing my booboo.

Mom and I share this special bond. The kind when you have only one parent left, and she has only one child left. The kind of bond where you have to have been hurting an enormous amount of pain together to know that you need the other to survive. That you are all you both have left.

She grabs my backpack off my shoulders, and I run back to the bus to grab my small suitcase. We throw my stuff in our old red pickup and I hop in the passenger side.

In the car back to the house, mom tells me all the gossip I missed while I watch the huge mansions as we drive past them.

Stoneview is...wealthy. That's the least I can say. Only the elite of the elite makes it to this town. And by elite, I mean footballers or their freshly divorced wives, politicians,

Chapter 1

CEO's, founders of billion-dollar-companies, senators, ambassadors and so on.

Naturally, they come with their lovely 'I've never been refused anything in my life' children. And these children go to school with me at Stoneview Prep. I am surrounded by people who wear $800 dollar uniforms during the week and snort cocaine on Chanel powder palettes throughout the weekend. They always make sure to cut their powder with their black amex. The lifestyle of the rich and famous.

The only reason I'm in Stoneview Prep, or that we're still living in Stoneview at all, is because dad was the Sheriff and the town pays for the children's education up to five years after the Sheriff passes away.

Mom works at a café on main street and that pays for the rest of our lives. It's not much but once we relocated to a two-bedroom house it turned out to be enough for rent, food on the table, and a trip to the movies every now and then. That's all we need.

Stoneview is not only wealthy but also small. Not too small, because we still have to drive pretty much everywhere, but small enough to know who you're talking about when you mention a last name. Like, who the parents are, what they do, how many kids, what *they* do, their reputation.

Mom is currently updating me on the Joly's. Judge Hope Joly, her husband – who owns one of the biggest law firms on the East Coast – Carl Joly, and Emily, my best friend, their one and only 'miracle' child.

Just as she starts telling me about Carl and Hope's latest parade of Emily at a summer junior debutante, I feel my phone buzzing in my pocket and pull it out to see a text from my friend.

> Emily: Please come get me. This is what they want me to wear for the Christmas ball.

She's attached a picture of herself in a long white dress. She doesn't look terrible but it's definitely hiding her gorgeous curves.

Emily's parents are working hard on getting her an invite to the International Debutante Ball in New York for next year and she hates it. She is the furthest thing from a debutante. Whatever the opposite of a debutante is, that is Emily. Her passions are all about sports and exercise. She dances, cheers, runs, gyms...anything that has to do with being fit, developing your muscle and looking the opposite of those poor starved girls on a juice cleanse that parade during the debutante balls. The only sport Em hasn't picked up in our school is lacrosse. This one is my jurisdiction. She's always there to support me on the sideline, though.

I smile and shoot her a quick response about helping her tear the dress to pieces with her dad's shredder.

"...anyway, needless to say Hope wasn't pleased with her when she signed up for that Triathlon. I say she needs to let the kid do whatever she wants," Mom keeps going. I've missed half of the conversation. Mom notices and changes the topic quickly:

"School is going to start quicker than you think, 'Me." Mom's voice is always soft when she uses the strange nickname I've come to love. "Have you thought of how you're going to train your team this year?"

My team. I like the sound of that. I've been elected lacrosse team captain for the second year in a row. Not that the team actually likes me, but I'm good. Last year, I took us to the top of the mid-Atlantic top ten, so I was made captain again this year despite being completely unpopular at school.

Now, have I thought of how I'm going to take us to national number one this year? Of course I have, I'm surprised mom even has to ask. She knows I am the kind with plans A, B, C to Z. I'm not 'work hard, play hard', I'm 'work hard, then work harder'. I'm top of the school, ready for college, and captain of the team. I don't need popularity; I need to meet the conditions for my scholarship to UPenn. I want to become a surgeon, not miss America.

"'Course," I reply to mom with a smile. "Hey, so I applied for a scholarship to Harvard when I was there."

"Oh, Did you? Change of mind?" She turns to me for one second with a raised brow.

"No, but it can't hurt, right? They insisted."

"Of course, 'Me." I can hear the smile in her tone. She was never good at school; she didn't go to college and she never wanted to. My mom was always about living on the wild side until she met my dad. Now she has a daughter who was offered multiple scholarships from the colleges close to us, one full ride to UPenn, and possibly to Harvard.

"I probably won't get it but still-"

"Oh please," she cuts me off, "I hate when you do this. I hope you don't do this at school."

I can't help a laugh. I do do this at school. To my defense, I truly think I've always done my worst at a test even when everyone around me knows I've done fine. I keep my expectations low to avoid disappointment. Call me pessimistic. This uncontrollable behavior and my respect for every single rule have earned me the nickname 'Goody' for goody two shoes. I don't care though, like I said, I'm not there to be the most popular. I've got Em and Mom and that's all I need.

We park by our small cottage and I get my suitcase while mom brings my backpack inside. I bring the suitcase up the four steps leading to the tiny porch and pull the screen. After a long journey, I finally push the door, and enter our humble home.

I breathe in the smell of Filipino food coming from the kitchen as I pass the door. Dad's parents were from the Philippines and although mom is not the best cook, she does her best to learn the dishes I miss since he passed.

"God mom, that smells so good."

Our front door opens straight into our living room that also serves as a dining room and any other room other than a bathroom or bedroom. Our house isn't big, to say the least. From the door I can see the small open plan kitchen separated by a short counter with two stools around it. The sofa is a few steps to the right when you walk in, facing the wall perpendicular to the doorway.

I walk in, past the entrance shelves with old pictures of when we were a full family and turn left to a narrow hallway leading to the two bedrooms and the one bathroom.

After showering and throwing my dirty clothes in the laundry basket I join mom back in the kitchen.

"Where's my souvenir?" She asks as she puts rice on two plates.

"Ha. Do you know how much anything costs in the Harvard university shop? I don't even study there for real. You'll get a UPenn sweater shipped to you if you're sweet."

Mom laughs and adds chicken adobo to complete our plates. "It probably won't taste like anything close to your dad's, but I do my best," she says as she passes me my plate.

We settle on the sofa and put some reality TV on. Our dirty little secret is our obsession with anything reality TV. From the Kardashians to the Real Housewives, we've watched them all. I think it definitely is linked to my toxic curiosity with other people's lives. Maybe I'm *that* unhappy with mine that I can't stop looking at others. Apart from Em, no one knows my vice and for some reason, I like to keep it that way rather than fit in with all the other girls at my school that watch them. Weirdly, I like keeping this image of miss perfect. Probably because that couldn't be further from the truth.

The next day, mom wakes me up early for my shift at the café. I should really work somewhere else if I want to be able to afford anything or save any money. The Bakers pay next to nothing.

"'Me, I'm going to need help behind the counter," mom says as I'm wiping a table. "It's overwhelming at this time of the day".

"Sure," I shoot back. I hurry and pull an apron from behind the bar.

I put my apron on and call the next person without looking as I try to tie it around my waist.

"Hey, what can I get you?"

My problem here is that being the progeniture between a small Filipino man and a tiny Southern Belle with a ballet dancer's body, I ended up being a five-foot creature that still fits in children's clothes at soon-to-be eighteen years old and I'm having a real struggle with this apron. Two times around the waist is leaving way too much string and it doesn't fit three, so I have to choose between looking ridiculous or stop breathing for the rest of the day.

"Do you need help over there?" A voice asks as I still try to tie the apron. I settle on two times around the waist, so I don't pass out during the day, and finally look up just to be met with the most heart-melting honey eyes.

My gaze locks with his for a moment before I drag my eyes to the boy's beautiful caramel hair with slight curls that almost reach his ears. He runs a hand through it, pushing it back, and smiles at me with his gorgeous shy grin. His slightly chipped front tooth has always made my gaze linger on his smile.

Christopher Murray. Six foot four of pure perfection. My ideal man, my childhood crush that has turned into something way too hot to be a boy anymore. The most perfect thing about him is that the personality that accompanies his manly body is kind, intelligent, and respectful. I know he is smart because he is my main competition at being this year's valedictorian. And I know he is kind because we've known each other since pre-school, he's always been good to me, has never called me 'Goody' and has never succumbed to the peer pressure of not talking to me because I'm not cool enough to fit in.

Until seventh grade, we were good friends. Not best friends but at least friends. Then one day he showed up with the twins and we slowly drifted apart. Nonetheless, he's always been nice to me.

Christopher is everything I want, or at least wanted. In fourth grade, I declared my undying love for him in a letter I put on his desk in class. He didn't love me back but at least he had the balls to come to me and say it to my face. And this is the story of how I know that Christopher Murray is everything I want but I'm most definitely not everything *he* wants. It's a good thing now I guess because the height difference that has progressed over the years would have been awkward.

Chapter 1

You go, Jamie, keep telling yourself that to make yourself feel better.

"Jamie? Are you okay?" His voice suddenly brings me back down to earth and I shake my head to push away the memory of the ten-year-old me getting her heartbroken by Christopher Murray.

"Oh my God, I totally zoned out. Hey Chris," I reply feeling the embarrassment creep up my chest.

A laugh escapes his lips and he shakes his head slowly. "I said, how was Harvard summer school? I also asked if I could have two black coffees but I'm more interested in your summer."

I smile at him, because his laugh just does that to me, and start preparing two coffees. "It was amazing, thank you. Now I'm even more sure I want to go to UPenn, but it was a great experience."

"That's good to hear."

I look behind him for the rest of his gang. Chris is always surrounded by his friends, you rarely see them apart. Meaning wherever Chris goes, Luke and the twins go and wherever the twins go, trouble follows. I turn my confused look back to him.

"Have you managed to get rid of the twins during the summer? Do you need help hiding the bodies?" I ask half-joking as I put the two coffees on the counter.

He gives me a cheeky smile, drops money and grabs the cups. "You'll never guess where they are," he says.

"Jail?"

He laughs but manages to answer, "School."

"School? Why?" It's impossible to hide the surprise in my voice.

"They've been offered to skip a grade. They didn't care until they realized they would be sharing classes with Luke and me, so they accepted. Late, but they finally accepted. My parents took them to school this morning to finalize it."

"What?" I almost choke on my own spit.

Chris and I share pretty much every class. I don't want the twins there. They're noisy and disrespectful. Add Luke to the mix and they're unbearable.

"Gonna be a fun year, huh?" he jokes. I know he doesn't believe a single word he's just said because he doesn't find their troublemaking *fun*. He finds it annoying but loves them too much to do anything about it.

I stay shocked at his statement as he turns around. I notice the amount of cash he left on the counter. There's enough to pay for ten coffees on here.

"Chris that's way too much ch–"

"See you on Monday!" He shouts, facing the door and waving a hand in the air.

I watch him meet with Luke outside. Well, I can only assume it's Luke, judging by the blond, almost white, hair reflecting the sun and blinding me.

This conversation leaves me with an uneasy feeling settling in my stomach. I don't think the twins skipping a grade is going to make my year fun. In fact, I'm pretty sure it's the opposite.

2

JAMIE

Find What You're Looking For – Olivia O'Brien

In my opinion, Monday comes way too fast. I haven't really swallowed Chris's news. I don't particularly know the rest of his group personally. I'm pretty much like everyone else, I know *of* them. That's all everyone talks about at Stoneview Prep. They're loved by the entire school, the teacher's worst nightmare: rude but smart without having to put in any effort.

Chris and his friends rule the halls without really trying. Our school made them kings of everything and they don't even give a shit about it. Of course, Chris is always his calm self, he's a pacifier when Luke and the twins push too far. He's just so perfect.

I'm usually excited about school. Coming from an average background – rather than being born with a silver spoon in my mouth like the rest of Stoneview's teenagers – I've learned to enjoy the things that make me privileged. I love our pretentious campus, our education is top-notch, we have amazing sport facilities – including a gym we can access 24/7 – our teachers are some of the best in the country, the food in the cafeteria compares to a restaurant. Even our cafeteria tables are beautiful mahogany that makes it look like you're eating anywhere but at school. Our library is straight out of Hogwarts and all in all the population of students is not that bad. I ignore them, and they tend to ignore me. I've heard horror stories of kids from poor backgrounds that were bullied in Prep schools, but my life here is pretty normal. I wouldn't go as far as saying I'm in with the cool kids, but my best friend is one of the popular cheerleaders and she is the kindest person I've ever met. Screw the clichés.

I'm usually buzzing for school, but today I stand on the perfectly manicured front lawn, in front of the red brick building, watching the students pass the four white pillars before the front doors, and I can't seem to find the strength to take a step further. I don't even know if Chris and his friends are going to be in my classes, but already, I know I'm not going to enjoy this year. I don't know why his news bothered me that much. Just that kind of feeling.

I don't have time to think about it further as a strong body suddenly jumps on my back almost making me fall forward.

"Ohmygodohmygod, OH MY GOD! I missed you so much," Emily shouts in my ear as she hooks her legs around my arms.

"Em, I missed you too but you're so heavy. Please, I don't have the strength of your cheer friends."

Emily unhooks her legs and falls back on the floor before stepping in front of me and shaking her head in disbelief. "How dare you say they're my friends. They just throw me in the air and catch me. No more. No less."

I laugh at her serious statement, I missed her so much. I

hug her tightly and go on my toes so my head can level with hers. This is pretty much the technique with everyone except children. Em is not *that* tall, she's about 5'5 and she's built of muscles and curves in the perfect places. I truly look like a child next to her, with my tiny body and almost non-existent boobs.

Her light brown hair and Chanel scent tickle my nose and I take a step back to look into her big hazel eyes. She holds me at arm's length, her hands on my shoulders, and inspects me.

"You look so tanned. I'm jealous." She looks at her pale arms in front of herself with a scowl.

"I tan easy. Mixed girl advantage, you know it." I shrug and smile in arrogance.

"And you look like you've lost weight."

How is she so observant?

"I just lose weight when I'm not at home."

"Oh my God, did you get taller?" The cheekiness in her voice and the smile that tugs at her lips make me laugh heartily. Jokes about my height never get old, eh?

I push her arms off my shoulders. "Yup, now you're making things up."

She smiles at me and messes my deep brown hair with one hand. "You just keep hoping, kiddo. Let's get to class." She turns around and we walk side by side into the building.

"So, I heard you signed up to do a triathlon..."

Emily barks a laugh. "Yeah, you should have seen my mom's face when she opened my confirmation letter at home. This woman needs to leave my mail alone."

I join her laughing and we make our way to our lockers.

Emily is leaning with her back against her locker while I'm dropping some books when she decides to change our conversation topic from the cheerleaders she's not looking forward to seeing again to...

"Holy mother of all guacamole. That's it. You thought Jake was hot before? No, my friend, it happened. He's clearly had a full glow up this summer. Aaaand, of course, Rose got hotter too. Who knew that was possible? Not me. I didn't."

I chuckle at her inanity. "I didn't think Jake was hot before," I lie as I turn around to look for her favorite people to fangirl over.

"Alright missy," she says with an eye roll. "You keep telling yourself that. Oh no, wait, that's true, you're all about Chris, our beloved bookworm."

Jake *is* hot. Only a blind person would think otherwise. He's always been and, although some people are in my way right now and I can't see him, I'm sure he is just as hot as he's always been, if not more.

The problem is that he is so aware of it that it would probably *kill* me to admit it. It's not just his arrogance. I've always had a bad feeling about him. His golden boy act feels *off*. I'm not the only one who feels it, it turns my fellow prep girls on the way it looks like he's hiding something. Like his nice side is fake. I can understand the need to find out more, the need to know the secrets behind the façade. It might be all a lie though; he might pretend there's a bad boy behind it all for the sole purpose of making himself interesting to girls. To me, Chris's intelligence and more average looks are much more attractive than Jake's hotness and egotism. Too bad I'm getting neither of them.

The two girls in my eyesight move out of the way and my gaze lands on Chris and his group of friends; him, Luke Baker and the twins – Jake and Rose White – are all gathered around Chris's locker, laughing at whatever stupid joke one of them has just told. Jake is looking at the people in the halls like he is searching for someone and seems slightly worried. Looking at him again, I am getting a strong reminder as to why so many girls fall at his feet and why the name on their lips is always 'Jake'.

Jake and his deep blue ocean eyes, his jet-black hair. Emily is right, what we all thought impossible happened: he had a glow up this summer. His jawline is harder and that makes him look tougher, it contrasts with his long lashes that soften his strong face. His arms are more muscular and his shoulders broader. They make his white shirt from our uniform look perfect on him. I'm probably not the only girl who has dreamed of having his strong arms hold me tight.

Rose whispers something in his ear and he suddenly looks the other way in a scare then back at her before shoving her in the shoulder, between playful and annoyed. Luke and Rose laugh at him while Chris just shakes his head. Christopher Murray is so tall compared to all of them and that feeling in my stomach comes back, tugging at my insides like every time I see him.

Jake and Rose are standing right next to each other, emphasizing their resemblance. They are so similar for fraternal twins, it's almost scary. She's got the same blue eyes as him and her long wavy hair that drops almost all the way to her waist is just as black. She's the kind of girl that's just too beautiful for her own good. She's model beautiful. I'm talking 5'10 with legs for days and a face that makes everyone who crosses her path fall in love with her. She slightly looks like Kendall Jenner if Kendall had naturally long lashes, plumped lips, and blue eyes. Here I am with TV reality references. If Rose was from LA, she would be part of Gigi Hadid's group of friends. For sure. Probably without even trying.

That's the thing with the Whites: they don't try, they just

are. The hottest, the smartest, the wittiest. They rule over everyone without really wanting to. Rose is not even a case of 'boys love her, girls hate her but want to be her'. Everyone is just in love with her. God knows why, because just like any naturally incredibly beautiful girl, behind the façade, she's just all kinds of fucked up.

Stoneview prep might be easier on people like me than other prep schools, but it still has to keep up with the other bitchy schools and for that, our rumor mill is probably the most active in the country. Chris and his friends are the water keeping that mill running. That's how I know Jake and Rose are not in the human realm when it comes to respect for their peers.

According to the rumors, last year someone walked in on Rose and Jason Simmons at a party, fucking in the bathroom. All would have been fine except Jason, who is also the Mayor's son, has been engaged to Bethany Lam pretty much all their lives.

Rose and Jake are simply unstable. You just have to look at the state of their dating lives and you know there's something wrong with them. Some kind of total lack of empathy or something. Physically they're perfect, they have a beautiful golden, tanned skin tone all year long like they're from Italy or some other Mediterranean country. There is no way to know though, because part of the reason everyone finds them so mysterious is that Jake and Rose are orphans. And, boy, do they use this excuse right, left and center. They both joined our middle school when they were in eighth grade and we were Freshmen, after the Murray's, Chris' family, took them in. They quickly proved that you can get away with anything when you use the right excuse.

As Jake's gaze is scanning the halls for whomever he is looking for, our eyes meet.

Shit.

I quickly look away, but I can see his cocky smile from the corner of my eye, and I want to slap it off his face.

"Should we go?" I ask Em.

"Jake White is looking our way. I repeat...Jake White is looking our way."

I laugh at her and grab her arm to drag her to class.

"Don't bother taking a seat," Mr. Ashton's harsh voice cuts through the students dragging their feet around the class as he walks in. "I've re-organized the class this year. I'm too old to deal with hormonal teenagers with a two-minute attention span." I notice he's also re-organized the desks and put them in pairs.

"Isn't he like, thirty years old?" Emily mutters to me. I chuckle but calm down as soon as Mr. Ashton's cold eyes land on me. Everyone walks back to the front of the class as we wait to be told our assigned seats.

The door opens again right after Mr. Ashton closes it, and Chris and Luke walk in closely followed by Jake and Rose. Chris whispers a quick apology on behalf of the group.

I watch Jake as his gaze locks with Camila Diaz's, she looks like she's about to jump him and disfigure him with her claws she calls nails. Not in a good way.

Mr. Ashton looks confused for a second as he watches the group then seems to remember.

"Oh, right, you two are seniors now," he says irritated. The twins both give him their most innocent, charming smile and he looks down at his piece of paper muttering to himself something that sounds like a very sarcastic 'fucking great'.

"Alright," he starts, "Baker and Harris..."

Luke grabs his bag from the floor and walks towards a front desk with Rachel Harris as Mr. Ashton keeps listing the duos. Rose watches them go and Rachel gives her a quick shy smile. Emily nudges me in the ribs to show me she notices their quiet exchange.

"I bet they're together again," she whispers low enough for Mr. Ashton not to hear her.

The beautiful Rachel is Rose's on and off girlfriend. If you can call it that. If I was someone's girlfriend, I don't think I would appreciate the countless boys and girls Rose sleeps with in-between their moments of exclusivity but, I don't know, Rachel seems fine with it? I'm not involved enough to understand their dynamics. I only catch up with these things when Em gets gossipy about them. According to her 'Rachel is the only consistent thing in Rose's life outside her group of friends and she never, *ever* cheats on her when they're together.' Does this only sound wrong to me? Am I that boring and inexperienced that I can't understand how us teenagers date?

"...Williams and White..." My heart suddenly skips a beat as I'm brought back down to earth by Mr. Ashton saying my name. Did I hear this right?

"Which one," the twins reply in unison.

Mr. Ashton rolls his eyes before tracing down a few rows of names on his sheet. He lets out a long huff. Like any other person of authority in this school, he struggles dealing with the twins, and their reputation usually precedes them.

"I don't know...any...Jake," he says, lazily gesturing to Jake.

Fuck. My. Life. Is this actually happening?

Chapter 2

Emily watches me with eyes as wide as saucers and mouths a silent 'Oh my God'.

Jake leans towards Chris and I can vaguely hear him asking about a name. Of course he doesn't know my name. Why would he? Chris slightly leans his head to the side to reply discreetly. Jake nods and his cocky half-smile appears back on his face. Chris notices me looking at them and gives me a sorry smile. *Thanks.*

My hand tightens on my bag strap as I walk toward a desk, closely followed by Jake. We both sit down, and Jake turns to me smiling. God, does he have to be so hot? I can feel my heart beating a hundred miles an hour from our current proximity.

"Ready to compete with my genius, Jamie?"

I can't help a scoff escaping from my mouth. It's a mix of the tension in my body and the ridiculousness of his words.

"Are you even planning on showing up to class?" I ask, "I'm pretty sure you have about the same attendance record as an alumni."

His smile extends and he leans towards me, his mouth *way* too close to my face. He smells of expensive cologne. Like pine trees, wooden with a hint of something spicy.

"I think you mean alum*nus*," he insists on the end of the word to point out my mistake.

Really Jamie? An alumni? You had to make the easiest kind of mistake in front of Mr. Cocky?

"It's nice to know you keep track of my attendance though," he adds. I can feel myself blushing at his statement. He leans back and looks at me from my toes to my blushed face. "I think we're going to have fun this year, Jamie,"

I ignore him and look ahead to notice only Rose, Chris, Emily, and Camila are left standing. This is just not going well for either of us. Emily has always had this weird crush on Rose. She's not interested in girls, God knows she's all about boys, except for Rose. It seems like it's the case for a lot of girls.

Em is staring at Rose and the latter catches her. Instead of looking away, her eyes widen, and she mumbles a few words looking for an excuse to justify herself.

"I...I..," Emily scratches her throat. "I really love your shirt."

Oh Em... I shake my head feeling bad for her. Rose looks down at her crisp white shirt, the exact same one everyone else around the class is wearing, then back up at Emily with a cocky smile. It's identical to Jake's.

"I wore it just for you," she replies in her raspy voice. She adds a quick wink and Emily's face dots with red patches. I shake my head as Jake lets out a low chuckle.

"Joly and White, and Murray and Diaz. Come on get to your seats."

Camila huffs and barges Chris' shoulder as she gets to her seat. He only rolls his eyes at her attitude, showing that they still don't particularly like each other. Emily quickly follows Rose to their seats, her face still blushed from her interaction with her.

I knew it. I knew this year was going to be anything but fun.

By the time Em and I are sitting for lunch, I'm exhausted. Jake and Rose are in my English class, science *and* calculus. In English, I couldn't focus because Jake was too close. His masculine scent was disturbing me and my heart beats too fast when he's close. My eyes kept drifting to his long lashes and the way his Adam's apple goes up and down when he chuckles at something. I think it also has to do with sitting next to someone popular. I'm not used to it.

In science, he was sitting next to Rose and I can't stand how noisy they get. They don't care who they disturb, and his laugh is too loud, too enchanting. In calculus, he was next to Chris who forced him to stay still and keep quiet. Jake was so focused on the class and taking notes, his jaw kept ticking every time he started losing focus and Chris had to tell him to get back into it. Too close, too loud, too... hot. I simply can't focus when he's around.

As I dig into my food, I notice Jake and his friends are at the table right behind ours, I'm facing them while Em is facing me.

"You're drooling," Emily mocks, still looking at her plate. I let out a small laugh and look back at her. "Which one are you looking at?" she adds.

I can't help but roll my eyes, why are we all so into them? Are the girls and boys in this school really that weak and unoriginal to just *all* be in love with them?

I'm not in love with them.

I just can't deny undeniable attractiveness. Especially Chris. Even if he made things clear a long time ago.

As if Emily could read my thoughts she starts again. "He rejected you in fourth grade, 'Me, that was practically eight years ago."

"He's not interested. Otherwise, he would at least try to spend time with me," I reply.

"He's just too busy being a babysitter for the rest of his group. Being responsible for the twins is a full-time job."

"He's not responsible for them. His parents are."

She looks at me intensely until I admit, "Yeah, ok he is but if he was even slightly interested in me, I would know."

"Please, 'Me, this is our last year, I beg that you make it more interesting than studies and lacrosse."

"I-" I'm cut off by the loud sound of something hitting the floor. Jake is looking at his tray on the floor in shock. Luke is sitting next to Jake, and Rose is facing Luke, both almost falling off their chairs laughing. Chris, sitting opposite Jake, is looking at the situation shaking his head.

"You're an absolute bastard, you know that?!" Camila is whisper-shouting at him, and we're close enough to hear everything.

Em's gasp matches her widening eyes. "I'll be too obvious if I turn around, are they breaking up?" she whispers.

I shrug, still looking at them. "I don't know."

Camila and Jake have been a thing for years. The whole school is well aware that he cheats on her constantly. Every time she catches him, they go through a very public argument, break up for half a day, and get back together. I think the last time they broke up at lunchtime, they were back together by the last period. She usually does something to make him jealous and he comes back running.

Camila is a gorgeous Latina with caramel eyes and long dark hair. Her body comes straight out of a photoshopped magazine. In short, her family is from Dominican Republic and her dad is a big property developer who basically built everything that is new in Stoneview.

Her mom is a court shark aka a defense attorney for all the bad guys around. No one can become rich enough to live in Stoneview *and* stay clear of illegal business. The wealthy are power hungry, and power comes with secret handshakes, dishonesty and criminality. Stoneview is full of illicit businesses, and run by rich gangs who control politicians and leaders. Camila's mother, she defends those people. She defends the underground circle of our town.

Her parents own Stoneview, her big brothers still have their playboy and tough boys' reputation in this school even a few years after leaving and she's got their protection. She's their queen and Stoneview Prep is her kingdom. It's only fair that the king of the school is hers.

Camila's beauty is above other girls, and she knows it. If Jake messes with her, he's got serious competition and she has no problem making him aware of it. As a true Queen Bee, she has scared every girl in our school into not even *looking* at Jake.

Because the girls here have grown terrified of Camila, Jake goes and gets his shots from the baddies on the wrong side of Silver Falls – aka North Shore of the Falls – the city attached to Stoneview. The only two girls that don't feel threatened by Camila's importance are Rose (*obviously*) and Rachel, her best friend, since she's too interested in the former.

"You fucked up, White. Good luck getting over me," Camila spits her words at Jake like they're never going to get back together.

"Yup, it's happening," I inform my friend.

Jake gets up from his seat to try and explain himself to his not so ex-girlfriend.

"Cam, please don't be like this," he starts his monologue. "I was not myself this summer. I was lost, you know I grew up without a father figure, it fucked me up. I swear." *Oh, here we fucking go.* His favorite excuse is just a few words away. "Do you think it was easy being abandoned as a baby? I fuck up sometimes because I get in these states where I don't know who I really am anymore."

Chris is scowling at Jake from his seat and Luke and

Rose have stopped laughing and are silently watching the action unfold. Jake just keeps going with his bullshit. "I guess…I'll never really know who I really am, but you keep me grounded, I promise. Please…"

Camila gives Rose a quick look and Rose nods with a fake sad look on her face. God, they're so good at this. Always in on each other's lies.

Camila crosses her arms and pops out her hip to look like she's in control. "I'm so sick of your orphan excuse, Jake. It can't work every time." She walks away, her heels clicking on the floor of the cafeteria. They didn't attract everyone's attention, but they definitely attracted mine and Jake catches me looking. He gives me a big smile and a wink.

I stand up and grab my tray, feeling myself blush from being caught.

"I'm stopping by the bathroom before history. Are you coming?" I ask Em.

"I've got Spanish next period, you go ahead I'll see you in gym," she replies before digging into her yogurt.

"Cool," I quickly smile back at her and escape the cafeteria.

I'm about to push the door to the girls' bathroom when I hear a deep voice behind me.

"Did you enjoy the show, Jamie?" I quickly turn around to face Jake.

Why did he follow me out? I left so I wouldn't have to deal with the embarrassment of being caught watching him. I raise my chin at his condescending tone and cross my arms across my chest.

"Your arguments with Camila are a daily occurrence. It's getting boring," I reply.

He lets out a genuine laugh and looks at me from my

toes until his gaze locks with mine again. "I couldn't agree more. Again, glad you're keeping track of my life."

I roll my eyes at him. How can he be so full of himself? "Please, just because you argue with your 'girlfriend' publicly every day of the week doesn't mean I keep track. It only means you're loud." I make sure to air quote the word 'girlfriend'. His wide smile turns lopsided as if he's annoyed at my words but knows he is still winning.

Winning what Jamie? You're not playing a game with him.

He takes a step closer to me and looks down at me before darting his tongue across his lower lip.

"Don't roll your eyes at me, Jamie." His voice is low and assertive, and my heart can tell it's in trouble. Jake's voice holds a certain darkness to it, like a promise to ruin me if I'd let him. He leans down, his mouth close to my ear and his voice is now a low rasp. "I would hate to have to punish you for something so silly."

What?

My heart skips a beat, or probably ten, and a strange sensation bubbles in my lower belly. I suddenly struggle to swallow my own saliva as he straightens back up, his stupid smile still on his face. From this close, I can see he has a dimple on his left cheek, and I think I might die right here and now.

"Wh-what?" I sound like a kid caught doing something wrong.

Why am I being like this?

He explodes laughing and reaches out to me, ruffling my hair. "You should see your face. You look like you just heard the word sex for the first time. So fucking cute."

My mouth drops open, I am lost for words and probably look like a fish out of water. *Is this guy for real?* I open and close my mouth a few times, unsure of what to say.

"Jake," a familiar voice calls out from behind him. He turns around and I see Chris walking towards us.

"Go annoy someone else. Jamie has no time for you."

Jake raises an eyebrow at his friend's statement. Is Chris really coming to my defense?

"I'm sorry," he puts his hands together in front of him as if praying and bows slightly. "Miss is too *busy* for me." He accentuates on 'busy' to show his sarcasm. He winks and takes a few steps backwards still looking at me before turning around and walking away. In the background, I can see him join Rose and Luke.

What is actually wrong with this guy? He is so hot and cold.

"Are you okay?" Chris asks.

"Huh?" My eyes move from Jake to focus on Chris. I look up to face him. "Yeah...yeah of course. We were just talking, no harm done."

Chris gives me a reassuring smile. "He can be really annoying and there's nothing wrong in admitting his jokes are shit. He met a pretty girl that wasn't on his radar before and that's his way of hitting on you."

Jake White? Hitting on me? Ha. I doubt it.

I let out a chuckle. "His jokes are pretty crap. And feel free to tell him I'm not interested in being on his radar."

Thankfully, the bell rings signaling the end of the lunch period and I get an excuse to escape this weird situation. A wide smile lightens Chris's face at my words. "Good then, I'll see you around Jamie." He turns around and joins his friends.

Good. Chris said 'good' when I said I wasn't interested in Jake. And he just expects me to not freak out over this.

Luckily, in the afternoon, Jake is neither in my gym, history nor physics classes. By the time I get to the gym

Chapter 2

lockers for lacrosse practice, I've finally stopped over-thinking the whole situation. Jake met a new girl he wasn't aware existed, he had his little fun, it's over. And Chris... Chris is my friend.

I finish putting my lacrosse kit on and grab my stick. I close my locker and turn around to face Emily who is finishing putting her cheer uniform on.

"He said 'good'?" She asks for the third time. "You said you weren't interested in Jake, and he said 'good'. First of all, why would you say you're not interested in Jake? That's a lie and you know it."

I roll my eyes at her. "Em, I'm just not interested. Stop it."

"Fine, Fine. Fuck, it's always so hot in here." She fans herself with her hand.

Our locker room is always the equivalent of oven temperature.

"Alright, what about Chris?"

I pause for a second. *What about Chris*?

"I don't know," I shrug.

She smiles at me cheekily. "Look I'm going to suggest something. I know you're going to say no but please think about it. Please."

"Oh God, what?"

"Friday, there's a back-to-school party at Camila's. Everyone is invited. And by everyone, I mean *everyone*. Like, every senior in this school and that includes you, baby. It's going to be our year and all these college people, friends of her brothers. It's going to be big, fun and, you know," she shrugs her shoulder and tilts her head to the side, giving me an innocent smile, "Chris is going to be there for sure. He's always there looking out for the twins."

I blink at her a couple of times before realizing what she just said.

"You want me to go to Camila Diaz's party?"

"Damn right I do. 'Me, her parties are great, and I promise you it's not what you think. I know you imagine a crowd of bitchy cheerleaders judging other girls, left, right, center. Really, it's just a bunch of people getting drunk, admitting things they wouldn't sober, and making out with their crush in the heat of the moment. I want my best friend to make out with her crush! And if her crush doesn't want her, trust me those college boys will want that bod."

Of course that's what she thinks because she is part of the cheerleaders and doesn't realize that not all of them are as sweet as her.

I let out a long huff. "I don't know, Em." I start biting the inside of my cheek, a nasty habit I have when I start stressing out.

She notices and adds, "Look I'm not saying decide now. We can talk about it later, just saying think about it, please. It's our senior year and I really don't want you to go off to college having never attended a party. You deserve to have fun"

I nod but I'm not sure. Camila and I have never been friends. I'm a small person in her kingdom and the only times she ever addressed herself to me were in elementary school when she would make fun of me. Now she simply does it behind my back. My only friend there will be Emily and she's got her own girls she usually hangs out with at parties. I know I won't be comfortable there.

"Just go to the tryouts. You pick that team, babe. We'll talk about it again," she concludes.

I smile at her and head outside to the lacrosse pitch wondering how an introvert like me ever became best friends with an extrovert like Emily Joly.

3

JAKE

Perfectly Wrong – Shawn Mendes

Luke and I make our way to the bleachers. We climb the stairs and sit a few rows behind a group of girls who keep turning around to smile at us. Luke winks at one of them he knows well. And by that, I mean he fucks regularly. His phone vibrates and he looks down at it.

"Chris said he's heading home. He doesn't want to watch the tryouts," Luke says as he looks back up. "I want to watch the tryouts."

"Sure you do, a bunch of girls running around in small skorts. Where else would you be?" I mock him.

He looks right at me and raises an eyebrow. "Are you here for something else? Trying for the team maybe?"

"I will always be part of the team. Even when I'm gone to college, my name will still be the most famous one on this team."

Stoneview men's lacrosse team does their tryouts at the end of the year rather than the beginning so seniors can help pick the team. I had to do it when I was in 8th grade to make sure I could be part of the team as a freshman and that is nerve-wracking for most of the guys. It wasn't for me. I'm good at this and nothing can throw me off my game. I play the same position as my sister, straight attack. I'm a scorer. We both love the pressure and the fame that comes with it. This year I was made captain of the team and Luke and I can't wait to terrorize our freshmen.

"Of course, Cap'." Luke winks at me.

I laugh and look at the pitch, my gaze goes to Jamie straight away. Jamie Williams. This morning I didn't even know who she was and right now I'm struggling to tear my eyes away from her. I think back to how she squirmed under my gaze in the hallway after lunch and my cock tightens. Fuck, she's hot.

Chris drew the line straight away. He didn't appreciate me fucking with her and he's made himself clear about leaving her alone. He said he didn't want to watch her get her heart broken, especially by me. I wasn't planning on breaking her heart, just playing with it a little bit. Nothing too serious. Chris isn't the boss of me, but he can be a scary fucker when he loses patience. And when he cares about something, I know it's important. He cares for his friends and if Jamie is one of them then I'll leave her alone. He doesn't have to know I watched her play lacrosse though, right?

"Why are you drooling over Goody?" Luke cuts my thoughts short.

"Goody?" I ask, turning to him.

"Jamie Williams? The girl Chris asked you to leave alone."

"I'm not drooling over her. She *is* hot though. How did I not notice her before? Chris said she's a friend of his."

"She is, they were really good friends until you and Rose

Chapter 3

decided to take over his life completely. I think she's got a thing for him."

Oh. So, this is why my friend has put her off-limits. "For Chris? He never mentioned her, how do you all know who she is and I don't? Is he into her too?"

Why am I getting so interested in her relationship with Chris?

Luke chuckles. "Dude, she's 'Goody' of course you know who she is, you just haven't associated they're the same person yet. She was lacrosse captain last year, every time Rose complained about early morning practice that 'Goody' added? *That's* Jamie."

I guess I have heard of Goody. Camila constantly makes fun of this girl who works at the Bakers' café and, according to her, doesn't get that clothes twice her size is not a fashionable look. Except when Camila talked about Goody, I imagined a geeky girl with boy clothes too big for her and no social skills.

I never would have imagined the gorgeous half-Asian girl with golden green eyes and tanned skin who's currently running around in a tight skort. I remember clearly Cam and Beth saying she got the unlucky beauty genes but from here I feel pretty lucky having a great view of her round, plump ass. Every time she bends down to pick up the ball with her stick, I can see the shorties under the skirt that hugs her tight cheeks.

Fuck, that's Goody?!

"You didn't answer my question," I say to Luke, watching her straighten back up and run towards the goal.

"Huh?"

"Is Chris into her?"

"Nah, man. He just cares for her. But could you blame him if he was? She's hot. You know you like them tiny and breakable." He wiggles his eyebrows at me, and I can't help but smile at his knowledge of me. "And you know who's even hotter? Her cheerleader friend." He points at the cheerleaders learning a routine on the other half of the field and I watch the toned, brown-haired girl Luke is pointing at. She breaks in a tumble alternating hands and feet until her two feet hit the ground in a thump, and she raises her arms, grinning proudly. The other girls and boys clap and gather around her.

"Hot," I admit but I don't feel anything that I feel when I watch Jamie.

"Hot?" Luke chokes out, "Dude, she's hotter than hell."

I shrug my shoulders and automatically go back to my main topic. "How can Chris do this to me though?" I complain. "If he's not even into her, surely she can't be off-limits."

Luke laughs at me. "Trust me on that one, you have no chance with her. Do you even know why we call her Goody?"

The fact that Luke thinks I couldn't get in her pants is tickling my ego.

"Why do we call her Goody?" I ask lazily.

"She's little miss perfect. Perfect grades, perfect plan for her future, lacrosse captain, never seen her at a party, goes to Church every Sunday morning. You know what, I don't think I've ever seen her have fun, like ever. Even on the field, she's there for one thing only: the win. A control freak like her, believe me, she's not the kind to let a boy get in her way. Even for a hot piece like you." He winks at me. "Chris was probably doing *you* a favor by telling you to stay away."

'I highly doubt that,' I think but don't say anything.

I turn back to watching Jamie again. I've thought about her all day. My thoughts were so busy with her that I forgot to find Camila to apologize for making out with Rose's friend, Ciara.

I don't know why she got so mad, Ciara's gay and had never kissed a boy. I was only trying to help her experiment. We were drunk, it just happened. The rest kind of just happened as well, suddenly I was in her room, and next thing I knew I was fucking her. And so was Chris. Except Chris doesn't have anyone to justify himself to when this happens. Smart guy. Ciara said she was gay, she fooled me. So really, I'm the victim here.

I know I fucked up a few times with Camila, but it would still hurt to lose her. We're good together and I know deep down she really is in love with me. I hate seeing her with other guys, it drives me fucking crazy and she knows it. It has always felt right with her but sometimes I can't help looking elsewhere. Right now, Jamie Williams is definitely keeping my mind away from my Latina girl.

"Fuck this shit. What the fuck does she think she's doing?"

I turn back to Luke to check what is suddenly making him so angry and I can't help a laugh.

"You knew that was going to happen. Ella's just as hot as you, what did you expect?"

Luke is looking daggers at his little sister and the guy hitting on her at the bottom of the bleachers.

"I'm not gonna be able to enjoy senior year if my 15-year-old sister keeps getting hit on by Stoneview's douchebags," he spits out.

Funnily, Ella and Luke are exactly three years apart and they both retook 8th grade. Their parents' wedding anniversary is in November, which might explain why she turned 15 on August 3rd, the exact same day Luke turned 18. Just a theory.

She's now a Freshman in our school and the only problem for Luke is that, while he doesn't see it, his sister is more than a ten. She takes from him with her long blond almost white hair and her big aqua blue eyes. They both have soft, innocent features.

Ella is the perfect girl next door. In fact, she *is* our girl next door since the Bakers live two doors down from us. Only in Stoneview, two doors down is a good five-minute walk. Now that Ella is at Stoneview Prep, surrounded by older guys who only have eyes for her, she gets hit on every two steps she takes. I think she was trying out for the cheer team and Scott Johnson pulled her out to 'talk'. We're now witnessing Scott, our lacrosse teammate, putting a hand around her waist while she smiles politely, trying to get away from him. Poor Ella. Like my twin would say: boys are trash.

"Scott looks like he's very much enjoying his senior year," I reply to Luke.

"Fuck this shit," he repeats getting up. "I'll see you tomorrow, man, I'm taking her home. You got a ride?"

"I'm all good, Ozy's got her car."

I watch him go down the steps two at a time. He taps on Scott's shoulder and when Scott turns around, I hear Luke say something about talking to girls his age and cutting his balls off. *Nice.* Ella seems relieved that Luke is getting her out of this situation, but she loses her cool when he grabs her hand and drags her away. She's shouting about cheerleading tryouts and wanting to be on the team, but I doubt he's listening.

I focus back on lacrosse and catch Rose, aka Ozy, scoring a goal. Some girls on the bleachers cheer her and giggle, trying to get her attention. She winks at them and I can't help a smile. *That's* my twin, talent runs in the family.

Chapter 3

Jamie

I zip up my sports bag and grab my stick. Most of the other girls have gone. I stayed slightly late to write down some notes about everyone's performance that I'll have to give to Coach Thompson. I only have twenty spaces on the team and about thirty girls showed up to tryouts. He's going to have his own notes too so we'll see what he thinks. I have my team from last year, but Coach T was adamant a spot last year didn't secure one this year, so I have to make sure I give a fair chance to everyone.

I hear a girl laugh out loud behind some lockers by the door. I put my stick in my locker and as I walk around, I spot Rose and her friend, Ciara, still chilling. Ciara is still getting changed and Rose is sitting on the benches fully clothed, her hair still wet from her shower, rolling a joint on her lap. The sleeves of her shirt are rolled up and I can see the half sleeve of tattoos on her left forearm.

"Hey, Goody," Ciara smiles at me. "Thanks for practice today."

I eye at Rose's joint, but she doesn't give a shit and doesn't even try to hide it

"It wasn't practice, it was tryouts," I reply. "I'm glad you enjoyed it."

"Tryouts?" Rose raises an eyebrow. Her raspy voice makes her sound constantly disinterested.

"Yeah, tryouts. I sent about a dozen emails about it. I only have twenty spots on the team and showing up fifteen minutes late didn't help you get one. You didn't have to fight me on tying your hair up either."

She looks at me, chuckles, and gives Ciara a look. "I already have a spot on the team. And I don't tie my hair up, Goody. You ask me at every practice knowing you'll get the same answer. Seems like you're the one fighting me on this." Her cocky lopsided smile glued to her face.

"Right, but I mentioned that a spot last year didn't mean one this year. Ciara you saw that, right?" I ask as I turn to her.

If Rose wants to act like she's not interested in anything, fine. But I won't bite into it. Like, what the hell is it with her and not wanting to tie her hair up when she exercises? Is she scared her fan club will complain?

She licks the paper of her joint, rolls it, and puts it in her pack of cigarettes before slowly getting up. Gradually her face goes from right in front of me to well above mine and I have to look up to keep looking in her eyes. She's so tall and intimidating. *And gorgeous.*

"Don't be silly. I know you wouldn't want to lose your best scorer, you're a smart girl." She picks up her bag and makes sure her locker is locked before turning to me again. "You want to take us to the top? Do yourself a favor, keep me on the team."

I'm about to reply but she puts a condescending hand on my shoulder and smiles. Her straight Colgate white teeth are so perfect I almost want to punch them. "I'll see you at practice, Goody." She turns to Ciara and gestures towards the exit with her chin. "Gotta go, Jake is waiting. See you tomorrow."

I watch her leave in shock and turn to Ciara who is grabbing the rest of her stuff. "The nerve she has."

"To be honest, she *is* your best scorer," she says in a shrug. She doesn't wait for a response and leaves me behind.

Yes, Rose is my best scorer and I know Coach T would

Chapter 3

never let me kick her off the team. It would still do her good to humble herself.

I'm biting the inside of my cheeks and re-run the conversation in my head as I head out. That's something I do a lot. I think it's part of being someone who constantly tries to better themselves. Or maybe it's just part of being anxious and overthinking everything.

I push the huge front doors of our school open and head straight to the bike racks. As usual, there is only one bike here: mine. All the other kids at Stoneview Prep are happy to drive their latest sports car that mommy and daddy dearest got them to fill the void they leave when they're on business trips. Don't get me started with the kids who have drivers.

I unlock the chain on my bike and look up to check out how many of these gorgeous cars are still parked. Only two, and I recognize one of them as Rose's: her black convertible Bentley Continental that makes me so jealous it almost gives me a headache. I turn around with my bike and stop in my tracks.

Not too far from me, Jake and Rose are talking to another guy. He's taller than both of them and what I would most definitely describe as dark and handsome. His dark brown hair is short on the sides and long in the middle, gelled back in a sleek way. While he's got a cocky grin on his face, his black eyes are saying the opposite. He's wearing simple dark jeans and a black tee, tight around his biceps and chest, and showing his tattooed arms as well as tattoos creeping up from his chest and all the way to his neck.

I recognize one of the tattoos on his neck straight away, having just seen it on Rose's forearm. It's of a thin 'X', big enough to fit a small crown just above where the two lines cross and a 'W' right under. On the left side of the crossing there is the number '19' and on the right side '33'. I've never really wondered what it meant until now, seeing it on this guy's neck.

I quickly see the tension between the twins and the mysterious guy could be cut with a knife. Rose and Jake have lost all their sassiness and I've never seen them so serious. That mysterious guy, he's got something malicious about him. Even from here, I can feel it brings something odd about Jake. That dreadful side he seems to hide so well.

Jake looks my way and I suddenly duck down behind a knee-high wall. I have no idea why, I just have this feeling that I don't want to get caught spying on their conversation. And while I don't want to get *caught,* I am still curious to know what's going on. Old habits die hard.

I leave my bike on the floor next to me and duck-walk closer to them, making sure I stay low enough that my head won't pop up. With my height, it's not too hard. I finally get close enough and I slowly look around to check on them while I eavesdrop on their conversation.

"You can't stay here. We don't want to see you and the Murrays surely don't want to hear about you," Jake says in a cold voice.

"Is this how you welcome me back into your life, Jake?" the stranger asks with a firm British accent. "I've been looking forward to seeing you two again. I found myself quite lucky that business brought me here."

"Business," Jake sniggers. "You can't bring that to Stoneview."

"Oh, but I am. I'm overtaking Stoneview actually and you're more than welcome to help. I would love nothing more than that."

"You're *overtaking* Stoneview?" Jake spits. "This city's got its own shit, what are you tryna do? Start a fucking war?"

Chapter 3

The stranger just smiles back at him before turning to Rose. "You're amazingly quiet, love."

Rose takes her time taking a pack of cigarettes out of her pocket, then takes out the joint she rolled earlier out of the pack. She brings it to her mouth, grabs a lighter in her other pocket, and lights it. She takes her time to inhale and finally exhales the smoke in the stranger's face before replying.

"Don't talk to me."

He lets out a genuine laugh. "God, if–

"You better not say his name in my presence, Sam," Jake cuts him off. "That would be a very stupid mistake."

Sam keeps the smug smile on his face. "If he could see you right now. He would turn around in his grave."

Rose freezes for a split second then her deep blue eyes almost turn black. "Fuck off, Sam. I'm serious, you're not getting back into our lives."

Jake quickly adds, "Make this the last time you try to get in touch with us. Let's go, Ozy."

I quickly duck all the way down behind the wall and sit down, my back against it. My heart is racing a hundred miles per hour.

Who is this Sam guy? And why are Rose and Jake so angry about him being here? I've never seen him around. Stoneview is not too small but you usually have an idea of who's who, especially if he shows up to school. I place a hand on my chest to try to calm my nerves and wait.

I hear one car leave and wait until I hear the sound of the other before standing back up. I lean over to grab my bike, still trying to get my head around what I just saw despite the fact that it has nothing to do with me.

As soon as I am back up a hand clasps around my mouth and drags me back until I hit a hard chest.

It all happens so fast I drop my bike without a chance to

scream for help. After a beat of realization, I try to scream but the sound is muffled by the big hand. I attempt to break free, fight, kick but my size against what feels like a giant behind me is leading me nowhere. This has to be the guy they were talking to. He looked dangerous, he caught me watching.

My nails are scratching against the hand on my mouth and I suddenly feel a breath against the side of my face. I close my eyes tight as the guy's other arm snakes around my waist, holding me tight. Just as I try to push the arm away from my waist, I recognize a smell. That mix of spice and deep, dark forest. Automatically my body half-relaxes as if it isn't in danger anymore. Before I can put my thoughts together, Jake's deep voice is reverberating in my ear.

"Did you enjoy the show, Jamie?" The same words I heard playfully earlier in the hallway send a chill down my spine as they take a threatening turn.

What is he playing at?

I try to reply, to justify myself but my words get stuck behind his hand on my mouth. I shake my head trying to show that I need him to move his stupid hand if he wants an answer. He doesn't. Instead, his voice resonates around me like darkness falling onto me.

"Listen to me real close. If you talk to *anyone* about what you've just seen, I'm going to turn your life into your own personal living hell." He pauses and tightens his grip around me making me squirm under his touch. His anger is palpable and right now he is not the popular guy everybody knows. No, right now it's that side of him everyone thinks he hides, and I feel like he could break my body in two if he wanted.

"You won't be able to go to work, school, or a party without having me on your back ruining your life. Hell, I'll even torment you in your own house if I have to. I don't want you to tell your bestie, your parents, or even your pet. Clear? Nod if yes."

I struggle for a few seconds before he brings me closer and tighter to him, enhancing his threat. My heart is beating so hard in my chest I'm scared it's going to break my ribs and jump out of my body. His breath is hot on my ear, his scent destabilizing and his strong arms around me are making my lower belly tingle.

"I *said*," he's now talking through clenched teeth, "Am. I. Clear?" I nod a few times. What else can I do? I'm in no position to negotiate right now. "Good girl. Now go home and forget what you saw."

He releases me and takes a step back, the sudden lack of warmth from his chest against my back sends a shiver down my spine. I hurry forward and away from him before I turn around. I'm breathing fast from the adrenaline and the closeness we just shared.

"Are you out of your mind?!" I pant, trying to catch my breath.

He simply smiles back at me, lips tight. *Who is this guy?* He looks devilish and his threat is still ringing in my ears.

"Go home, Jamie." He turns around and walks away, hands in his pockets as if not a care in the world.

I take a moment to catch my breath and process what just happened. Jake White is one scary guy, that's for sure, and I can't believe I've just let him terrorize me like that.

I realize Rose's car is gone, as I thought. I did count two cars leaving the lot. Jake must have stayed behind. I get on my bike as quickly as possible and head out of the parking lot. A few blocks down I see Jake getting into Rose's car. She left to fool me into thinking they were gone, and he stayed to give me a freaking heart attack. The two bastards.

If they really think they can scare me into keeping my mouth shut they've got another thing coming. I wasn't even thinking of telling this to anyone. Maybe Emily, since we share literally every single thing that happens in our lives and because I was curious to see what she thought. But I wasn't planning on sharing their weird interaction with the whole school. A random scary guy talked to them. So what?

4

JAMIE

Swim – Chase Atlantic

In the evening, I keep replaying the events of the afternoon in my head. I hate that I keep doing that. I should just let it go but I'm just not the kind of person who *lets go*. I'm lying in bed thinking of that stranger, 'Sam'. What did he want and what is his business?

Mostly I keep thinking of Jake's change in behavior, how furious he got at me when he caught me listening. How suspicious was that? Sam was obviously someone from their past and Jake's reaction was a desperate act to avoid anyone finding out anything about said past. But what is he hiding?

Jake White is the golden boy of Stoneview Prep. No matter how much trouble he gets in, he always gets away with it. Everyone, *everyone* loves him. If they knew how cold he can turn, I'm sure that would be a different deal. I saw a side of him earlier that no one knows about. At least no one that isn't close to him. I can't help wondering if his friends know about this. Chris? Is that why he told him to leave me alone? Could Jake actually be dangerous?

Okay Jamie, you need to calm down.

The next day, I walk into English with a heaviness in my stomach. I'm not scared of Jake but that doesn't mean I particularly want to confront him either. I'm really not a confrontational person. I prefer pretending something hasn't happened and never talk about it again.

Luke is sitting on his right, in my seat, chatting with him.

"I'd be more than happy to sit next to Rachel, but I don't think Mr. Ashton will appreciate us messing with his seating arrangements," I say to Luke. He and Jake both turn to me smiling.

"And I know you would never want to cross a teacher, Goody," Luke tells me as he gets up. "Don't let me get you in trouble." He grabs his backpack and turns to me again. "Hey, so Camila's party on Friday...are you and your friend coming?" I can see from the corner of my eye that Jake is waiting for the answer as well.

"Uh, I'm not sure," I admit. Mr. Ashton chooses this moment to enter the class and I take my seat as Luke walks to his.

Jake leans close to me as soon as my butt hits my seat. "You shouldn't go to Cam's party. It's not for girls like you. It's all booze, drugs and, oh, S. E. X." He spells it out as if I'm a child and he has to watch out what he says around me, and then he puts on a fake shocked face.

Screw this guy. Who does he think he is?

"You know what, Jake," I reply, feeling the anger building in me. "I think I might go to Camila's party. Hey, is your friend Sam going? He's cute," I ask with a big smile on my face. *Eat that, asshole.*

His eyes turn black and his face hardens. In a split second he turns from cocky to evil. His gaze is intense. It screams violence and ferocity. I feel like little Red Riding

Hood about to be eaten by the wolf. My mouth feels incredibly dry as regrets sets in.

No, Jamie, don't let him destabilize you.

He turns back to face forward but slowly adjusts his chair to the right, toward me. My left arm and his right are almost touching.

It takes all my strength to not move an inch, to not bend to the fear. Especially when he wraps his right arm around the back of my chair. I gulp but do my best to keep looking straight at the board. Mr. Ashton is writing on it and everyone is quietly taking notes apart from the few people here and there whispering to each other or on their phones.

I swallow the lump in my throat. I feel so tense I want to jump off my chair and run away. The scent of Jake is tickling my nostrils and I realize I'm holding my breath but can't seem to get myself to start breathing again. He's not saying anything, though I can feel the furious anger emanating from him.

Why isn't he saying anything?

I can sense his arm on the back of my chair starting to move and he suddenly grabs my right arm in his big hand. I let out a sharp breath and bite back a whimper. His fingers are wrapping around my upper arm so tight I'm sure it's going to leave a bruise.

He leans a little closer to me and starts whispering in my ear. "You're gonna pay for that."

He's still looking straight ahead to not attract attention, but his icy voice is focused on me. I twist under his hand and he tightens his hold.

Okay, I'm officially destabilized.

"Mm..." I can see his tongue licking his lower lip from the corner of my eye and he lets out a low chuckle. "I don't think there's a better thing in the world than feeling you squirm under my touch, Goody."

I freeze on the spot.

He needs to stop.

My arm is starting to ache but that's not the worst part. The worst thing is the heat in my belly and the electricity from his touch. It's white-hot on my skin and I feel like I'm going to combust any minute now. I try to compose myself and turn my burning face to him.

"You're hurting me," I hiss.

"Am I now? It's not like I didn't warn you yesterday though, is it?"

"Jake, let go of my arm."

He finally turns to face me and fake pouts. "But my skin on yours feels so right."

"I'm serious, let go. You're hurting me." Our whole conversation is whispers. My voice is slowly going from ordering him to let go, to begging him to.

My arm is burning under his hand and if I don't melt from his touch, there's a chance I won't be able to play lacrosse if he keeps going like this.

"I haven't heard the magic word Goody, c'mon, you know you're not a rude girl."

My heart picks up and my breaths are coming out sharper. I want to slap the smile off his face and claw at it until he bleeds. I hate him. This is the problem with the people in this town. They think they can get away with anything.

My mind hates him so much it's in complete contradiction with my body. I take a deep breath before letting out the words I'm pretty sure are going to scrape my throat coming out.

"Let go of my arm, *please*."

Chapter 4

"Mm..." he thinks, and I can see him moving in his seat. The bastard is still not letting go and the blood drains from my face as I see him adjusting his hard-on under his jeans.

The fucker is getting off on this. Is it hurting me? Is it the begging? What is wrong with him? Actually, *what is wrong with me?!* Seeing him adjust himself again, I can't help my mind wandering to places. I want to see what's under his uniform. My fucked-up thoughts are cut short by Jake's phone vibrating on his desk. He quickly looks at it and back at me in a smile.

"Saved by the bell, Goody," he says as he grabs his phone and shows the screen to me. It's a text from Chris, simple but efficient.

> Chris: Let her go.

My head snaps to Chris a few rows behind us. He's watching us like he wants to annihilate Jake. Chris's eyes go back to his phone between his lap and his desk and Jake's screen lights up again.

> Chris: Now.

Jake finally lets go of my arm and turns to Chris, flashing him his most innocent smile. I massage my arm trying to get the blood flowing again and Jake turns back to me.

"I don't know why Chris is busting my balls to leave you

alone, but I stand by what I said. You're going to regret this. Watch your back."

He goes back to writing some notes and ignores me completely until the end of the class. As soon as the bell rings I jump off my seat and run out of class.

I realize when I burst into the ladies room that I didn't even wait for Emily. I'm out of breath from running across campus to the furthest bathroom possible from where Jake was. I'm shaking when I look at my arm in the mirror. I'm wearing the summer uniform and my shirt has short sleeves. I have red patches, dots where his fingertips were. *Fuck*. What the hell just happened? Jake has no limits, he just hurt me in class in front of everyone and only Chris noticed.

Chris. Surely if he came to my defense, he knows how Jake can get, there are no other possibilities. He's always on the twins' backs, keeping them in line. What if it's more than stopping them from playing stupid pranks on people and causing trouble at school? What if it's to stop them from hurting anyone? No one knows their background. They might as well have been assassins before they joined our school.

They joined at fourteen years old Jamie. Calm down.

I remember how they were covered in bruises when they showed up, in the middle of the school year. I remember wondering what that was about back then. Chris and Luke shut down stupid rumors, Jake got in some fights and life went on without anyone ever knowing what had happened to them. Who were they with before they went to live with the Murrays?

I shake my head trying to stop the thoughts from flowing. I'm overthinking and biting my inside cheek so hard I can taste blood in my mouth. I need to keep Jake off my mind and as far away from me as possible.

I spend the rest of the morning sitting far away from Jake and he seems to be back to ignoring me. I hate what I'm doing but I am actually watching my back, exactly like he wanted. Emily catches on that something is wrong by lunchtime. I don't have the mental strength to explain what happened. I still haven't decided if I want to tell her about Sam and the dark side of Jake or if I want to keep it to myself. I want to tell her because Jake threatened me not to and I've got too much pride to follow threats from overprivileged Stoneview kids.

On the other hand, he was clear this morning and every time I look at my arm I can't help thinking: do I really want to involve Emily in this?

"'Me, are you going to answer my question?" she insists. I have no idea what she just asked.

"What?"

"Why are you so out of it today? Did something happen?"

"I..." I'm about to lie but I change my mind at the last second. I look around the cafeteria and notice Jake and his group not far from us. "Hey, can we talk about this later?"

Emily frowns in confusion and nods, "Sure, come home with me tonight? I'll drive you."

"I've got my bike. I can meet you there."

She shakes her head at my statement. "When will you drop that old bike and let me drive you to school?"

"My house is out of your way to school and I like biking, especially at this time of year."

"'Me, that bike is as old as you and I know you're tiny, but it looks like it's going to break under your weight. Come on, let me drive you to school. That's what every bestie does. Camila drives Rachel in her stupid bimbo Lambo every morning, I want to do that with you."

"Em, you've got a Lambo."

She scoffs at me as if I've just insulted her. "Don't compare my beauty to her piece of trash. Hers is sport and gold because she's an attention-seeking bitch. Mine is black and it's an Urus, babe, sweet and classy like me. Let me take you to school goddammit."

"Em!" I'm not crazy about God, but I do enjoy my time at the church. I tend to avoid all sorts of cursing and blasphemy. Except when I talk to myself.

"My bad, my bad sorry."

"Look," I start. "That bike is way older than me. It was my dad's, he had fixed it for my brother and then, you know, I took it from Aaron." I shrug as if it wasn't a big deal, but it is.

I love riding my brother's bike. I still remember when dad fixed it for him. I was so jealous of it, Dad said he would buy me one, but I didn't want one from the shop, I wanted to repair a bike with him and bond like he did with my older brother. Dad promised we would fix a bike together, but time ran out before we could get around to it.

Emily is looking at me with sorry eyes and I know I shouldn't have said anything.

"I... I'm sorry, I knew that. I didn't even think about it." Em goes fully quiet and now I feel horrible looking at the sadness in her eyes.

Around three years ago, Emily and Aaron started dating. We were 14 and he was 17, and they were in love, real love. It was beautiful, we all thought they were going to be the kind

Chapter 4

of couple that lasted forever. High school sweethearts who get married and have kids. Except Aaron's forever got cut short less than a year into their relationship.

I subconsciously run a hand right under my bra strap, on my left shoulder. The bullet wound is almost three years old but when I talk about Dad and Aaron, it burns just like the first day. Emily's heart is just as broken as mine when it comes to my brother and I can't blame her for not wanting to talk about it.

"Hey," I say, putting my hand on hers. "How about tonight I bring that bike home but tomorrow you pick me up in that beautiful Lambo of yours."

We share our pain for a few more seconds followed by a smile.

The next morning, I hop in Emily's car with new confidence. Jake White can shove his threats up his ass. If even Chris thinks he's out of line, then he's got no one to back him up in his shit. Except for his stupid twin but she never addresses more than one word my way.

"Hold on, hold on, he turned psycho," Emily points to my arm, "because you talked about a dude he doesn't want you to talk about? What the actual fuck is wrong with this guy?!" She takes a deep breath. "Alright, before I conclude if I'm going to kill him painfully or not, what do you know about the mystery guy? Was he hot?"

I can't help a laugh. "He was good looking. He also looked about as nice as a gangbanger."

It's Emily's turn to explode laughing, "Alright, I see. What was his name?"

"Sam, I believe."

I've barely finished my sentence when Emily hits the brakes hard enough to come to a stop in the middle of the road. A few cars behind us honk as they suddenly have to overtake our car.

"Oh my... Em!"

She puts the hazard lights on and turns to me. "Sam you said?"

"Yes Sam, why? Please start the car."

"Dark and handsome with a British accent?"

I can't believe she knows who I'm talking about. "Do you know who he is?" I ask. "I had never seen him before."

I can see she is thinking, as if trying to put memories back together.

"I," she hesitates. "Well, you know I always dig into my mom's files, I can't really help myself."

"Yeah..." I try to encourage her to keep going but I'm not sure what she's getting at.

Emily's mom is a famous Stoneview judge. She deals with anything that happens in Stoneview and the surrounding areas. One thing that has always linked my best friend and I is our lack of boundaries when it comes to our curiosity. I remember bonding with her in kindergarten because we both loved to roleplay detectives while others wanted to be moms and dads. I can't count the number of times we both looked into her mom's files because we heard of a story on the news that was going to court.

She nods and continues. "When the twins moved to our school and we learned they were in the system, I knew there had to be some trace of them in my mom's files. And there was. For the Murrays to become their legal guardians it had to go through my mom. On the day they went to court they were accompanied by a guy called Samuel Thomas."

"What? What do you mean he accompanied them?" I ask, confused.

"I mean he was there with them. I read the whole transcript; Samuel was there protesting them going to the Murrays but he was a minor back then so he couldn't do anything concrete."

"How do you know he's got an English accent if you read the transcript only?"

I can see there is much more she wants to say but doesn't.

"Em, come on. What did you do?"

"I may or may have not started looking for him online. He was hot so I investigated his social media, and I may or may have not um..." she gets her phone out as she slows down her talk and starts typing.

"Oh Em, you follow him on Insta. Are you for real?"

"I don't know, was it this guy?" She shows me a picture of the exact same guy that was talking to Rose and Jake two days ago.

"Yep," I pop the 'p' as I nod at the picture.

"Cool. Cool. Great. Tiptop," she says slowly.

"What? What is it?"

"I have such shit news right now," she keeps going. "Believe me when I say you can learn a lot from people when you've stalked them for years."

"Em, spill it."

"I'm not too surprised you thought he looked as nice as a gangbanger."

I widen my eyes already knowing what's coming next.

"He *is* a gangbanger, 'Me," she says, concern edging her tone.

She frowns at me as if I'm in big trouble.

"You can't learn that from Instagram, Em. Surely he'd be arrested by now if he put anything on there."

"You're so naive when it comes to social media, babe. And it's not so much what he posts, he's kind of lowkey. It's more what others post about him."

So that's why Jake doesn't want anyone to know about Sam? He used to be in a gang?

Impossible. He was too young.

Something else comes to my mind.

"But...he talked about doing business in Stoneview. Everyone knows Stoneview is Volkov's jurisdiction."

There aren't many criminals who can get away with anything and *everything*. Vladimir Volkov is one of them. His gang, the Wolves, overrules underworld crime in almost the whole state of Maryland, including Stoneview.

Rumors have been going around that their men on the ground here are the Diaz boys. It is known that Camila's brothers are the go-to people for overly privileged teenagers looking for drugs, but who knows how involved they really are with Volkov. What I know is that when you're the gang who does business with politicians and billionaires, you don't have to worry about getting caught or being overridden by another gang. Some people say they keep Stoneview safe and don't mind admitting the city belongs to Volkov. I know without a doubt that I hate them with every inch of my soul.

"It is Volkov's territory," Emily confirms. "And if Jake and Rose's bestie wants to come to do business here, they're going to be in serious trouble. You don't want to be involved in any of this, 'Me."

Silence falls on the car as we both get lost in our thoughts. A honk makes us both jump.

"Shit, we need to get to school," Emily puts the car in gear and starts driving away.

My head becomes its own enemy as thoughts rage in my mind.

Volkov. Volkov. Volkov. Volkov. My inner voice repeats, my heart pressing against my ribcage.

Gorgeous villas and mansions unroll before my eyes one after the other. Huge fences, beautiful bushes. Gardens straight out of home magazines.

Find him.

Emily takes a corner. The last one before we enter our gated preparatory school.

Don't do anything. Stay out of this. Danger warning.

The houses have disappeared. We're now driving along the huge red brick wall behind which is Stoneview Prep. A place where I'm safe. A place where Volkov doesn't belong. Where I can pretend I'm not still desperately trying to understand what happened that night.

Volkov is a ghost. This might be your one and only chance. Do something!

The gate opens quickly as the security guard sees the sticker on Emily's car.

Breathe, Jamie. In. Out. In. Out. What is it you really want? Is it worth the risk? For answers? You wouldn't just be looking into Volkov. You'd be looking into Jake's past. He's obviously hiding something dangerous.

Think.

Just. Think.

"We need to find out what Sam wants with Volkov," I admit as we park in the school parking lot.

"Uh, no we don't. We just agreed you should stay out of it."

"Em," I shake my head slowly trying to show her I'm

sorry.

"Please, 'Me, promise me you won't."

"I can't," I say closing my eyes for a few seconds. When I open them, I am determined. "I can't possibly not get involved when it comes to this gang, Em, you know it. I'm sorry."

"Jamie, these guys are dangerous! You don't need to be told this, you've experienced it firsthand," she insists. I automatically bring my hand to the scar under my bra strap. "Please, as your friend, I'm asking you to stay away."

"Em, try to understand! How can you ask me this?" I flip.

I can't and I won't stay away from anything including Volkov. It's hard enough to ever get close to something the Wolves are involved with, I finally have something to hold onto and adrenaline is thumping in my veins right now.

"I'm asking you because I've already lost one person to them, I'm not going to lose another because she's too stupid to stay away!" She opens the door, gets out of the car, and slams it in anger. I jump at the strength she put in it and stay another minute to calm my nerves and boiling anger.

Emily and I ignore each other all morning but by lunch, I find her at our usual table. She's looking apologetic and I know I have just as much apologizing to do as her. If not more.

"I'm sorry," I sigh as I drop my tray on the table and let myself fall in the chair.

She looks up at me and takes a deep breath. "I'm sorry, 'Me, but I'm scared. They went after your family once. What's stopping them from doing it again if you put your nose in their business?"

"I shouldn't have said anything. I know how you feel about this. And I would never want to scare or hurt you…" I continue.

"But," she insists, knowing there's more I want to say.

"But I lost my brother and my Dad, Em. I almost lost my life. The pain I see in my mom's eyes when she talks about it, wondering where Aaron is or if he's still alive...It's killing me to watch her live a life without answers. I owe this to her."

She's about to say something but I cut her off.

"Look, I'm not putting myself in any danger. I won't get even remotely close to Volkov's gang. I just want to know more about Samuel Thomas' business. If he's going against them, you know what they say."

"The enemies of my enemies are my friends," she concludes in a big sigh.

I give her a nod in confirmation. She shakes her head for a few seconds before replying, "Ugh, fine. I'll help you. Where do we start?"

"I guess for now our only link is the Whites."

"Isn't this great," she replies in a sarcastic tone. "You're gonna have to befriend your favorite people in the whole school."

"Wonderful," I deadpan

"And you know the best way to start getting into their circle..."

"Please don't say the p–"

"The party on Friday, yes my friend, you guessed it," she beams. "And once we've become their best friends, I'm calling dibs on Luke Baker."

"Party on Friday it is," I reply with as much motivation as a kid who has been asked to tidy their room.

"Oh yes, that's my girl." She does a little dance as she picks at more carrots on her plate and I roll my eyes. God, I love this girl.

5

JAKE

Darkside - grandson

By Friday, Ozy and I are in complete disagreement regarding Sam being in Stoneview. The problem with my twin is we rarely agree on anything. She one hundred percent believes we shouldn't tell Chris and ignore our old acquaintance. In fact, Sam *has* been quiet since he showed up after school. That's the kind of guy he is though, the dude talks once a year. At least that's how I remember him.

I think we should warn Chris and get rid of Sam as soon as possible. Chris and Luke are the only ones who know how our life was before coming to Stoneview and I want to keep it that way.

I could use the guys to kick him out of Stoneview. I don't know how exactly but I'm thinking something like beating the shit out of him, tying him up, throwing him in the trunk of my car and literally driving him out of Stoneview. I will definitely need at least Chris' muscles for that.

I also need Jamie fucking Williams to stay the hell out of

it. Although I could think of advantages in having her tied up too.

This girl is trouble, I can see it coming from miles away. The way I lost control when she mentioned Sam. This is not good. I can pretend it was because she mentioned him, or I can admit it was because she defied me. I lost it and I loved it. The way her skin felt under my hand, it burnt under my touch. The way her small arm fit perfectly in my grip. The way she flushes every time I get too close to her...*Fuck.*

I need to control my cock; it can't keep making decisions for me. I scared Jamie enough that she didn't mention Sam again but who knows how brave she believes she is. I'd be more than happy to show her not to defy me. Break her down and build her back up, complacent, and answering only to me. Teach her to appreciate the roughness and beg for more.

And I've derailed from the topic again.

Kick Sam out of Stoneview. Keep Jamie quiet. That's it.

I can think of so many ways to keep her quiet, one being my dick in that gorgeous mouth of hers.

Fuck! I need to get her out of my mind and I shouldn't have these thoughts in the middle of class. There's a party at Camila's tonight, it's time I make it up to her and keep my cock busy.

I poke my twin in the back with my pencil, but she doesn't move. I whisper so our science teacher can't hear me.

"Ozy." I use the nickname only I'm allowed to use for her to catch her attention. She turns around and raises an eyebrow at me.

I give her a cheeky smile. "Take your car tonight, I'm staying over."

She laughs at me. "Dude, I'm picking up from Roy. I'm

going to be on another planet tonight. I don't think it's wise for me to drive."

"Chris it is," I conclude.

She smiles at me and turns back. I wonder how long my sister will be able to avoid Sam. She's even more pissed than me that he's here...for now. This is another reason I need him out of this town. Rose isn't going to be able to stay away from him.

It took her so long to get over him the first time we got separated, if she falls back, she won't get over it this time. I know it's affecting her more than she lets on. She keeps things inside, like me. Bottles it up until it explodes or eats her up from the inside.

Sam knows how to push her buttons, he knows her by heart, and he won't hesitate to use it against us. No matter how much it breaks my heart, the truth is her loyalty used to lay with him and the bastard knows it.

I turn to the other side of the room and watch Jamie for a few seconds. She's focusing on taking notes and biting her cheek. Her brows are slightly furrowed, and I want to run my thumb between them to soften them. She looks up and our eyes cross.

To my surprise, she offers me a wide grin. I frown back at her and give her my most threatening look. She needs to know I'm not fucking about and to stay in her place. As soon as she drops the smile, I miss it though. It's like she was lighting the room and it suddenly got dark. She looks away from me, but I can't take my eyes off her lips. A sudden urge to kiss her overtakes me and I have to look away. It's always like that when a new girl gets my attention, I just need to fuck her out of my system.

But first, I need to re-focus.

Kick Sam out of Stoneview. Keep Jamie quiet.

Chapter 5

When Ozy and I walk out of school, trouble is waiting for us outside. Unsurprisingly, Sam is back. What takes me aback is to see him waiting by his car, chatting with Camila and Rachel.

"The fuck," I say watching him put an arm on the small of Rachel's back. She looks slightly uncomfortable, but I know she's too shy to say anything. "I told you we should have gotten rid of him straight away," I mumble to my sister.

Ozy notices right after me and she chuckles to herself, but I know what this chuckle means. It means shit is about to go down.

"Keep your cool," I warn her but she's already hurrying down the stairs, her hair flying behind her.

When I reach the group, Ozy is unexpectedly keeping calm. Or as calm as she can keep.

"Rachel might be too nice to tell you to fuck off but I'm not," she says smoothly to Sam.

He smirks at her and takes his arm away from Rachel. Rose automatically puts a hand behind her neck possessively.

"My bad, just trying to meet some decent girls. I heard Stoneview was full of them." I know he's acting up to piss us off. This is probably the most I've heard him talk in my entire life. He hates making conversation, he hates everyone, and he never pretends otherwise.

So why is he outside our school trying to make friends with ours? How did he even get in? Our gate keeper is the most annoying person I've had the pleasure to meet in my life. He takes his job way too seriously and yet Sam gets past him twice in the same week? I guess when you look like Sam does, it's easy to scare people off.

"You do what you have to. Just next time keep your

hands off my girl," Rose says quickly. It's like she's trying to get rid of her words before she snaps.

Sam laughs and puts his hands up in a peaceful gesture. "You bite. I don't want any trouble. Promise. But if you girls want a little fun, I'm all yours."

My nostrils flare at his words. I fucking hate him. Everything about him makes me want to punch him. The way he thinks he's above everyone, his stupid British accent, the fact that my own twin used to love him more than anything. And worst of all, the fact that he's trying to win us back, no doubt for his own benefit.

Fuck. Him.

Rose laughs in his face and talks as she turns around, still holding Rachel and guiding her away.

"What for? So you can get a free pussy-licking lesson?" she sneers.

A mocking chortle escapes Rachel's lips. Rose doesn't wait for a reply and walks away with her. She's leaving me alone with Sam and Camila but I'm not mad at her. I know there's only so long she can spend in his presence without losing her shit completely.

"What's with her today?" Camila asks. "Jake, this is Samuel. He's a friend of Roy and Carlo."

I try to keep my face as expressionless as possible, but this is big news. The fucker actually knows people here.

"Cool," I reply disinterested.

I can't really add anything else because Rose's car stops right beside us on its way out of the parking lot. It's a nice day and she's got the roof down. Rachel is sitting in the front passenger seat, the one closest to us.

Rose takes a cigarette out of her pack and lights it before turning to us and smiling at Sam as she puts her right arm around Rachel's shoulders.

Chapter 5

I walk over to her to get in the car. Rose's gaze doesn't leave Sam's. She wants to make him angry and I can see he's biting when his face turns cold. Rose winks at him and flips him the bird with her hand holding Rachel's shoulder. As soon as I hop in, she leaves screeching her tires.

"You made him mad," I say when we reach the road. I'm not too worried about talking in front of Rachel. She's a quiet and nice girl, she hears shit all the time being around Rose, and she never talks about anything.

"Don't care," Rose replies. "Hopefully it'll push him away."

"Or he's gonna get back at us."

"He can try," she shrugs.

"Ozy, don't play with him," I try to warn her. She can't get into his games, not her.

"I won't if you won't."

That's easier said than done but I concede anyway. "Sure," I reply.

I don't know if I really believe it or just want to talk about something else. The fucker's got no right to walk back into our lives.

Ozy drives us past the huge iron gate of the Murray's estate and drives all the way to the top of the hill where the mansion stands. She parks in the garage full of expensive cars and we all get out.

I need to drive to school more often, I think as we walk past the Audi R8 Chris's parents got me for my sixteenth birthday. This family swims in money and they never hold back when it comes to our gifts.

We walk out of the garage and around the house. We go through the garden, past the huge rectangular pool with a hot tub on one side and an island with a palm tree in the middle, and head straight for the pool house.

The Murrays have about ten bedrooms in their house. Still, they always allowed Ozy and me to live in the pool house. I think they knew we needed the space and didn't want to act too much as 'parents' to us. They never adopted us, they're only our legal guardians. They just wanted to get us out of the mess we were in. To be honest they're not too parent-y to Chris either. To our luck, they have the kind of jobs where they never spend more than a few days at a time at home. The house is massive, and we end up spending most of our time in the pool house. Except for parties of course.

I push the door open; we never lock it. Stoneview is way too safe for that and if someone ever makes it past the gate and up the hill, they will probably go for the huge house, not the cute pool house next to it.

I walk in to find Chris and Luke are already here playing video games on our sofa, music playing in the background. Ella is watching the game, settled on the other side of the guys. The place is simple but out of all the foster houses we've ever been in, it's the one that feels the most like home.

I walk in straight into the living room area with a sofa facing the left wall and a TV mounted on the wall. At the back, there is a kitchen counter and a small kitchen behind it that we never use, and the right wall opens to a hallway leading to our rooms and a shared bathroom. Everything is new. After almost three years it still looks untouched. But it's the people here with me that make it cozy and homey.

I fist-bump my friends hello and mess up Ella's hair.

"What are you doing here, little gnome?" I ask.

"She truly believed she was going to Camila's tonight. I had to keep an eye on her," Luke explains.

Ella sits up and scowls at Luke. "Luke, because of you I couldn't finish the cheerleading tryouts, they're never gonna let me on the team. Now you want to stop me from going to a party all my friends are going to. Why are you trying so hard to kill my reputation?!"

I think if Rose had been my younger sister like Ella is to Luke, I would have been the same kind of brother. Annoying, overprotective, controlling. Sadly, Rose is my twin and the little shit doesn't take orders from anyone.

I can't help chuckling at Ella. "I thought it was seniors only. You're too young to go to Camila's parties," I tease her.

"You're sixteen, Jake. I'm fifteen," she replies.

Being born in October has always been a pain in my ass. Like having to skip a year to be with my friends. We were born the same year, we should have been in the same classes straight away. Especially since we arrived in Stoneview passed October and we were already fourteen.

We couldn't join Chris as freshmen when we arrived in Stoneview because then we wouldn't have been fifteen by the time we were sophomores and so on, and god forbid we started college at seventeen. That's a pretty stupid system we have, especially now that they offered us to skip a year to raise their success rate.

"I'm turning seventeen in a month and you've just turned fifteen. But really in our heads, you turned five yesterday. We need to protect you from the big bad world, El'," I smile at her.

"Give her a break, everyone will be there," Chris drops.

We all look at him shocked. Luke's jaw is hanging so low I think it's going to hit the floor. How is it that the dad of the group is saying this is fine?

"Don't look at me like that," he continues without even glancing at us. His gaze is still on the game in front of him. "It's not like we all didn't go to parties at her age. We'll be there to keep an eye out, let your sister have fun," he concludes.

"Whatever," Luke mumbles, crossing his arms.

Everyone at school thinks I'm the leader of our little group. Because I'm the captain of the lacrosse team, I'm the most popular, I get the most girls and especially because I broke a few noses when I arrived. I've got the image.

Between us, we know the quiet Christopher Murray is the one who calls the shots. Not because we fear him though. Yes, on the outside Chris imposes respect, he's the tallest and biggest but, internally, we simply know he's the wisest and it's always better to go with his plans.

"Look at that, El'. It's your lucky day, boss said you can come out," I keep teasing her as I mess up her hair again. I hear Chris growling at the fact that I called him boss.

"Go away," Ella mumbles grumpily as she tries to put her hair back in place.

I catch her hands playfully to stop her from rearranging it and I can see her blushing at my touch.

I instantly let go. I don't want Ella to think I'm flirting with her. We're only two years apart, she's hot, and clearly into me, but I don't feel anything more than physical attraction toward her. While this wouldn't be a problem with any girl, Ella is not any girl. She's Luke's sister and he would cut my balls off if I broke her heart.

The more I think of why I don't want to get involved with Ella the more my mind drifts back to who I *want* to get involved with and a precise face gets pictured in my head.

Those almond green eyes, sparkling with gold when she smiles. The beautiful deep brown brows that furrow when she focuses. I remind myself of her tight body and my cock twitches. I bet her boobs are perky and would fit perfectly in my hands.

Chapter 5

"Where's Rose?" Chris's question cuts through my indecent thoughts and hearing my sister's name is like a cold shower. I look behind me, towards the front door.

"Probably smoking outside." Right on cue, Rose and Rachel walk in.

"Well, well. Looks like she just can't stay away from you, Rach'." Luke smiles and winks at Rachel.

She lets out a shy laugh and nods to say hi. Ozy takes her hand and walks in the space behind the sofa. She slaps Luke at the back of the head before leading Rachel to the rest of the house. They close the door to the hallway behind them and a few seconds later we hear Rose's door slamming.

Luke, Chris and I give each other an awkward look in complete silence. After a few seconds, I'm the one who breaks. "Should we just leave?"

They both jump off the sofa in a rush. "Good idea," Luke says as we all head out.

"Wait for me," Ella shouts after us as she gets up.

Just before 9pm, Luke parks his G-Wagon besides countless other cars in Camila's driveway. Rose and Rachel disappeared on us by the time we headed back to the pool house. My sister has a tendency to disappear in general and apparently, she never learned that when phones ring, they're meant to be picked up.

We can hear the bass from out here. Mid-September in Stoneview is still warm enough that some people are hovering in front of the house. We walk through the double front doors and the heat and noise of the place hit me.

It smells like drunk people and fun in here. Excitement

builds in me as the loud music reaches my ears. We walk through the grand foyer, full of people drinking, and head for the living room. The couches have been pushed to the side and the room turned into a dancefloor. Ella spots her girlfriends straight away and makes a beeline for them. I turn to Luke with a cheeky smile.

"They grow up too fast," I say in an exaggerated sigh.

He laughs, taps my shoulder, and points with his thumb at the door that leads to the kitchen.

"Let's get drunk so I can forget my baby sister being at one of our parties."

We go to the kitchen and stop by the island that has been turned into an open bar. I fucking love rich kids' parties. I got used to the elite life quicker than I thought I would.

We pour ourselves some drinks and Chris gestures with his chin towards a corner of the room.

"Found her," he declares unimpressed. I look around taking a sip and roll my eyes.

Ozy is sitting on the kitchen counter. In front of her, Roy and Carlo, Camila's older brothers, are drinking her words.

"That fucking traitor," I grumble. She knows they hate me. They'd decapitate me and offer my head on a platter to Camila if they could.

"Can you blame them though? You fuck around with their little princess, of course they're gonna try to get back at you and hit on your sister. How many times do you think Camila's cried to her big, bad brothers about you?" Luke explains. Derision glints in his eyes. I don't care what Rose does with boys, but Luke knows karma would be hitting me real hard if she had a thing with one of the Diaz brothers. I know my sister though. The only reason she gives them

Chapter 5

hope is because they're our local drug dealers and she loves a good party.

"This is nothing to do with me, trust me. She loves having them two wrapped around her fing–" My words die in my mouth when I see Jamie and her cheerleader friend walk into the room.

She's wearing a short high-waisted black leather skirt that she's had to tighten with a red belt around her tiny waist. She's tucked in a simple white tee that's too big for her and is slightly overflowing on all sides. *Fuck*.

My cock hardens in my pants at the view of Jamie in leather. Two guys in the kitchen turn around when she walks in and look at her ass. I barely refrain a growl at them but throw them my darkest look and they both look away when they catch me. They can grab the leftovers when I'm done with her.

I look around for a second and realize a lot more people are looking at her. She's never come to a party before. She's fresh meat and I can't stand the interest she brings out in the guys. She needs to go back home and go to fucking bed like she usually does on a Friday night.

This is my territory, baby, you're just a little sheep that walked right into the wolf's den.

6

JAMIE

Nails – Call Me Karizma

"Let's get you something strong," Emily says as we walk into the kitchen. I can sense the two guys we just passed drilling holes in my back. Or at least I hope it's my back.

"Em, I told you I'm not drinking," I reply. I must have told her about fifty times by now.

I'm so uncomfortable. The music is loud, the skirt I borrowed from my mom is too big at the waist and I keep having to rearrange it. I also had to take a white t-shirt from Emily because I dropped my matte red lipstick on mine while I was applying it. As a result, I'm now wearing a t-shirt twice my size and I definitely don't fill up the boob part.

Mainly, I'm dreading the moment Em will bump into her cheerleader friends and leave me to fend for myself. I guess I'll just head home at that point.

"Will you stop being so grumpy?" Em turns back to me from the kitchen counter holding two red cups. As if she just heard my thoughts, she adds, "I told you I'm here for you and with you. You can meet my friends, if you don't feel comfortable, we'll just hang the two of us."

I force a smile and grab the cup. "I promise I'll make an effort. What's in this?"

"Oh, it's just…"

I don't hear the end of her sentence. My gaze locks with Jake's and I'm suddenly short of breath. I don't know if it's because he looks more handsome than ever – his black jeans and black tee hug his perfect muscles, especially his chest and arms, making him look like the sculpture of a Greek God – or if it's the current look he's throwing my way.

His eyes are darker than the ocean in the middle of a storm. His jaw is ticking and there is pure hatred in his look. I instantly feel uncomfortable. There's always that energy around him. It's a mix of danger and fascination. I'm pretty sure this is what the devil looks like. Forbidden, desirable, magnetic.

I want to look away, but he's got a hold on me and I can't seem to move. I want this to end and, at the same time, I don't want the warmth in my lower belly to ever go away. I'm completely under the spell and I wish I could just walk over and put my lips on his, but I know better. He's not doing this because he wants me to walk over to him. In fact, he wants the opposite. He wants me to turn around and walk out the door. Well, guess what Jake. I'm here to party and party I will.

"Uh, remember we're trying to make friends with them, not get ourselves killed. Why is he looking at you like that?"

"Because I threatened to spill about his little friend Sam," I say between gritted teeth.

"I don't get if he wants to kill you or fuck you. Maybe both."

I turn to grab the cup Emily is handing me and when I

turn back to him, he is still looking daggers at me. I give him a smile, tilt the cup toward him in a 'cheers' movement, and drink a few sips. This shit is strong, what the hell did she put in here?! I try to keep my face as normal as possible as the alcohol burns down my throat. Jake's nostrils flare up and he takes a step towards me, but Rose suddenly gets in his way.

"You'll never guess who's here," I hear her say.

Emily walks into my line of vision and offers me her widest grin. "Ready to have some fun baby?"

I take another sip of my drink and smile at her, the alcohol now soothing my throat instead of burning it. She takes my hand and leads me back to the living room where everyone is dancing. The music is not my style, but it still makes me want to dance.

Emily and I start dancing with each other. She's a good dancer and attracts a lot of the boys' attention. Her curves move to the rhythm of the music like she doesn't care who's watching and a few minutes later we're surrounded by multiple guys trying to get her attention. She doesn't even look at them, not giving them an ounce of hope, and focuses on me. She grabs my hips and helps me loosen up to the rhythm of *Taki Taki*.

A few songs later, we're dancing close to each other and laughing at the guys' jaws dropping to the floor. Emily notices something behind me and leans down to talk directly in my ear.

"Don't turn around but Chris is coming our way." She talks so close to my ear that I can hear her over the music while no one else can. The only fact that I hear the name 'Chris' coming out of my friend's mouth sends my heart into a frenzy.

A second later I feel a hand squeeze my arm gently and

Chapter 6

I turn to Chris as he slides his hand from my arm to between my shoulder blades. He says something but I can't hear him, and I point at my ears and shake my head. He smiles brightly and points at the door leading to the patio with his thumb. I turn to Em hesitantly and she nods excitedly.

In a wave of braveness, I put my left hand around his bicep, nod to him, and mouth 'let's go'.

Oh my God, his arm is huge.

Once in the never-ending backyard, we sit down at a table on the wooden patio and watch for a few seconds as some boys throw some girls in underwear in the pool and jump after them.

"It's so nice to see you at a party for once," he grins at me.

"I couldn't do senior year without at least going to one, could I?"

He chuckles. "No, you couldn't. I hope I'll see you out more." His eyes are tracking my body movements and I shiver. I cross my legs, trying to act confident as I straighten my spine.

"You never really struck me as a party guy," I admit, "I mean we've been competing for top of the school all our lives and my life consists of school and homework. I'm starting to get really jealous that you party every weekend, make zero effort, and still are making me work for that first place."

This time he laughs out loud, it's deep and light at the same time. I'm brought back to the feelings I poured out on the letter I had given him when we were ten.

"I promise you, I spend a lot of time studying to keep up with you. Neither of us stand a chance anyway now that Rose is in our year." He shrugs. "And these parties must be what keeps me in second place, I guess. I don't even enjoy them that much. I think I'm more like you."

"Like me?" I ask. "What does that even mean?"

"You know, staying at home with a good book"

There's a flash of something in his eyes, it's almost like envy. Does he envy me because I have no social life? I move my chair closer to him and put a hand on his knee. The alcohol must have made me crazy brave to go beyond the first rejection.

"Hey, you're more than welcome to read a book at home with me anytime. It's thrilling," I reply with humor in my tone. My brain is somehow scared he's going to think I'm serious. I mean, I am but I don't want him to think I am. Please take it as a joke.

He lets out another laugh and I feel like I want to hear this sound forever. He puts his hand on mine holding his knee and squeezes gently before locking his gaze with mine. His beautiful amber eyes are so sincere compared to Jake's deep blue ones. Jake's are freezing and cruel. Chris's make me want to bathe in their warmth.

"You're so precious, Jamie," he states. "Honestly, there are no other girls like you in our school and, I just want to say, I'm always here for you, whatever you need."

I swallow his words and my gaze drops to our locked hands against his jeans. It's my right hand on his right knee and I'm twisted in a way that I'm almost facing him. I place my left hand on his arm and, in a final act of courage, I lean in slowly. Before I can close my eyes and get too close to his face, Chris lifts his hand from mine and cups my cheek, stopping me in my tracks.

"Jamie," he hesitates.

He frowns and the look in his eyes says it all.

Oh no. This is not good. Not good at all.

Chapter 6

I can tell he's looking for the right words not to hurt me. *Kill me. Kill me right now.*

I'm about to get turned down by Chris Murray for the second time in my life.

"I'm so sorry," he shakes his head as he talks, "I've completely sent the wrong signals. I– I meant I'm here for you as a friend."

"Oh God," are the only words that manage to pass my lips.

"Please don't be upset. You're an amazing girl, any guy would be so lucky to have you. I– just...not me. I promise you, you don't want that."

"This is fourth grade all over again," I mutter more to myself than him.

"What?" he asks surprised.

"In fourth grade, I wrote you this–"

"Letter, I know," he cuts me off. "But this is nothing like it. In fourth grade, I was just a stupid boy who didn't want anything to do with girls."

"Now you don't want anything to do with me." Tears form in my eyes and I will them not to drop.

What is wrong with me? This shouldn't make me cry but within seconds a single tear leaves my eye and lands on his hand cupping my cheek. *This is so embarrassing.*

I can see he cares and starts panicking, he fully turns to me and grabs both my cheeks in his big hands. He runs his thumb under my eye and wipes away my tear. I'm just here, helpless, a prisoner of my own emotions and speechless at my stupidity.

"No, no, please don't cry. I'm so sorry. That's not what I meant. I meant back then I hadn't realized what an impressive girl you would turn out to be and I was just too blind to see it. Now it's different, I appreciate you more than you think, Jamie. You're smart and stunning and I'm the one who's not for you."

I shake my head and get out of his hold, anger boiling in my chest. "I understand you're not interested, Chris, but don't be that kind of guy. 'It's me, not you'. I know you're trying to be sweet but I'm no charity case. I can handle a guy not liking me."

"Look," he admits. "All I'm trying to say is; you're great but I'm not looking for anything. My life is school, these stupid parties and making sure the twins stay in line and aren't sent back into the system. I can promise you that's all my energy goes to."

"They don't deserve you. Your life shouldn't be all about them. Rose is cocky and rude, and Jake is full of himself and..." I hesitate for a second. The alcohol has gone to my head and I'm blurting out information. "...dark." I conclude.

"He is," he concedes after a few seconds. "They both are."

"Why did you defend me against Jake if you've no interest in me? Why would you do this?" I ask annoyed. I know it doesn't make sense. He defended me because he's my friend and I'm the one being stupid, but I can't help it.

Not every guy being nice to you is hitting on you, Jamie.

"Because Jake is not just fun and games. He's got a shady past. I like you, you're my friend, you're a good person and I don't want him to involve you in his life. He's my best friend, fuck, he's my brother, but you deserve better, Jamie. Don't let him drag you down his fucked-up slope just because he's haunted by demons he can't handle"

I bite the inside of my cheek for a second, hesitating to tell him what I know. He cares for the twins, it shows, and they're going behind his back, hiding things from him.

"What?" he asks worried. "What do you want to say?"

Chapter 6

"Nothing," I smile. Not only is this not my business but I'm not exactly looking to be on the wrong side of Jake right now.

Chris is anything but stupid though, and he senses something is up. His gaze alternates between both my eyes, dancing a sidestep as he tries to figure out what I'm thinking.

"Why did I have to intervene?" he asks.

"What?"

"In class, the way he was holding you. Not okay. But why was he doing it?"

"Uh..." I look for an excuse with an alcohol-slowed brain.

"Please, tell me," he insists.

My silence makes him continue. "Are they in trouble? If you think it's bad, just tell me, Jamie. Please."

I take my cup on the table and down it in one go, giving myself more courage. I lock my eyes with his and finally let it out.

"Do you know who Samuel Thomas is?"

His expression shifts from empathetic to confused in a split second. "Where did you hear this name?"

"Monday, after school. When Jake and Rose were talking to him in the parking lot."

"No, you must have gotten it wrong."

"Tall, dark hair, British accent. They call him Sam. I know what I saw."

He gets up from his chair with such force it falls back. The confusion has been replaced with fury. He points at me in a schooling way. "You. You stay away from this shit. You get me?"

"What? Why?"

He leaves the patio with a determined walk, not bothering to answer me. That's when it hits me: he's going to tell Jake.

Shit!

I jump from my seat and run after him but as soon as I'm back inside the crowd overtakes me. Chris is nowhere to be seen and the party has gone out of control. The music is loud and thumping in my ears, a couple are in their underwear against furniture, getting down to business in front of everyone. A guy is snorting coke from a girl's belly on the dining table. People are dancing, crowded and sweaty, jumping to the beat.

I need to find Em. No, I need a drink. No, I need to pee first. I need a quiet place to gather my thoughts and calm down. I also really need to pee so bathroom it is.

I spot Jake on a sofa. Camila is straddling him, kissing his neck, and his hands are holding her ass tightly. A wave of jealousy overtakes me, and I feel sick to my stomach.

You knew that would happen, Jamie.

Of course, I knew. They broke up on Monday. They were bound to be back together by Friday. It doesn't matter that Jake gave me attention during the week and that my body responded to it. Ultimately, he's Camila's.

At least Chris hasn't gotten to him yet. I'm going to the bathroom and I'm leaving this party. I need to text Emily and let her know.

I struggle to turn away from Jake and Camila but when I see her taking over his mouth and him gripping her hair possessively, it's too much. I turn around and make a beeline down the hall. The bathroom must be one of the doors I passed on my way back to the living room.

I try the first door but it's a closet and I can hear moans coming from behind the coats. People need to get a hold of themselves, is everyone just *that* horny?

Chapter 6

I close the door in a hurry and walk to another one, the music has turned clubbier. Beat and bass are ringing in my ears and I'm suffocating. I'm hot from the alcohol and while I'm not *drunk,* I'm definitely not sober.

Where is this fucking bathroom?!

A door opens on my right and I see Rose stumbling out of the bathroom. I expect to see someone after her but she's on her own – Stoneview rumors tend to include Rose, sex and bathrooms. She wipes her nose a few times and stashes a tiny plastic bag in her back pocket. *Oh.*

"Goody," she smiles at me, her voice raspier than usual. I realize that she's dressed exactly like Jake except her black jeans are skinny and her black t-shirt is falling off her right shoulder, showing her black lace bra and making it all in all a lot more feminine than Jake's outfit.

"Are you okay?" I ask worriedly. Is she going to die? Overdose? Does she usually take drugs? *Why do I care?* When she learns that I've told Chris about Sam she's going to kill me.

"I'm perfectly fine," she replies, slowly walking to me. At least she can walk in a straight line. "Hey, can I tell you something," she says as she stops right in front of me. She's so close I can smell her. It's unbelievably sweet for someone with her personality.

"Uh, yeah," I hesitate, my throat drying up from the closeness.

She looks down at me and locks her ocean eyes with mine, a cocky smirk plastered on her face. God, she's tall. I have to look up to meet her eyes. The heat from her closeness is starting to warm me. She smells like whiskey and flowers in the spring. This defines Rose just right, the perfect balance between badass and feminine.

She slowly raises her hand and glides it in my long hair.

Her other hand tilts my chin higher before sliding to my neck, my arm and finally settling on my waist.

"That leather skirt looks very good on you," she says, her eyes not leaving mine and slowly licking her upper lip with the tip of her tongue.

My heart is beating a hundred. million. miles. per. hour. *This*. This is the Rose White effect. You hear it from everyone at school. She's so seductive everyone falls for her. Hell, people fall for her when she's not trying and right now, she's definitely trying. I'm speechless and I'm surprised the heat radiating from my body isn't burning her hands.

Wait. *Am I gay?*

Surely, I would know by now, wouldn't I?

"I–" I lick my bottom lips, why does my mouth feel so dry? "Thanks."

She chuckles. "No, thank you. Really. Bathroom is all yours." She steps back and I feel the spell lifting. I shake my head like crazy, not really understanding what just happened. I make a beeline for the bathroom and lock the door behind me.

I'm not even into Rose. I'm just drunk. My stomach tightens at the embarrassment. I push my back against the door and slide down to the floor. What is wrong with me? I need to start learning to read the signs.

You know what? People need to stop sending me the wrong signs!

Parties are just not for me. This is the first and last party I will go to. I feel sick thinking about what Chris just told me. He's not interested. He never was. How could I have been so stupid to think that Chris Murray wanted me?

Chris is into girls that are the total opposite of me. I hate to give into the rumors but this one feels too true to ignore.

Too many girls at school have talked about Chris and Jake's 'sexcapades'. They like sharing.

That's why Camila hates Chris. When she started dating Jake she thought, Chris, being the nice one of the group, would have her back if Jake slipped. Instead, they're always having their fun behind her back.

Chris likes girls that are wild enough to have threesomes. Too bad for me I'm just a regular 17-year-old who doesn't take drugs, indulge in sex parties and live the high life like Stoneview's finest. I guess I thought if he cared for me, I might be able to change him.

But who am I kidding? Why would it be different with me? Chris is wrong, I'm not smart. Not smart at all. I'm pretty stupid actually.

I hear a familiar voice behind the door and stand to attention.

"Hi, love," the British voice says, and I distinctively recognize it as Sam's.

I'm brought back to the beginning of the night. 'You'll never guess who's here' Rose said to Jake.

I stand up and put my ear to the door.

"Please be kind and *piss off*." She says the last two words in her best British accent, and it makes him chuckle.

"Come, we need to have a chat," he replies in a more serious voice,

"Do I look like I want to die? Go away."

There's a few seconds of silence cut by Rose's furious voice.

"Ow...fuck, let go. Sam. Let go..." her voice dies down and a few seconds later I don't hear them anymore.

Tonight is my night of braveness – or stupidness however you want to call it – so I open the door and look around. Surely, they didn't go back to the busy living room. I follow the hallway in the direction opposite to the party and go up a flight of stairs that are too narrow to be the main stairs.

I reach another hallway, it's much quieter than downstairs and no one seems to have wandered to this bit of the house. This part looks slightly older and there are three doors. I open the first one and enter what looks like a studio apartment. I quickly realize that I'm in the help's quarter. Is this really a thing rich people have? How 18th century.

I leave the small studio as soon as I understand it's completely empty. I hear two voices down the hall and follow. There's light coming from a door that's been left ajar. I silently walk to the side of the door, giving myself access to see them without being seen.

'Curiosity killed the cat, Jamie' I hear my mom's voice. I smile when I remember what six-year-old Jamie used to reply. '*I'm not a cat, mommy. I'm a detective.*'

You're a nosy bitch, that's what you are. My inner voice reminds me.

Rose is standing in front of Sam and for once she's got a serious face on. He, however, is looking at her with a sneer on his face.

"I can't believe you're avoiding me. That hard to admit you missed me?" he states.

"If you think I missed you, you're even more fucked up than I thought," she replies through gritted teeth.

I can see her jaw ticking and she's holding her fists tight against her side. He takes a few steps to be closer to her and grabs her chin tilting her face up. Rose is tall but Sam is a giant. He gives Chris a good run for his money when it comes to height. She looks in his eyes for a few seconds. I know this look, it says everything, tells a thousand stories. Mainly it portrays the truth: she likes him. She quickly snaps back into her role and slaps his hand away before shoving him in the shoulder.

"Don't," she growls.

"Fuck, Rose, you were so much more fun when you were in love with me. What happened to you? Is it because I never gave you a chance? It's not too late to admit it."

"I wasn't in love with you. It was just a kid's fantasy. Get over yourself."

He chuckles at her, mocking her. "Right, you tell yourself what you can to forget about me, love." He grabs a phone from his back pocket. "Did you score from Roy and Carlo tonight?"

She shrugs and avoids his gaze.

"Rose. I just asked you a question. I know you're high off your face right now. So tell me: did you get it from Roy and Carlo, yes or no?"

"What if I did," she tilts her chin up in defiance.

"Don't. They're still selling Volkov's shit. By next week they'll be selling mine and you can go back to your dirty habit."

Her eyes widen in shock. "They will...what? Are you out of your fucking mind, Sam? You turned the Diaz brothers on Volkov? Are you trying to get them killed?!"

"They'll be fine," he shrugs. "They've got my protection now."

Rose runs her hands on her face and in her hair in a stressful gesture. "Are you done? I'm leaving"

"Nope. Take this." He hands her the phone he just got out and she takes it lazily.

"What do you want me to do with that?"

"It's a burner. Got a few errands for you and Jake to do. Make sure they're done on time," he orders.

She frowns, slowly understanding. "No, no, no. Sam,

you're not getting us involved." She tries to pass him the phone back, but he grabs her wrist, pulls her to his chest, and grabs her jaw with his free hand. She twists but he holds tighter.

Should I burst in? But if I do, I might miss important info and I have to keep an eye on my ultimate goal. I need to know how to find the Wolves.

"Rose, love, listen to me. You guys are involved. Period. You were involved before coming to Stoneview. Running away to a rich family doesn't change shit. You two do what you're told, and we'll discuss keeping you out of future shit."

He lets go of her and she takes a few steps back, looking daggers at him and massaging her jaw.

"Your family needs you. Don't disappoint."

He turns to leave, and I sprint back down the stairs.

This is worse than I thought. The twins are neck-deep in this.

I only stop running when I'm out of the house, past the driveway, and back on the street.

I need to talk to Emily about this. I need to bring her home with me and tell her what I just saw. There is too much information for me to handle on my own. I turn around to walk back to the house and hit against a hard chest.

"Ow," I exclaim and take a step back looking up as a hand grabs my arm tightly.

Fuck.

Jake is looking down at me, furious. The hate emanating from his body is burning through his hand and on my arm.

"You," he growls.

He knows I told Chris.

My brain goes on high alert and the drunken feeling I had completely disappears.

Chapter 6

"Wait, let me explain," I say, helplessly shaking my head.

"Yeah, you've got a lot of explaining to do." He drags me with him up Camila's driveway.

"What are you doing? Wait!"

He doesn't listen and doesn't let go until we're by a black G-Wagon. He opens the passenger door, throwing me inside. I barely have time to pull my arm away before he slams the door.

I look around the car and take three deep breaths. Each one makes me tremble a little more and Chris' words ring back in my ears. 'Don't let him drag you down his fucked-up slope just because he's haunted by demons he can't handle.'

What kind of demons? The kind that had him involved in Sam's gang when he was barely a teenager? The kind that you pick up when you've been in the system for too long? When you've been in so many families that you lost the meaning of it? Seen too much that forced you to age too early?

The slamming of his door makes me jump out of my thoughts.

"Seatbelt," he says coldly as he starts the car.

"This isn't your car," I reply.

Really, Jamie? That's what you're worried about?

"Shut. Your. Mouth. Do you know what that means? Clearly not since you went and told Chris about Sam. Out of all the people you could have told...Chris," he seethes. A cold chill runs down my spine.

I slowly fasten my seatbelt as he backs out of the driveway and onto the road. He speeds down Stoneview and I hold onto the door.

"Have you been drinking?" I ask worriedly. I don't want to die because the bastard doesn't get it's not a good idea to drink and drive.

"If you don't stop talking, I'm going to hurt you, Jamie." The way his voice stays calm when he says this makes me shiver. It's *so* calm.

I swallow the lump in my throat and try to quiet down the voice in my head that screams, *he's going to hurt you anyway!*

After minutes of driving in silence, he finally stops the car. I recognize where we are straight away. It's the parking lot at the bottom of the trail that leads to Stoneview lake. The lake in the middle of thick, dark woods. He gets out of the car, slams the door, and walks to my side to open my door.

"Out."

I unlock my seatbelt with trembling hands as I try to compose myself. He won't hurt me. He's not that bad. He just wants to scare me because he's mad but really, how far can he go?

He was part of a gang, Jamie. He's probably killed people before.

Of course he hasn't. Don't be ridiculous.

I ease out of the car, my eyes slowly adapting to the darkness.

"Why are we here?" I ask.

He doesn't answer and shoves me forward toward the start of the trail instead. "Be quiet and walk."

I take a step forward then stop. "Jake, I'm not walking with you to the woods in the middle of the night. If you have something to say to me, you can say it here."

He's still standing behind me and I'm about to turn around when I feel something cold at the back of my head.

In a split second, my heart free falls from my chest and a heaviness settles in my stomach.

Chapter 6

"Who said I have anything to say to you?" he says in a mocking tone.

He can't. He can't possibly have a gun. *Please let it not be a gun.*

As if he heard my thoughts, he pushes against my head. "Usually when people have a gun to their head, they execute orders, Jamie. Now shut that beautiful mouth of yours and walk."

I start walking. Because what choice do I have?

We walk in silence for what feels like fifteen minutes and all I can say to myself is that he's doing this to scare me because my brain simply won't register that I'm going to be shot dead in the woods.

The trail slowly disappears, and he guides me off-track completely until we're so deep in the woods that the moonlight barely makes it through the thick tree branches. I don't know if I feel cold because I'm in a skirt and tee in a forest in the middle of the night or if it's because I don't know if I'll still be alive in five minutes.

"Stop here," he orders. "Turn around".

I stop and turn around to face him. I wrap myself with my arms to try and stop my body from shivering but at this point, I think there's no use.

Jake looks at me and shakes his head in disappointment. "I told you to keep your mouth shut about Sam, didn't I?"

"Really, Jake? You're going to do this because I told your best friend about some random drug dealer you used to know?"

I know he's not just some random drug dealer but I'm trying to minimize the problem here.

"I asked you something so simple, Jamie. And I warned you about the consequences. This is serious shit and you took it as a game."

"What's your plan here? Scaring me into backing off? You don't want to lose your golden boy image so bad that you just eliminate whoever knows the truth about you? I'm not interested in your life, Jake, but if you think you can intimidate me into *anything* you got me all wrong. It'll take a little more than an unloaded gun and a dark forest to scare me."

He chuckles but it only lasts a split second. "You're playing brave with the wrong person here."

I know I am. But I can't just let him frighten me into keeping my mouth shut. He does it once and he'll think he can do whatever he wants with me.

"I have a game for you, Goody." He slides the magazine out and looks at the bullets inside, proving me the gun *is*, in fact, loaded.

He's doing this to scare you. Just to scare you. Stay strong.

It's easy to think, it's harder to act out on it. My heart picks up so hard, my eardrums tremble.

Jake slams the magazine back into place. "If you make it to the car before I catch you, I'll let you off with a warning." He slides the top, loading a bullet. "If I catch you…we're gonna have a lot of fun before I kill you."

I can feel my eyes growing in shock before I register his words. Shock? It's not just shock, it's terror. Absolute. Terror. My blood is slowly freezing, milliliters by milliliters.

He takes a slow step toward me before whispering, "Run."

I don't think. I act. My legs move before I can take in a breath and I'm running through the dark forest.

Before I was born, my parents used to live on the North Shore of the Falls. Aaron lived there for the first few years of his life. Me, I've only ever lived in Stoneview. We never went on holiday, dad was just too busy, so my whole childhood was spent in these woods and I know them like the back of my hand. It doesn't matter that it's dark and silent. I could find my way out of here in my sleep.

I sprint through the night like my life depends on it. I think it does.

I don't have time to let rational thoughts in my head. I don't have time to weigh if a high school teenager would really be capable of putting a bullet in my head. I know nothing of Jake White's background or past and I'm not going to take my chances anymore tonight.

I run for my life. I run because Jake was involved in a gang. Because he is dangerous. I can think of the humiliation later. Once I'm at home safe and alive.

Years of playing center on the lacrosse field has given me good endurance and speed but I can't compare with someone twice my size. Soon enough I can hear Jake's running footsteps behind me and his cruel laughter make it past the wind in my ears.

"Quick, Goody. You're almost there," he exclaims behind me.

I see the parking lot at the edge of the woods and double my speed despite my lungs begging me to stop. When my feet slam on the asphalt, I bend to the right to reach his car. I need to get in, lock the door, call the police.

I'm close enough to touch the car when I feel a weight slamming into my back. My legs can't take it and I'm pushed to the ground. My hands and knees take the fall, the rough ground peeling at my skin. I whimper at the sharp pain before rolling on the floor. Miraculously, I manage not to hit my head.

"Got ya," Jake smiles as we stop rolling. He managed to get himself on top of me and in a split second his gun is below my mouth, pointing up. "How did you like the run? So much fun to give you false hope, isn't it?"

"You're a psychopath," I pant. I'm out of breath, completely exhausted and he looks like he didn't break a sweat.

I don't wait for him to reply. I need to get myself out of this situation. I should have done this when we were still in Stoneview and people were around. It doesn't matter. I have to try. I take in a deep breath and let out a strident scream. I scream again for help and another time, almost breaking my vocal cords before Jake gets to slam a hand over my mouth.

"Are you stupid? No one is going to hear you here."

"Please, let me go," I beg once his hand is off my mouth. The lump in my throat gets bigger and I struggle to swallow back the tears. "You can't just kill me."

"Not so brave now, are we? Are you scared yet? Or does it take more than a gun and a dark forest?"

I flinch at the words I used a minute ago. I was scared then, I'm terrified now.

The click of the gun brings back horrible memories and I shake my head to make them go away. My scar is burning through my skin. I look away from him as the tears start rolling down my face. "Jake-"

"What?" he cuts me off. "If you're not about to finish this sentence with 'I'm sorry for disobeying' then you can save your breath."

I can't look at him. He's so heavy, I'm struggling to breathe, and the tears are now freely flowing.

I can't believe I used to find him attractive. Just like any girl in our school, I've spent my high school years fantasizing about Jake White. But there is nothing attractive about a sociopath like him.

Chapter 6

He runs the barrel of the gun up and down my cheek smearing my tears over my face.

"Are you? Sorry?"

I nod multiple times because I'll do anything to not meet the same fate as my father. Is this how dad felt when Volkov's man killed him? Was the last thing he saw the hatred and coldness in his eyes?

"Then say it," he orders.

"I-I'm sorry," I sob.

"Mm...look at you, you're such an Angel." He thinks for a second. "You're so hot under me, Goody. You know that?"

I bite back the insults I want to throw in his face and look behind him to avoid looking at him. There's something curling inside my gut, lower actually. It's my lower belly. It tingles with excitement and grips at me, but I'm forced to ignore it as fear takes over.

"So, tell me now. Are. You. Scared?"

I nod multiple times because, fuck, I'm so scared.

"Good," he smiles. He gets off me and puts the gun at the back of his jeans. "It's called survival instinct. Don't forget that feeling when you're around me."

He offers his hand and I grab it to help myself up, shaking like a leaf.

I don't know what I would have preferred, dying with my dignity or being alive and live with the humiliation of what just happened.

"Let's go, Angel."

He puts a hand on the small of my back as he helps me inside the car. I get in without complaining and wrap my arms around my body. I feel like the shivering is never going to stop. I'm cold to the core. I hate him. But I hate myself most, because now that I'm not overtaken by fear of death, I know exactly how my body was reacting to having him so close. To having his bodyweight crushing me. It was exactly the same as all the other times it reacted positively to Jake this week. I refuse to spell it out to myself, but my heart picks up at the idea of pleasure.

I need to see a shrink. A therapist. Someone needs to tell me that all of this was wrong, and that a game of cat and mouse is *not* sexy. It's dangerous and stupid. And with the wrong person, I could end up seriously hurt.

Jake starts the car as his phone rings. He connects it to the car speakers and starts driving away.

"Hey, babe," he says sweetly.

"*Where are you?*" Camila's voice resonates through the car and I break down in a silent sob against the door. Jake is back to his school's favorite boy act.

That's what Camila gets. She gets the sweet guy whose worst flaw is that he struggles to stay faithful.

I get the devil that drags you to the woods and threatens you with a gun.

"I just went to drop Rose home. I'll be back soon," he replies.

"*Ok, hurry I miss you. Party's still going but I'm ready to take you upstairs.*"

"Mm, I can't wait." He hangs up and talks to me without even glancing at me. "Where to, Angel? Wanna go back to the party and keep hitting on Chris?"

"Home." My voice is raspy and my throat hurts.

He turns to me and raises his eyebrows. "Is this really how you're going to talk to me? Did our little time together not teach you anything?"

I hit my head against the window in frustration. "Please, Jake, just take me home...please"

He smiles and turns back to the road. "That's more like it. Address."

I tell him my address and he lazily puts it in the GPS.

I try to look at anything but him and finally settle on a dirty spot on the passenger window.

When he parks on the sidewalk in front of my house, I open my door as quickly as possible, but he grabs the back of my neck and drags me back in before I can get out fully.

"Are you gonna talk about Sam again, Angel?"

"Please don't call me that."

He tightens his grip and I wince. "I'll call you whatever the fuck I want. Now answer my question."

I take a deep breath, "No. No, I won't."

"Good girl. Really, that's all I wanted from the beginning. It didn't have to get to this point." I can't reply to him. Maybe I should have listened since the beginning?

No. No, Jamie. Don't let him turn this around.

"You should get some rest. And you know what, I think those parties really aren't for you. Let me not catch you at another one."

He doesn't release his grip and I shift in my seat. "Can I go now?"

In an unexpected gesture, he pulls my head closer to his and drops a soft kiss on my temple.

"Goodnight, Angel," he says as he finally releases my neck. I don't move for a few seconds, frozen by the shock of his gesture.

Images of the woods flashback in front of my eyes and I jump out of the car before sprinting to my front door.

Jake White has officially shown his true form to me and it's not a pretty sight.

It's cold, scary, dangerous. And despite my reluctance...

Exciting.

7

JAMIE

Call It What You Want – Taylor Swift

The shower I take before bed doesn't stop the shivering, neither do the warm pajamas, nor going under my huge comforter. Sleep comes easily but I know it's going to be a tormented one by the way my body won't stop shaking.

My dad is on his knees, wearing his Sheriff uniform and his badge, begging Volkov's men to let me and Aaron go.

"Please, please you'll get back the money you lost. I'll pay back every last dollar. Just not my kids. Please. Kill me. Take me but not my kids."

The man in the dark hoodie turns to Aaron and me in the corner of the room. We're sitting down against the wall, knees to our chest. Aaron is holding me to his chest and running his hand up and down my back to calm my cries and shivers.

"It's okay," he whispers. "It'll be fine. We'll all be fine. I promise, 'Me."

The man approaches us slowly and I can't breathe. The room smells of sweat and blood and the scent is crushing. I hold Aaron tighter at every step the guy takes. I'm only looking at his feet, not daring to look up.

"I think one of you is going to have to serve as a lesson to your old man, kids," he says in a mocking tone. "Get up. Both of you."

Aaron slowly gets up, I know he must be looking right into his eyes, daring him to do something. I can't. I can't look up. I just want to leave. I just want to go home.

As my brother gets up, he grabs my arm, his other hand still on my back.

I struggle to stand still on my shaking legs, and he whispers to me again. "It's okay. I won't let anything happen to you."

His height means he can wrap me against him, my head against his chest, and protect me. Like he always does. He protects me. Everything is going to be fine.

I finally look up, my brother's courage overtaking my fear.

The last thing I see is his face, his pale face, steel grey eyes, and the scar that runs from his left eye all the way to the bottom of his jaw.

"You sure kid?" the man says to Aaron. "You sure you can protect her?"

White light blinds me, and I scream. I scream so hard it burns my throat. My shoulder is on fire. I can feel Aaron's arms tightening around me. My head is against his as we both fall to the ground. His body is heavy on mine. So heavy I can barely breathe. I'm suffocating, his weight is crushing my ribs and I can't take another breath. Stars start dancing in front of my eyes and the room slowly darkens. I just need to take a breath. Just. Another...

I wake up gasping as I sit up.

I take three long breaths and put a hand to my scar. It

hurts, too deep for my touch to change anything but damn it hurts. I scratch my throat trying to ease the stinging pain, but it still hurts from screaming in my sleep. I wait a few seconds, expecting mom to burst in the room like she always does when I have night terrors.

When she doesn't, it hits me. The woods, the gun…Jake. I didn't scream in my sleep. My throat hurts from screaming for help.

I take my head in my hands and wipe the tears that are spilling uncontrollably. I should have never gone to that party. I should have never told Chris. What good did it do anyway? He's probably given Rose and Jake a good scolding and on Monday they'll be the solid group they've always been. They're family. Who am I? No one. Just the girl Jake terrorized in the woods before going back to his girlfriend.

I check the time, four am. I can't sleep and I'm going to look like a zombie at the coffee shop tomorrow.

I'm cold. I can't seem to warm my hands and my feet. I don't think it comes from the temperature in the room. It comes from me, from my core.

When mom bursts into my room on Sunday morning, wearing her Sunday outfit, she walks all the way to my bed.

"Sweetie, I let Saturday go because you went to a party, and the shop wasn't busy, but I won't let you skip Church. Hangovers aren't meant to last two days. Come on, get up."

Yesterday, I found the stupid hangover excuse to avoid going to work. She wasn't happy but it was better than to say I didn't want to get out of the house by fear of bumping into Jake or any of his friends. Emily called and texted, but I don't have the strength to take that either.

Chapter 7

I squint my eyes when my mom opens the curtains. "Mooom!" I whine as she sits on my bed.

"I'm taking you out for lunch after Church. Wear something nice, Pastor Gilligan is doing our service today. You know how he is," she rolls her eyes. Really, she loves him.

I sit up in a sudden movement. "Oooh Pastor Gilligan," I wiggle my eyebrows, teasing her. These two have always gotten along. Since dad passed away, he's been helping mom with everything. I know she likes him more than friends, but she would never admit that to herself. She doesn't want to do this to my dad. I'm sure she will move on, in her own time.

"Get ready please," she sighs at my silliness.

She leaves my room and I start looking for a dress in my wardrobe. I find a floral dress tight around my bust but that flows from my waist to just above my knees. That's church-y enough. There are still scratches on my knees from Friday night and I shiver at the memory. When I'm done getting ready, I shoot a text to Emily:

> Jamie: Can I call you after Church?

> Emily: Thanks for letting me know you're alive. You disappeared on me at the party and haven't picked up your phone since. Thank God your mom knows how to use a phone, unlike you!

I silently thank my mom for keeping Em in touch. I'm about to reply when she sends another text.

> Emily: I'm mad btw, in case you hadn't noticed.

Another beat before I see the three grey dots on the screen again.

> Emily: But yeah, call me after Church. Pray well my little angel. [praying emoji] [angel emoji]

My heart drops when I read her last word and Jake's voice rings in my ears. I grab my handbag and put my phone in it before hurrying out of the house, joining mom in our old red truck.

Mom parks in front of the Church and waves at her friend in the courtyard.

"I need to discuss something with Tricia. Can you bring the potato salad inside, sweetie?"

I nod. "I'll see you inside."

She hops out of the car and I take my time getting the salad for the get together after mass. We don't often stay but mom always brings something. She's very attached to this Church, it's the one where she got married. It's where we used to come every Sunday as a family.

Chapter 7

I open the truck door, put my bag on my shoulder and grab the salad from my lap. My hands still feel terribly cold and I shudder despite the sun shining and the clement temperature.

As I get out with one bowl of potato salad, I realize there's another one on the middle seat. *Really mom? Two bowls? We're not even having lunch here.*

I hug the first bowl against my left hip and grab the other one with my right hand. I take a step back and go to close the car door with my hip but my bag falls from my shoulder and I almost drop the bowl in my right hand.

"Damn it!"

"You might want to keep the blasphemy down," says a voice behind me.

I turn around and raise my eyebrows at the man in front of me as he continues talking in a whisper. "I'll let you in on the secret, that, right there," he points his thumb at the Church, "it's a Church."

I chuckle and take a few seconds to take him in. He's taller than me, my eyes level with his chest. He's wearing a white button-down shirt with the two top buttons opened and I can see tattoos creeping up. I can imagine his chest covered in them.

I look up to his face and get struck by the deep blue eyes. They are framed by thick, square, black glasses with a rounder edge at the bottom.

He has dirty blond hair pulled back and into a tight bun at the back of his head. A strand has escaped and is resting against his square jaw. He has a light, dark blond stubble spread on his cheeks and jaw. His plumped lips are in a small smile and he suddenly flashes me a gorgeous smile straight out of a Hollywood film.

He looks like Thor. My stupid brain giggles.

Only in a leaner way, more like a professional boxer rather than a big guy. The mix of the smart glasses, the haircut, the elegant suit, the tattoos and the strong physique are so opposite but somehow work perfectly on him, giving him a smart, leader vibe.

"Can I help you with that?" he asks, bringing me back down to earth.

"Oh, yes. Please. Thank you." I smile at him and let him grab one of the bowls. "As you can see my mom is planning on feeding the whole Church. I hope you're hungry."

As he grabs the bowl, I notice his hands are covered in tattoos too. All the way to his fingertips. They continue up until his shirt sleeves cover them and I'm guessing up his arms. He bites his lip for a split second and his gaze goes up and down my body.

"I'm starving actually," he says with a grin on his face.

I almost giggle like a silly girl but manage to turn it into a normal chuckle.

"I'm Nathan by the way." He extends his hand and I shake it.

"Jamie. Nice to meet you. You don't usually come here, do you?"

"No, I just moved here."

"I see. Well, you might want to button up your shirt. Pastor Gilligan is a bit...conservative. Not much you can do about the hands I guess."

"Oh, right." He grabs the other bowl from my hands, holding both of them in each hand. "Do you mind giving me a hand?"

I chuckle and shake my head. I start buttoning up his shirt and lock my gaze with his. "Is that how you hit on girls? Get them to button up your shirt and touch your chest," I tease.

"I don't know...maybe. Is it working? You don't have to touch my chest by the way, unless you really want to."

I let out a loud laugh. It feels so natural that I feel the weight of the weekend's events lifting off my body.

"I think it's working," I conclude as I finish the last button. I pat his chest and *damn* it's hard. I close the truck door and grab one of the bowls back.

He thanks me and we walk together towards the entrance when something suddenly hits me: I'm not cold anymore. The warmth creeping up from my body as Nathan holds the door to the Church open for me makes me feel light and comfortable. Above all, it makes me feel safe.

During the service, I don't think of Jake and what he did, I don't think of Friday night, of what I heard Sam say, of finding what happened to Aaron. My scar doesn't even burn anymore. No, the only thing that occupies my mind is the blond handsome guy sitting a few rows before me and mom.

I can't focus on any word coming from Pastor Gilligan. All I can focus on is Nathan's tattoos creeping up from his sleeves, his defined arms and his bun. I want to undo his hair and run my hand through it. I want him to pick me up and hold me against his strong chest. The heat building between my legs makes me shift on my seat. I imagine his mouth on said heat and-

"'Me! Are you listening?" I jump in my seat at my mom's voice.

Oh my Gosh, you're in a Church, Jamie, what is actually wrong with you?!

"What? What?" I say looking around as if I'd said my previous thoughts out loud.

"I'm going to talk with Pastor Gilligan, help set up lunch please."

I nod, desperately wanting to get up and get busy. I

hurry towards the long tables set on the side by the entrance and start unpacking all the food people have brought.

"So, are you here every Sunday?" a warm voice asks me.

I turn to Nathan as he helps me unwrap platters and bowls. "I am yes," I confirm. "Will I see you here again?"

He passes me a few serving spoons and we both dig them in the food. "I think, now that I can use it as an excuse to see you, yes."

I feel the heat building up my chest, quickly followed by my cheeks.

We look at each other's eyes for long seconds before I break it. I could let myself drown in his deep eyes but the intense intimacy we're sharing is starting to make me blush too much. I move a few steps to the side to put napkins on plates and he follows, his hand now in his black suit pants. He surely dressed smart for Sunday service.

"Will you go to school here? I go to Stoneview Prep," I try to say as casually as possible.

"Oh," he laughs. "Fuck. I'm so sorry. You looked...older." He takes a step back from me and runs a hand behind his neck before putting it back in his pocket.

"What?" I suddenly snap.

What?

I look up at him and it hits me. His traits, his stubble, his behavior, his *everything*. He's older. Older than me. Too old to go to school with me.

"I'm....eighteen. Almost," I say, trying to sound mature before I realize it has the opposite effect.

"And that's cute," he replies. "I'm sorry, I didn't mean to come onto you so hard earlier. The buttons, and the chest... You must think I'm some perv now."

I shake my head intensely. "No! No, of course not." It hadn't even crossed my mind that he could be older. An awkward silence falls on us and I try to pretend this revelation hasn't affected me.

"So, uh, how come you're moving to Stoneview?"

Silver Falls is the big city attached to Stoneview. Emily and I go when we want to go to a real mall rather than the shops on main street. Young adults usually prefer living in the big city rather than in expensive, unaffordable Stoneview.

"I have friends here I'm trying to reconnect with," he replies calmly. His behavior has shifted and he's clearly not hitting on me anymore.

"'Me! Let's go!" my mom shouts by the door.

"'Me?" he asks.

I shrug. "That's just how my friends and family call me. Ja*mie*, 'Me," I insist on the last syllable of my name to explain.

"And your boyfriend, does he call you that too?"

Ok maybe I was wrong. Maybe he's still hitting on me.

The warmth I've been feeling in my chest comes back and I smile at him. "No boyfriend in sight but I'd hope he would," I reply.

He gives me a lopsided smile and grabs his phone from his pants pocket. He unlocks it and gives it to me. I instantly get the message and write down my number quickly.

"I'll see you around, 'Me," he says taking a few steps back. He grins before turning around.

"Jamie Williams!" mom shouts from the door.

"Alright, I'm coming!"

Mom and I sit down at a booth in our favorite diner. It's a rundown place in-between Stoneview and Silver Falls. It's too cheap and old to be frequented by Stoneview's population, and it's just a little too out of the city for Silver Falls' population. There are so many restaurants, fast food and cafés in Silver Falls that no one would bother coming all the way down to Silver's. Still, this place runs on the regulars' visits and the fact that it has the best loaded nachos in the state of Maryland, according to my professional opinion.

Iris, the 60-year-old waitress, comes over to us straight away.

"Hi, Iris," I say in a bright smile.

"Hi doll, how have you been? Haven't seen you two in a while."

Mom shrugs, avoiding saying she couldn't afford taking us out for lunch and Iris understands straight away.

"Loaded nachos and a vanilla shake for you, doll?"

I nod excitedly, I've been having the same thing since I was nine years old.

"What can I get you, Caroline?" she asks my mom.

"Just a black coffee thanks, Iris."

She writes our order on her small pad and walks away. I don't even ask mom why she isn't ordering any food. She grew up being sent to debutante balls and forced to watch her weight despite having always been rather skinny. These sorts of things stay with you. Sometimes if she's a bit stressed or sad, she won't touch food for a few days.

Once I'm halfway through my nachos, mom slides her arm on the table and squeezes my hand tight.

"Sweetie," she starts.

"I knew there was something wrong," I cut her off.

She looks at me with a sorry face and anxiety overtakes me.

"What? What is it? Is it money? I can take up a real part time job mom. I can bring money back too. And I don't have to go to Stoneview Prep. I know dad saved a lot of money for me and Aaron to attend private school but I'm happy to go to Silver Falls High."

"The city pays for school, Jamie. Will you calm down?"

"What is it then?"

She hesitates a few seconds, avoiding my eyes. "I, um, Aunt Ruby is very ill."

"Oh no, I'm so sorry mom. What is it?"

I don't know my aunt very well, except that she's my mom's twin who still lives in Tennessee. Mom moved away to Maryland after meeting dad and once they had kids it was always the four of us. When she married him, mom's family stopped giving news and slowly, as time went, they stopped talking altogether.

I think they were more bothered by the fact that he was Filipino rather than him being ten years her elder. My grandparents both died before I met them, and mom would always say it was better this way. I guess they weren't too keen on meeting their mixed-race grandchildren. I know mom isn't close to her sister but I'm sure it still hurts to know your twin is ill.

"She's got lung cancer. It's too far ahead to do anything at this point. She's only got a few months left."

My heart aches at her tone. She sounds so sad.

"Mom..." I put my hand on hers, trying to soothe her. Tears start cascading from her usually sparkling green eyes, the same I inherited from her, and I get out of my side of the booth to sit on hers. I take her in my arms.

"I'm so sorry."

She calms down in my arms for a few seconds then pulls away wiping her tears.

"Sweetie, she asked me to be by her side in her last months."

My eyes widen at the nerve my aunt has to ask the sister she's ignored for years to travel all the way to Tennessee when she knows she's the only family member I have here.

"I'm going to go, 'Me," my mom blurts out looking at her hands twisting on her lap.

"Wh–what?"

My brain suddenly goes into overdrive. Am I going to have to move? Say goodbye to Emily? Go to live in the south because my aunt has decided she wants to make amends before dying? She probably doesn't even want that; she just doesn't have anyone else to call and take care of her and can't afford a carer.

"But mom, my school, my friends, lacrosse! I-I can't just leave it all. It's my senior year. Mom, I'm going to be valedictorian. How can we just drop everything? Our house…dad's town!"

I'm suddenly short of breath and mom shakes her head.

"Sweetie, sweetie breathe!"

I take three deep breaths and slowly calm myself down. I need to call Emily.

"'Me, I know all of that. That's why I'm not asking you to come."

My stomach twists as I swallow the news. "You're gonna leave me here? On my own?"

"It's up to you. Hope said you can stay over at Emily's as much as you like. The Bakers are letting me take an extended paid holiday from the shop and Pastor Gilligan said he'll pick you up from the house every Sunday to take you to Church. You don't even have to work at the shop if you don't feel like it. All you have to do is focus on your studies and let me take care of the rest."

The shop. We rarely talk about it.

Last year, I added together our bills and her wages and

quickly came to the conclusion that there was no way she could afford our rent, the food, my uniform, lacrosse, the car... When I confronted her about it, she didn't hesitate one second before admitting the truth. She stole from the till. More often than not.

Every lacrosse field trip, every hobby and extras in our lives were stolen money. The clothes on my back, the desserts on our table, the trips to the movies and our TV subscriptions. All. Stolen. Money. I never blamed my mom for what she does.

The Bakers pay her shit. They have chains of coffee shops and restaurants all over the country and my house could fit five times in theirs. They live a golden life and never gave my mom a raise. My mom lost her husband, she's raising me on her own. She's doing what she can, and a couple hundred dollars missing a month doesn't make much of a difference to them.

When she told me about this, she expected me to shame her because I'm a rule follower. Rules were *not* made to be broken in my opinion. But this was different, so I asked her to teach me.

Small town, no POS system, no cameras, and owners that never show up. It's just too easy. Now one order out of five paid cash we 'forget' to register on the till. We take the order, make the coffee and take the cash. If it's never been registered, the money can't be missing.

These stolen dollars are my pocket money. My trips to Silver Falls with Emily. My lacrosse kit. This meal is probably paid with the Bakers' money.

"How long will you be gone for?" I ask with a dry throat.

"I'm not sure, it could be six months, it could be one for all I know."

There's a long silence. It's so heavy that I almost

suffocate.

"You're almost eighteen, 'Me, and I trust you completely. I know you'll be fine on your own and if there are times you don't want to be on your own, you can go to the Joly's."

"I... guess."

I don't want to be on my own. I miss my dad and Aaron every day. I don't want to live without my mom as well. I know it won't be for long, but it still scares me.

"What if something happens?" I ask a lump in my throat.

This is what losing family members does to you. You live in fear that anything could happen at any time. I don't want to lose my mom. I want to keep her close.

"Aw sweetie, nothing will happen to me. I promise."

She takes me in her arms and holds me against her chest. If mom isn't here maybe it gives me more space to focus on finding my brother. I can spend more time working on this. Finding out what truly happened to him. I can make it my mission and when mom comes back, I'll have answers and, who knows, maybe more.

"Ok, mom." I pull away from her. "You go take care of Ruby. I'll stay here. But promise me that if you need anything you'll call? You'll ask me to come if it gets too hard."

"I promise, sweetie."

"When is your flight?" I ask.

"Oh, we can't afford flying, 'Me. I'm driving there."

"What? It's like a ten-hour drive from here to Franklin!"

"I'll do it in two days. Don't worry about me. I'm just sorry you won't have the truck."

I shrug, "Meh, what am I going to do with it without a license anyway? I've got my bike."

And just like that, I'm going to be all alone.

8

JAMIE

Trainwreck – Banks

I spent the rest of Sunday helping mom pack so she could leave this morning. It all happened so fast I'm not really realizing she's gone. I should feel more alone than ever but I'm not. All I'm thinking of is finding Aaron. I will not rest until I have answers. I will not rest until I know if he's alive or dead. And if he's alive I will find where he is, and I'll bring him back.

Emily and I are sitting outside, eating our lunches. It's such a beautiful day for mid-September. Jake didn't speak to me at all today, but it doesn't mean he ignored me. No, he throws me a knowing look every time he crosses my way. Like he's keeping an eye on me. Like he doesn't want to let go of the control he had on Friday night.

"Are you gonna spill what happened on Friday? I've got you at home every day now so don't think you're going to avoid this conversation."

"I'm not going to come to your house every day. Only

when your dad cooks," I joke and hope it will change the topic.

She laughs and pops a grape in her mouth.

"Hey, Em?"

"Mmh?"

"Please don't tell anyone my mom's not here."

She turns to me, raising an eyebrow as she swallows her grape, asking a silent question.

"I don't really want anyone to know I'm on my own. I know Stoneview is super safe but...we never know."

She nods. "'Course, 'Me. And you know you can come to mine anytime, really. Mom's getting another key cut today."

"You guys are amazing."

"Are you okay? Does you not wanting anyone to know have anything to do with your disappearance on Friday?"

I shrug. "I drank too much on Friday. Your drink was an absolute killer. I left early and spent Saturday with my first hangover ever. Not cool."

I lied to my best friend for the first time in my life. Jake's arctic eyes flash in my mind and I shiver. I can't. I can't tell her what happened. Because it makes it real. It makes the fear he put in me real. It makes my body's reaction real. The tingling in my lower belly and the shuddering coldness in my chest both opposite but very real.

Emily laughs and takes a few seconds settling back. "Alright, well next time make sure you text me. I was worried."

"I learned something though." I take a moment before I keep going. "About Samuel Thomas and the twins."

Emily straightens up and turns fully to me. "What did you learn?"

I run her through what I overheard Sam telling Rose and her eyes get wider at each sentence.

Chapter 8

"Jesus fucking Christ," she drops.

"Em!"

"I'm sorry. I'm sorry. Oh my Gosh, 'Me, this is huge! So, the Diaz brothers *do* work for Volkov. The rumors were true."

"At least until today apparently."

"Do you think the Whites used to be part of Sam's gang?"

I look away thinking. "I don't know...I guess. And now that he wants to take Stoneview from Volkov he's turning to them. You never really leave a gang, do you?"

"But they were so young," Emily pops another grape in her mouth.

"Yeah, that doesn't make sense," I agree.

"I guess they could have been put in a foster family that was involved in shady stuff and, you know, fall into it too. These things happen."

"Yeah," I confirm. "That's a possibility. No matter what happened, that's not my focus," I say trying to avoid talking about Jake. "My focus is knowing more about Aaron and so finding out more about Volkov. If Sam is stealing the Diaz brothers from the Wolves, then he must know *a lot* about them."

"Of course he knows about them, baby, you know what they say." She wiggles her eyebrows at me. "Keep your friends close, keep your enemies closer."

I don't reply as I look at the familiar G-Wagon parking in the school parking lot.

"We need to get our hands on that burner phone. How is the plan 'becoming friends with the Whites' going?" Emily asks as she looks in the same direction as me.

A chill runs down my spine at the thought of Friday night. "Not good. We're putting this plan in the trash."

"So, we're fully going behind their backs now? I know you, 'Me, you're going to get that phone one way or another."

"I will," I admit. "But I guess learning the twins might have been in a gang since they were kids is not exactly encouraging." And the fact that Jake would literally shoot me dead if he caught me. *Or worse.*

"We need it. Then we can communicate with Sam pretending to be Rose and we can ask whatever questions we want."

I think in silence, watching Chris, Luke, Rose and finally Jake getting out of the car. Rose gets a cigarette out of a pack and puts it between her lips before lighting it. Jake grabs her pack and quickly copies her.

They start walking towards the entrance and Jake catches me staring. He gives me a cold, calculated smile but doesn't say anything. When Camila hops off her bench to go meet him, his face switches completely. He becomes warm and welcoming.

Fuck this guy.

A new wave of hatred toward Jake engulfs me. I'm going to take whatever I want from him, just like he did with me.

"Let's do it," I say with renewed resolution. "Tonight, during lacrosse. I'll sneak into the locker room and get it from her bag."

"That's my girl," she exclaims happily, getting us the attention of the group not far from us.

Camila looks at me like she's ready to kill me. I want to go over there and shake her. Shout that her boyfriend is a psychopath but what are the chances that she'll think I'm just some jealous groupie?

Maybe I am.

Camila's friend, Beth, walks with her but separates from

her before they reach the group. She turns around and goes another way.

"I bet Beth doesn't speak to them because of Rose," Em says as she catches me watching.

"You've just heard rumors. You don't even know if she really slept with Jason."

She sighs dramatically. "I wish we could know if the gossip about this group is true. Especially the sexy ones."

I laugh as we walk back into the building.

By the end of lacrosse practice, my brain is in overdrive. I wouldn't be surprised if steam comes out of my ears from overheating. I left practice slightly early and I'm now going through Rose's sport bag that she left on the benches in the locker room. My cheek is practically bleeding from gnawing on it.

What do I do if I get caught? I wonder for what seems like the hundredth time. The burner phone is not in her bag. In fact, there's only her uniform. She must have put her precious stuff in the locker.

I face her locker and my brain is buzzing, wondering how I could possibly find her code.

There's no way you're going to break into her locker, Jamie. You're really not that smart.

I can start with her birthday. After all she does love herself and she loves her brother. Everyone knows the twins' birthday in this school since it's always the biggest party of the year. I roll my eyes at the thought as I roll the wheel of the lock. 1. roll. 0. roll. 3. roll. 1.

Oh, the irony that Jake's birthday is on Halloween since he's a demon.

Sadly, the lock doesn't move.

"Ugh, come on," I mumble to myself.

We have four rows of lockers in this room. The first two rows are perpendicular to either side of the doors and the other two rows are on the other side. This means that when someone walks in, there is a row on their left, a row on their right and they have to walk around the row on their right to find the other lockers. My locker is on the side of the room that can't be seen from the door. Rose's locker is right by the door. If someone walks in right now, I'm screwed.

I open the door to make sure no one is coming and close it again. My hands are so sweaty I have to wipe them on my skort. I'm not used to doing something illegal.

I need to try something else. I can't get my head around this girl. I thought she didn't do feelings, but I saw the look in her eyes when she was alone with Sam. Maybe she's not as heartless as she pretends. Her code might be the most random numbers, or it might as well be the date she met Rachel for all I know.

Just try something. Anything!

Alright let's try her birth year. I quickly roll to each number, but the lock doesn't bulge.

"Fuck my life."

Is there anything else I know about her? She's friends with Luke and Chris. I know absolutely nothing about Luke. I guess I know Chris the most out of all of them. He's like her brother...kind of.

I shake my head knowing this is not going to work and try Chris's birthday. He would always invite me to his birthday parties when we were kids. Now he does it for old times' sake, but I never show up. 0. roll. 9. roll. 1. roll. 5.

While this gives me a reminder that Chris's birthday is on Friday, the lock doesn't do anything. I let out a long huff.

Chapter 8

What was I thinking? I let my head fall and hit the locker in frustration. When I pull away, I look down at the lock again. I didn't roll all the way to the five. I stopped at four by accident. In a last attempt, I push to the five and let out a crazy laugh when I hear the click.

That bitch is so sentimental.

I hurry to open her locker and start searching through her stuff. *Oh my God,* who is stupid enough to keep weed in their locker? If we get searched, she's going to get kicked off the team and probably the school.

A thought suddenly crosses my mind. What if she didn't actually bring the phone to school?

I lift her school shoes, and something falls out. *The phone!*

I grab it in a hurry and unlock it. There's no password. I look through it very quickly. No pictures, no messages, no apps. This *has* to be the burner phone.

Just in case, I keep looking and find another phone. I try to unlock it but this one has a passcode. I can't help but look through the locked screen. That curiosity will get me killed one day. I scroll through the texts and missed calls on the locked screen and –

Jesus Christ who has that many people texting them?!

There are three missed calls from Chris, texts from Jake, Luke, Rachel – she saved her name with a heart, how cute – and I don't know how many texts and Instagram DMs from random people.

> Chris: Rose. I'm going to kill you. Pick. Up. Your. Phone. Where are my car keys?!

> Jake: Did you actually hit on Miss Randall? Keep your dick in your pants. Seriously. I'm paying for your shit now that she thinks she can hit on teenagers.

Ew what is wrong with her? Miss Randall is our career advisor.

> Jake: I hope for your life you didn't lose Chris' keys.

> Luke: Pick up your phone.

> Luke: Chris is going to kill you.

> Rachel ♥: I like that red bra. Wear it more often please. xoxo

> Unknown: Stop ignoring me please. I miss you.

> Unknown: Are you really back with Rachel? I can't believe you're doing this to me.

There are at least five or six different unknown numbers texting her about Rachel and missing her. Seriously, what does she put in their drinks?

I'm about to put the phone back when a new message pops up.

> British knobhead: If you keep ignoring me, I'm going to have to go to the police about your brother. Don't be stupid. x

A chuckle escapes my lips at the sight of Samuel's nickname but when I read the text my heart drops in my chest.

Going to the cops about her brother? What did Jake do? What did he do that's bad enough to use as blackmail?

I hear voices outside and put everything back in a hurry before putting the lock back into place. I jog around to my locker and throw the burner phone in my bag. The door opens and I let out a relieved sigh.

I grab my own phone and text Emily to let her know I've got what we needed. The girls flood in and get changed but I sit down trying to calm my racing heart.

When I finally decide to get changed there is no one left on my side of the lockers. I didn't hear Rose's voice when everyone walked in, but she must have come in and left already. I walk around to check and see her bag still on the bench. *Weird.*

I check the time to see almost an hour has passed. I'll just take a shower at home. I get up and put my uniform back on.

I hear the door open and close again. Rose must be back.

"Aah, just who we were looking for. The saint of our school," a voice says behind me.

I turn around, buttoning my shirt and frown when I see Camila and Beth standing just before me. Camila is still in her uniform with a skirt way too short to be allowed and Beth is wearing the Stoneview Prep cheerleading uniform.

"I'm sorry?" I ask as if I hadn't heard her properly.

"You heard me," Beth says. Her voice is so high it's actually painful to the human ear.

"Do you have anything you want to say to me?" I feign disinterest.

"I do," Camila cuts in. "I have a question actually. On Friday, you conveniently disappeared right at the same time as Jake and you guys were gone for a long time. Do you want to explain yourself? Because he said he was driving Rose home, except Rose was still at my house."

"Oh wow," I mock. "You really keep tabs on him. Trust flows in your relationship I see."

Beth gives me a shove in the shoulder, and it forces me to take a step back.

"Are you crazy? What is wrong with you?!" I fume.

I'm not the biggest girl and someone my size would most probably lose a fight, but I'll be damned if Beth Lam thinks she can scare me.

"Answer the question, Goody," Beth orders.

"I don't have to justify myself to either of you. The fact that your boyfriend can't stay faithful is not my problem. But if you want to know *that* bad, I didn't do anything with him. I hate the fucker."

Now that's a lie Jamie and we all know it. You're human, you have eyes, you're into him.

"Oh please," Camila chuckles, "You've been eyeing him for years. You just know he'd never be interested in a tramp like you. How do you even go to this school? I thought you were poor."

"Shut up," I growl. "You don't know anything about me."

"I know you're getting too close to my boyfriend and you're going to get hurt."

Camila shoves me and I have to take another step back. Beth is barely taller than me and doesn't do much, but Camila is a bigger girl and I struggle to stay in place when she keeps pushing me.

"You. Stay. Away. From. Him." She pushes me between every word and before I know it, I'm hitting the wall of the showers. "I think the tramp needs a good clean, Beth. Wouldn't you say?"

Beth smirks and takes a step towards me.

"Ugh fuck you," I say trying to go past them. They both push me back and Camila hooks her leg behind mine as they push. I fall to the floor of the shower in a loud thump. The fall is so hard it hurts all the way from my bottom and up my spine.

I refrain a scream, but it takes me a few seconds to get my bearings again and it gives enough time for Camila to turn the shower on. I yelp when the freezing water hits me, and I hurry to try and get back up. A sudden pain shoots in my stomach and this time I can't hold in a groan. Camila kicks my stomach another time, her pointy shoe hitting right in my solar plexus, and my breath gets stuck in my lungs. I roll on the floor of the shower, the strong jet of water hitting my face and body.

I can't really see them anymore, white dots dancing in front of my eyes, but I can feel when they pour shampoo and shower gel all over my body and head. I hear Beth laugh when Camila says, "I bet you've never had such a deep clean. Do you get running water at your house? You're welcome by the way."

The shampoo gets in my eyes and mouth and I bring my hands to my face trying to wipe away the stinging pain, but they keep pouring more. Both their laughs are ringing in my ears, making the humiliation a hundred times worse. I see a flash at some point and realize one of them is filming with their phone. The pain in my stomach and the sting in my eyes are completely stopping me from getting back up. I just lay there while they keep on throwing insults at me and filming the scene.

The laughs suddenly stop, and I hear a bang against a locker as Beth screams in surprise. A second later, the water stops, and a towel is thrown at me. Slowly, I manage to sit up and dry my burning face from the shampoo and water.

I open my burning eyes, slowly adjusting to the light in the room. My mouth drops open when I see Rose has pushed Beth against a locker and is now standing in-between the two girls and me.

"Are you two sluts for real?" she mocks them.

"The bitch spends her time hitting on my boyfriend, wouldn't you do the same if she hit on Rachel?" Camila whines.

"Oh Camila, you're such a fucking disappointment. I really don't get how Rach is friends with you. Your boyfriend spends his time hitting on anything with legs. You're nothing special. Neither is she."

The insult aimed at Camila cuts right through me. *Nothing. Special.*

Rose turns to Beth and puts her hand out. "Your phone. Now."

"Fuck you," Beth spits.

Rose looks at Camila raising an eyebrow. They seem to have some sort of understanding because Camila turns to Beth. "Beth, give her the phone."

Beth reluctantly hands Rose the phone.

"Atta girl," Rose smiles at her.

She takes a few seconds to go through it as I stand silently, still in the shower.

"Fuck. You two really think this is Mean Girls, don't you?" Rose laughs.

I'm looking at the exchange with eyes as wide as saucers. Is Rose White actually defending me right now? This is the last thing I would have expected from her. I knew there was bad blood between Beth and her, because of the whole rumor of her sleeping with Jason, but I thought she was friends with Camila.

Rose is doing this so casually I almost feel stupid standing there, helpless. There is not an ounce of fear in her body, whereas I'm trembling like a leaf.

"Alright. That's deleted. Let's hope for Camila's sake this little incident doesn't reach Jake's ears. You know how he is when you get possessive."

"Rose, please, don't be like that," Camila begs. She is actually begging her not to repeat this to her twin.

Rose shrugs. "Next time you bitches want to start a catfight, pick someone your size."

Camila drops her head in shame, but Beth is still fuming against the locker.

"You're pathetic. You just hide behind your three boys hoping they'll have your back because they have real influence here, but you're nothing without them. You don't run this school, Rose."

Rose laughs heartily at her statement. "I might not run this school, but I definitely run your fiancé's cock. What I'm still trying to get my head around is if you're jealous of me 'cause I fuck him...or jealous of him 'cause he fucks me."

Beth gasps and I can't help but laugh.

"Off you go, babe," Rose concludes and both girls scurry out of the locker room.

I guess the Jason rumors were true. Rose turns to me and hands me another towel.

"You alright?" she asks, disinterested.

I can't really look at her, the embarrassment is too big. I decide instead to focus on my hands twisting in front of my body.

"You need a ride home?" she insists.

I raise my eyebrows in surprise. She's offering me a ride

home. Rose White, the I-don't-give-a-shit-about-anyone queen of broken hearts is offering me a ride back home.

I must look like a fish out of water because she chuckles mockingly at me. "Don't get all wet, Goody, it's just a ride."

I snap my mouth shut and shake my head. There she is, sounds more like her.

"I'm okay, I've got my bike with me. Uh, thank you. Really. For what you just did. I'd really appreciate it if it could stay between us."

She shrugs and walks back to her side of the locker room. I'll take that as an agreement.

I quickly take off my wet clothes and put my lacrosse kit on. They smell but I guess it's better than my wet uniform. I feel a sudden rush of guilt knowing I have Rose's burner phone in my bag. Will she get in trouble for this?

On the other side of the lockers, I overhear Rose making a call.

"Fuck Chris I'm so sorry. No, they're in my bag. I know. Alright, stop shouting I'm coming home now." The way her voice switches when she talks to Chris reminds me that his birthday is her code. She truly cares for him and she cares what he thinks of her. It's cute. It reminds me of Aaron and me. Or at least what we used to be like.

I gather my stuff and walk around. Rose is changed, putting her kit in her bag.

I put my hand on the door handle but decide to turn around one last time. Rose is not like Jake, she just proved to me that they're opposites by taking my defense, and I get this feeling that I can trust her. I turn around and ask something I will probably regret.

"Why does Jake own a gun?" I blurt out.

Her head snaps up from her bag to me and she looks

worried for a split second but quickly goes back to neutral. "Jake doesn't own a gun."

"Yes, he does. I saw it." I shiver at the reminder before I focus back on Rose.

"I got you out of a shit situation, Goody. It doesn't mean we're friends and we're gonna share our deepest secrets. I don't know what led you to think my brother owns a gun, but I'd suggest you keep the information to yourself. That includes talking to me about it. Trust me, I'm telling you this for your own good."

She gets up, grabs her bag, and walks past me, out of the locker room. I give a glance at her locker and my stomach twists in guilt again. The girl just saved my ass and I stole her burner phone to spy on a guy she hates.

Am I just as bad as Jake?

9

JAKE

Bad Drugs – King Kavalier & ChrisLee

I'm sitting on the couch, coding a website on my laptop when the door of the pool house bursts open, and Ozy walks in. Okay. She's mad.

She looks around and I know she does that when she's checking if we're alone. I can feel she's going to tell me something she only wants me to know and I go to stop her. "Wait–"

"Did you pull a gun on Jamie Williams?" She cuts me off.

"You did what?!" Chris's voice comes from behind the kitchen counter as he gets up from under the sink.

I close my eyes, taking a moment to accept that Rose just blurted out information that is going to get me killed within a few seconds.

"Ugh, fuck," she mutters. "You should have said."

I open my eyes and give her an annoyed look. "I fucking tried, idiot."

Chris walks around the counter, holding a heavy-duty wrench. He was fixing the kitchen sink that no one knows

Chapter 9

how it broke since we barely ever use it. I get up from the couch and turn to him, knowing perfectly well I just earned myself a fucking long conversation.

"Jake, did you actually pull out a gun on her?" Chris says calmly. Too calmly.

"'Course not," I lie.

I did much more than pull a gun on her and it's too wrong for me to say it out loud. Let's call a spade a spade: I crossed the line and went so far beyond it that I'm surprised I even found my way back.

I went home that evening and spent the whole night having flashbacks of what my previous foster dad did to me to trigger my 'survival instincts'. He put a darkness in me. I spent the last three years acting like a good boy, following Chris' advice to stay under the radar, but Jamie brings something back up that I thought I had under control.

I had never gone that far into intimidating someone, but I have seen it plenty of times from the people I lived with. My actions were straight out of the gangster book and I'm a huge hypocrite for doing something I always claim I'm against. Scaring people to keep them quiet. That's just not how I should be acting.

"So, if I call Jamie right now and ask her what happened Friday night when you both disappeared, right after I told you about Sam, she's going to say you just took her home, right?"

"She's the one who told you about Sam? I didn't even know." Wow, it must be 'lie to your best friend' day.

"Spare me the fucking lies," he growls.

"Can you put the wrench down?" I ask.

Rose chuckles behind me and I want to turn around and punch her. Did she have to put me in so much shit?

"No, I can't because I think I might have to split your

head open to check if you actually have a brain," Chris replies.

"I can explain, there's no need to get violent." God knows I can hold my ground in a fight. Hell, I probably can fuck up most guys in this town, but Chris, I'd rather stay out of his way.

He's the kind that stays calm until he's pushed too far and when he snaps, it's not good to be around. No one wants to be on Chris's shit list. For now, it only holds one person, Sam, and I don't want to join him.

"What?" Chris asks me mockingly. "You're strong enough to threaten Jamie but you back down when it comes to me?"

"Fuck you, I only did this to keep her quiet. She's a sneaky rat and she snitches at the first occasion. Why do you protect her? You don't even like the girl!"

"I like her a lot actually. Just because I don't like her romantically doesn't mean I don't like her at all. She's my friend and I already warned you not to mess with her. What will it take for it to stick in that small brain of yours, for me to punch it into you?"

I can feel the anger boiling in my chest. Chris taking this girl's defense over mine hurts like a stab in the chest.

I walk closer to him and only stop when we're head-to-head. He's taller than me but I'm an angry motherfucker and I won't go down without a good fight. Nobody has the balls to start shit with me at school anymore after I beat up a few guys when we moved here, but I live for the thrill of it and Chris knows it.

"Alright big guy. Punch me then," I snarl.

Chris throws the wrench to the side and looks me right in the eyes. "Are you sure your pretty-boy face can take my fist?"

Chapter 9

I shove him in the shoulder. I know it'll take more to get Chris to hit me. He's years away from snapping right now and I want to push him more.

"Alright, alright, we get it. Big guys. Dangerous. Grr. Alpha," Rose says as she slips in-between the two of us.

She's facing me and putting her back to Chris. I could push her out of the way easily, so could Chris. Ozy is tall and she can be scary as fuck, but in truth, she's a skinny girl, and a gust of wind could snap her in two.

"Jake, you're in the wrong. Drop it," she insists.

She locks her eyes with mine and puts her hand on my shoulder. The simple gesture calms me down, her soft features in front of me drag me back from hell up to the present moment. The boiling anger in me slowly dies down.

"Stop grinding your teeth," she orders me in a firm voice.

When I'm about to snap, when it gets too much and I try to hold it back, my teeth take the fall. I've had so many trips to the dentist for a broken tooth or because I fucked up my jaw it's laughable. I listen to my other half and slowly relax my jaw.

"Here he is," she smiles.

She takes a step back from me, walks around me, and settles on the couch. Chris gives me one last look before moving to sit beside her. She lays down, her head on his lap, and her feet resting on the armrest on the other side. Chris starts playing with her hair. This girl is like a cat, she'll lay down anywhere expecting someone to stroke her hair. I can sense my friend is not over with this conversation, but Rose changes the topic.

"Sam gave me a burner phone," she drops as if all was fine. She's toying with the remote trying to turn the TV on.

Chris and I both snap to her. Chris's hand on her head

stops, she groans a complaint. I walk and stand in front of the TV.

"A burner phone?" Chris asks.

"When?" I add.

"Friday at the party. Told you he was there," she shrugs.

"What does he want?" Chris insists.

Rose throws me a look and I frown then nod to indicate she can talk about it in front of Chris.

"He texted me a few times, he wants us to pick up packages for him in NSF."

"Let me see," I hand out my hand, palm up.

The fucker wants us to do his dirty work for him on the North Shore of the Falls. The only reason my friends and I ever go to NSF is to attend North Shore High parties. They're more exciting than Stoneview and, mainly, I can do whatever the fuck I want behind Camila's back.

"I deleted them. Look, I'm just telling you because I won't ignore him anymore. Just so you know what I'll be up to."

"What?" Chris chokes. He gets up in a hurry making Rose jump up and forcing her to sit up.

"You're not going to do it, are you?" he questions her.

"It's just a bit of white. I won't get caught."

"Where's the phone," Chris asks.

"In my bag," she replies. "You won't find anything on it though, I delete the texts as I get them."

Chris goes to her bag by the door and starts going through it. I look at her confused. How? How has he dragged her back down already?

"Why," I blurt out without any emotions in my voice.

My face is a blank mask. The second I show her I'm worried for her she'll shut down, hide things, try to protect me.

Chapter 9

"He's saying he'll go to the cops, Jake," she sighs.

"He won't," I reply automatically.

"But he could. And we can't take that risk."

"He wouldn't do that, don't be stupid," I insist. She's looking up at me from the sofa and I'm looking down at her, scowling.

"I told you this purely for your information. At no point did I ask for advice," she growls.

I know I'm making her angry by getting in her way. Ozy and I struggle for power and protectiveness in our relationship. People assume I'm protective over her because I'm the guy, but hell will freeze over before she accepts anyone to be overprotective and make decisions for her, even if it's to keep her safe. Hence why she ends up in shit situations 90% of the time, although she'll never admit, it's because she refused help in the first place. Stubbornness runs in our blood.

The problem with the fact that she never accepts help is it clashes with the fact that I like controlling everything. Scratch that, I don't like it, I need it. It's the only thing that keeps me sane. That burning need to make sure everything goes my way and because I decided it would. This tug of war over control often ends up in clashes between us and I can see exactly where this discussion is going.

"Can you get out of the way? I'm in a binge-watching mood."

"Are you for real right now," I snap, not moving an inch.

"What?" she shrugs.

"Ozy, you're not doing any work for Sam. You don't give into Sam's threats, you don't play his games. You more than anyone else should know that."

Her lips press into a thin line and I can almost feel the heat from the anger bubbling in her head.

"Look," she smiles at me. I know there's no honesty in it. "I want to apologize because obviously I didn't make myself clear. I'm going to move a few bags for Sam. I don't give a shit about your opinion. Now move out of the way so I can watch Netflix."

"Fuck," I huff. "Old habits die hard." I regret the words as soon as they pass my lips, but I don't show it. Maybe she needs a bit of poking.

She gets up from the sofa in a sudden movement and gets in my face. Her jaw is ticking, and I almost want to laugh at how similar we are.

"Take that back," she growls.

"I can't. I said it and I meant it. Sam's not back for five minutes and he's already gotten a hold of you. You think it's because he's gonna go to the cops, Ozy? Don't make me laugh, you wouldn't take that threat seriously in a million years. You're weak to this guy and it's driving me crazy."

She gives me a big push, I barely move, and it makes me chuckle.

"Look at you, you're such a big dude trying to do the right thing while I take care of the problem and sort us out. You're right, old habits really *do* die hard," she spits at me.

I lose control. She knows she hit straight home, and I give her a push back making her fall back on the sofa. She doesn't back down though. She never does. Instead, she gets back up quickly and tackles me like a football player.

My back hits the TV behind me and I grunt as I push her back kicking the back of her leg, making her fall to the floor.

"You want to go back to being Sam's bitch? Fine. Make sure you don't take me down with you."

"Enough you two," Chris scolds from the other side of the room.

I look up to see he's emptied Ozy's bag all over the floor. I help my sister back up while we're both still shooting daggers at each other. She's driving me mad, but I can't really leave her on the floor.

"The phone isn't here, Rose. Where did you put it?" Chris asks.

"In my bag, I told you."

"It's not in your bag."

"Ugh, of course it is. I put it there before practice," she huffs as she joins Chris and picks her bag up from the floor.

She looks through it, picks up stuff from the floor, pats her pockets.

"Shit," she concludes. "Shit, shit, shit." She goes through the bag again but nothing.

"Are you sure you put it there?" I ask.

She's now running her hand through her hair in panic. "Yes! Before practice, I put it in my shoes and then I put my shoes in my bag. I didn't bother switching my sneakers after practice."

She grabs her everyday shoes on the floor and looks inside but nothing. "Someone's taken it," she drops. "It's gone."

"You lost it," I scowl. "Could you possibly get more annoying?"

"Fuck off, I didn't lose it, someone took it!"

"Jake, back off," Chris says calmly. "Rose, you put it in your shoe before practice, and did you check after?"

"No, I just threw my shoes in my bag," she admits.

She thinks a few seconds and seems to come to a conclusion.

"Fuck," she turns to me. "Jamie, that...ugh," she huffs in frustration. "She left practice early. It's her. I know it's her. No one would fucking dare steal shit from me. But that bitch? And she asked me questions about you and your gun. She knows shit, Jake. She must have gotten into my locker. She took it."

I don't need to question Ozy again. She's not stupid. In fact, she's a damn genius and if this is her conclusion there is no second-guessing her. It wouldn't be the first time Jamie Williams puts her nose in our business. I don't know for what reason she would do this, but I clearly haven't scared her nearly enough. And here I was, thinking I went too far.

"I'll handle it," I say coldly.

"No, you won't," Chris interjects. "I'll talk to her. You stay the fuck away, Jake."

"Sure," I mutter without meaning it.

He scowls at me. He knows I'm not leaving her alone but what is he gonna do about it?

Oh, Angel, you have no idea how bad you fucked up. No idea what's coming onto you.

10

JAMIE

Casanova – Allie X, VÉRITÉ

I'm in bed on the phone with mom when the burner phone beeps on my bedside table.

"Mom let me call you back. Love you." I hurriedly hang up and grab the burner phone.

> Unknown: This is your last chance. Friday night. V's strip club in Silver Falls. Roy will drive. Try to fit in.

Ew, this guy is sending a teenager to a strip club *and* asking her to dress the part. I'm instantly brought back to Sam reminding Rose she was in love with him. How? Why? You must be a certain shade of fucked up that I don't quite understand.

Don't you? You got hot and bothered when Jake tackled you to the ground and threatened you with a gun.

Yeah. I'm a hypocrite.

I Google 'V strip club Silver Falls' on my phone but nothing comes up. I type 'Volkov strip club Silver Falls' perfectly knowing it won't lead me anywhere. After almost an hour of googling strip clubs in the city and traumatizing myself with pictures I should have never seen, I give up in a yawn. I can't find which one he's talking about. I'll have to figure it out with Em.

Just before I fall asleep, my own phone beeps, and I have a look at it thinking it would be my mom wishing me good night. My heart somersaults in my chest when I read the text.

> Unknown: On a scale of 1 to 10, how bad is it that I can't wait until Sunday to see you again? N.

I instantly understand it comes from Nathan and I feel a rush of warmth going through me. *He texted me.* Tiredness dissipates from my body and I fully grab my phone sitting up slightly.

> Jamie: I'd say about 9 but I don't blame you.

I save his number in my phone and put it down next to me on the bed. A few minutes later it beeps again, and my head shoots up.

> Nathan: Don't tell me you can wait. You're going to hurt my feelings.

I can't help the smile from spreading on my lips.

> Jamie: No... I can't.

He doesn't reply for a while and my eyelids grow heavy.

When I wake up, my chest is swollen with happiness. I'm instantly reminded of my exchange with Nathan. I grab my phone with bubbling anticipation, it's uncurling in my stomach like a blooming flower spreading its fresh petals. As soon as the screen lights up, I jump off my bed and skip to the bathroom happily. This is going to be a good day.

I look at the text again as I'm brushing my teeth.

> Nathan: I'll think of a way to solve our problem. You go to bed, beautiful.

I reply as soon as I'm dressed.

> Jamie: Looking forward to hearing the solution.

An hour later, I'm hopping into Emily's car still in a conversation with Nathan.

"Where is this cute, cheeky smile coming from?" Emily notices my mood straight away. "You're either texting your mom or you're ordering breakfast to collect at Starbucks."

I laugh and shrug. "I'm just in a good mood. Am I not allowed?"

"This is not a happy smile, this is an 'I'm doing something I like' smile. I'd say it's an 'I'm getting laid' smile but we both know you're not getting laid. Or...are you?"

I laugh out loud and she gives me another look. "Girl, what is up with you?"

"Just texting this guy I met at Church."

It's her turn to laugh. "Oh, I bet he's a real bad boy."

I give her a nudge as she starts the car, and she gives it back in my stomach making me wince.

"What's wrong?" she asks, suddenly worried.

"Ugh, nothing. Turns out Camila should become a professional soccer player because she's got quite a kick."

"A kick? She kicked you?" My friend's voice goes up a few notches.

"It's nothing, honestly." I run her through my post-training altercation while searching through my bag. As I conclude, I pull Rose's burner phone out of my bag and present it to her.

"Anyway, ever heard of V's strip club?"

"Wait up, 'Me, are you okay?"

"I promise I am. They won't try anything again. Rose scared them enough to not try again in this lifetime." I don't exactly want to be getting into the details of my humiliation right now.

"Rose? As in Rose White?"

"I know. I was surprised too. Please can we focus on this damn burner phone?" I shake the phone in her face, and she glances at me before refocusing on the road. She finally clicks this is not something I want to talk about and nods.

"Yep. Yuh. Sorry. Go on."

"V's strip club. Does it ring a bell?" I ask.

"Should it?"

"Samuel is asking Rose to go there on Friday night."

She thinks about it as we park in front of Stoneview Prep. "The only one I can think of is the Vue Club but it belongs to Volkov. If they're opposite gangs, why would he send her there?"

"Yeah, that wouldn't make sen– wait, it belongs to Volkov? As in, that's where they hang out. Him and his guys?"

"'Me, don't even think about it. Suicide mission."

"It's a strip club. Anyone can go if they want to. I want to."

"You're a minor," she insists. "And you don't want any of them to see you, what the hell!"

"Of course I do. I want to talk to them. I want answers."

"You're being completely delusional. They're criminals.

They *will* kill you if you get nosy. You don't even know what they look like, how would you know who to talk to in the club? Even if you did, what will you do? Go straight up to them and ask where your brother is? Threaten them? Girl, I love you but look at yourself, you look like you'd fly away if someone blows on you. You don't look threatening in the slightest."

I stay silent, swallowing the bitter pill.

"'Me," she puts a hand on my shoulder, "when we get to this topic, you lose all sorts of rationality. Please, let's take this one day at a time, this is going to be a long process. You've got the phone. Great. Now, wait and see what other texts he'll send before running to Volkov's sex club."

"Sex club or strip club?" I ask as my gullible self.

"Guess," she rolls her eyes and gets out of the car.

As hard as it is to accept, Emily is right. Only, it's complicated to keep still when I've learned I'm so close to Volkov's men. In truth, they're never far, I could potentially get close to the bottom of their organization but there is always this fear of being recognized. I spend the day thinking this over before accepting that I must wait if I want to do this properly.

The week goes quicker than I thought. Jake and Rose have gone back to pretending I don't exist. Chris gives me a shy smile every now and then, but I can't gather the strength to talk to him after the humiliation at the party. None of this matters anyway when I'm on my phone talking to Nathan.

I can never help the smile and the warmth I get when I receive a text from him. We've been talking all week. Day and night. I can't put my phone down anymore and, clearly, neither can he.

I had never had this feeling of mutual attraction and addiction. He wants to meet on Saturday and have lunch together. He doesn't want to tell me where but says he's planned it all.

I can't wait to get lost in his deep ocean eyes again. I want to run my hand through his blond hair and rest my head on his shoulder. I want all the cuteness bullshit. I want to hold hands and I want to get inhibited with his elegant cologne. I just have to get through the week first.

On Friday afternoon, I'm walking towards Emily's car when Chris calls after me. I don't want to stop and turn around, dreading the conversation, but he quickly catches up and walks next to me.

"Hey Chris," I force my lips into a smile but keep my gaze ahead, trying to not engage too much.

"I've been trying to find a moment to talk to you this week," he smiles back.

I can't help but glance at him and take him in. God, he's handsome.

And unavailable for you.

He's wearing the uniform trousers, burgundy with double white lines running the length of the side seam on both legs. He picked the navy polo with Stoneview Prep's logo of an Eagle wearing a crown and wears the navy jacket sporting the logo too.

"We're matching," he says, stopping me in my observation.

I raise my eyebrows, wondering what he means, and he points at my clothes. I look down to my burgundy skirt with the double white lines just above the trim and the navy polo tucked in the high waisted skirt. We have a lot of options with our outfit. Every student can buy navy or burgundy polos, skirts, and pants with white button-downs. It's nice, it means we don't have to wear the exact same thing every day.

Chris is right, today, we *are* matching. Like a real non-dating couple. I only smile in response.

Please make this quick, I can only stand this so long before I start being reminded of last week's embarrassment.

"Look, I have a question and I really need you to be honest with me."

I stop abruptly and fully face him. Maybe this is not about last Friday. "Is everything okay?" I ask him.

"I–look, I don't know how to ask this and I want to apologize in advance if I assume wrong but…" he shifts on his feet. So typical of Chris, not wanting to hurt other people's feelings.

"I won't take it the wrong way," I encourage him.

He takes a deep breath and I suddenly feel uneasy. This is not good.

"Rose had something stolen from her locker during practice on Monday and she said you're the only one who left early. She wanted to mention it herself, but I insisted on talking to you first. She can be a bit…you know?"

"Hostile?"

"Right, I guess we can say that. I trust you, Jamie, and if you say you had nothing to do with it then I'll believe you."

My thoughts are running a thousand miles an hour. Rose knows her phone is gone. She thinks it's me. She wanted to confront me about it. I'm screwed.

I try to keep my face as blank as possible while my brain tortures itself. She mentioned me. Did she also mention what happened with Camila and Beth? Why wouldn't she, she probably hates me now and for good reasons as well.

"Jamie?"

How long was I out? I take an extra few seconds before replying, "It wasn't me."

He looks me in the eyes, and I can't stand it. I look away. Behind him, Rose, Jake, Camila, and Jason are walking out of the school's heavy wooden doors. Jake is holding Camila by the waist and Rose and Jason are walking dangerously close for a couple of friends. Her olive skin looks pale next to Jason's dark complexion. He says something in her ear and her raspy laugh makes me shiver. I need to stay away from her and her friends if I don't want to have Jake's gun to my head again.

A honk coming from the parking lot makes me jump and I turn around to see Emily popping her head out of the window.

"Hurry up!"

"I'm sorry I couldn't be more helpful," I say to Chris before heading away.

He quickly catches my arm and I turn back around.

"Jamie, are you sure? You can tell me anything. I won't get you in trouble. I won't let the twins get back at you. But I can only help if you're honest with me."

He keeps going after another long silence from me. "Come on. Don't lie to me. You know me, there's nothing I hate more than dishonesty between friends."

His behavior changes slightly from the sweet Chris to the powerful man he could be. His brows furrowed, he observes me, waiting for any kind of reaction. I take in his height and size. He looks taller and bigger than usual and I realize that it's exactly how he's trying to make himself look. Is he trying to intimidate the truth out of me?

I frown at him. He needs to get off my back. With what Jake has done to me, taking their phone is nothing.

But Jake isn't Rose.

Chapter 10 145

I don't care, they're the same.

And Chris doesn't know what happened.

I try to calm down, but Chris' behavior is riling me up and I can't help it.

"Drop it, Chris. I don't need you to keep me safe from the twins, okay? I'm not scared of them. They have no right or justification to bother me. If they want to, I won't go easy on them. You know what? I don't even owe you any explanation. I didn't take her stupid phone."

I snatch back my arm violently, even though he's holding it softly, and hurry to Emily's car.

I close the door in anger and wait for her to start the car while watching Chris. He takes his phone out. Jake and his group are joining him but Chris stares at me.

My phone beeps and I look down at it on my lap. I don't need to unlock it to see his short text.

> Chris: I never said it was her phone.

My eyes snap back up at him. He shakes his head disappointedly and walks away with his friends. I can feel the blood draining from my face. It's icy and goes straight back to my heart, making it beat too fast for me to handle. My eyes blink multiple times before my brain registers the situation fully.

No. No. No. No. How could I be so stupid?! I just snitched on myself. I just lied to his face and revealed it right after. What is wrong with me?

Emily reverses out of the spot while she talks to me. "Are you okay, baby? You're really pale."

"I-I'm not feeling well suddenly."

"'Me, come on you have a date tomorrow. Don't get ill now!"

I stay silent for a few minutes as she drives toward my house. Fear creeps in, mixed with the uneasy feeling of knowing that Chris doesn't have my back anymore. That any minute now he could be telling Rose I'm the one who stole her phone. That Jake will know I'm still looking into Samuel.

What will he do then? It doesn't take much to trigger Jake. Chris was putting himself between me and him. He said it himself, he didn't want me to get involved in his dark world. And what did I do? I jumped right into it.

"Em?"

"Mhm?" She replies, her gaze leaving the road. She seems lost in her own thoughts too.

"Can you stay with me tonight?"

This is the only thing I can think about right now. If I'm home with Em, nothing can happen, right? It's a short-term solution but it's a solution.

Your imagination is bigger than the threat. Calm down.

That's true. What are they going to do? Break into my house? They don't even know I'm on my own. Even if they did, they're not going to cross that line. I know it.

But the uneasy feeling just won't go away.

"I'm sorry, babes, I have a date tonight." Emily's light voice contrasts drastically with my dark thoughts.

"A date?" I ask surprised. "You never said anything."

"Because it's nothing really." She waves her hand. "Luke came to talk to me about his little sister, Ella, because she missed cheer tryouts. He said it was his fault and he wanted to make it up to her. Apparently, she's a great flyer."

"And he talked to you about it?"

"He thought I was captain. How cute?" She laughs. "I said I'd talk to Beth about it and ended up getting Ella a tryout next week. Anyway, he said he's taking me for dinner as a thank you."

"Em! Why are you not more excited about this! You've been into Luke Baker for, like, *ever*!"

She shrugs. "Because I know it's nothing. He just wants to say thank you."

I notice the guilt in her eyes straight away and put a hand on her leg.

"Em...please. You know you're allowed to date, right? It's been almost three years. No one will judge you."

Since Aaron disappeared, Emily hasn't dated anyone. She used to be the popular girl at school. All the guys wanted to date her, all the girls were jealous she was with a senior when we were freshmen.

About a year after Aaron's disappearance, guys considered she was back on the market, but she turned down everyone. Every. Single. Soul.

I know at first, she was too heartbroken to be into anyone else, let alone love them. With time, people started saying that she would never find anyone after Aaron, that their love was too strong, and they praised her for that. Now, while she still loves my brother, she is too scared to make any move. Too scared she will be judged by the same people who praised her for staying faithful to a guy that was gone.

"Look, I gave you *my* blessing. Shouldn't that be enough?" I encourage her with a smile.

She giggles but a single tear rolls down her cheek. She quickly wipes it and smiles back at me.

"It's not just that. I know what kind of guy Luke is. If I express interest, he's going to want to have sex. And, well, it's been a while. Like...three years while."

I laugh at her loudly. "Come on, who cares? Just say you don't want to have sex. He's not going to jump you. Please, I want you to have fun. Luke is clearly interested. Show it back."

She stops in front of my house. "Fine. I'll jump him then."

I laugh and hop out. "Have fun!"

"Have fun with Nathan," she winks at me.

I wave and hurry inside my house. As soon as I'm alone the uneasy feeling creeps back into my stomach and I double lock the door. Is it possible that I'm not truly alone?

Like a crazy woman, I start searching the house. Behind the kitchen counter, in the tub, under my bed, and in my closet. While in my bedroom, I hide the burner phone in my underwear drawer.

Samuel will be waiting for Rose tonight, but Emily made me promise not to act on it and I know it would be too dangerous. Once Rose doesn't show up, I'm sure I'll hear more from Samuel.

I open mom's room and look around there as well. Thank God I don't live in a mansion the size of Emily's or it would have taken me all weekend.

Once I'm sure there's no one, I drop my bag by the door and my phone on the counter before slumping down on the sofa and turning the TV on. Friday, it's time to binge-watch some crappy reality TV on Hulu.

I don't feel at ease, but I don't feel sick from fear anymore. Before I realize, my gaze stops focusing on the screen and my eyelids grow heavy.

My dad is on his knees. The hooded man grabs his Sheriff badge, spits on it, and throws it on the floor.

"You really thought you could stop us, Williams? You barely managed a dent in our budget. And unless you can pay that back.

One of your kids is dying tonight." His heavy Eastern European accent is thick in my ears.

"Breathe, 'Me. Breathe please."

My brother's voice echoes in my head, but I can't stop shaking. Am I holding my breath?

A shot rings and Aaron's body falls on mine. Again, his limp body crushes my chest. I can't breathe. I feel dizzy. I try to push him off but he's too heavy, he's holding onto me like he still wants to protect me from the man. My shoulder is burning, melting from hellish heat. My chest is too constricted for me to survive this.

Just another breath. It's just a dream. Breathe.

Breathe!

I wake up trying to take a deep breath but it's impossible. There's a dark form on me, one big hand covering my mouth and nose. I'm still dreaming. I'm still in a nightmare. My eyes are darting everywhere trying to understand my surroundings. It's dark, too dark to comprehend what's happening but I know I'm on my sofa. I'm at home.

I start clawing at the hand and the shadow straddling me when a face lowers to mine. Deep, dark blue eyes shine in front of me and an evil smirk inches closer to my ear.

"Wakey wakey, little Angel." Jake's voice floods through my veins, colder than ice, bringing me back to reality. I'm not dreaming, I'm wide awake and he's trying to kill me.

I try to scream and start twisting, kicking my legs, and pushing him but he doesn't move. He straightens above me and chuckles.

"It's fucking hilarious how weak you are. Like a tiny lamb fighting against a big. Bad. Wolf."

My eyes flutter as I try to inhale any oxygen possible but

it's not enough. I feel dizzy and my vision gets dotted with black spots.

"Unless you want to pass out, I suggest you nod at my next suggestion. If I take my hand off, promise you won't scream?"

I nod hard multiple times. I don't have time to think, I just need to breathe. He withdraws his hand from my face, and I take a huge gasp of air. It takes me a minute or so to regain sense of myself and the situation.

When I grasp what is happening and understand he's not getting off me I start trying to push him off. I push my hips up and down trying to throw him off and he starts laughing. I punch him in the chest as hard as I can, and he grabs my wrists.

"You're gonna tire before I do, baby. Better give up now."

I try pushing my hips up again and he tightens his grip on my wrists. "If you keep humping me, I'm gonna have to fuck you. I can only resist for so long," he lowers his mouth close to mine, "and I don't think you'll like it. I'm rough."

His breath burns my lips and all the way inside my body until it reaches my lower belly. His words have a one-way effect on me. A wave of warmth crashes between my legs and I stop moving. My inner thighs clench automatically while the rest of my body freezes. He sits back up.

"Now." His face turns grave and I know nothing good is coming. He releases my wrists, knowing full well I won't move after his threats.

"What do you want?" I growl.

"Less attitude and more answers. Where's the burner phone?"

My heart sinks and panic overtakes me again. I try to push him away again. "Get off, Jake. Get off me and get out of my house!"

Chapter 10

"Answer my question."

"My mom will be home any minute now, go away."

He pushes my hands away and grabs my jaw tightly. I can barely refrain a whimper and freeze in place.

"Your mom is in Tennessee."

My eyes widen at the revelation. How does he know?

"The phone, Angel. Where is it?"

I shake my head in negation. "I don't know what you're talking about."

He lets out a sarcastic chuckle. "Jamie, Jamie, Jamie. What am I gonna do with you?" He shakes my head lazily as he repeats my name. "How many warnings can I give before I start acting on my words, huh?"

A freezing chill crosses my whole body and I tremble under his hands. My brain is screaming at me: *he's a psychopath!* That must be it. How can someone be such a golden boy in front of everyone else and break into my house after school?

"You don't have to act on anything, I have no idea what you want," I lie.

"You know what the problem is with good girls like yourself?" He waits for a second to see if I'll reply and keeps going. "You're terrible liars."

"I – I'm not lying."

He sighs like this is only a mild inconvenience to him. I'm just a little bump on his way to retrieving the phone and he didn't want to act on his words but clearly the stupid girl in front of him is forcing him to.

What if he kills me?

He finally gets off me and I jump on the occasion to get up. I try to make a run for my phone on the counter, but he quickly grabs me by the back of my neck.

"Tsk, tsk. Not so fast. We're not done."

A shiver runs through me at his touch and he drags me with him to my room.

"I hope you're aware this is a home invasion. You can get in a lot of trouble for this. Leave now and I won't tell a single soul."

"Aw, how sweet."

"Jake if you don't leave now, I *will* take this to the police as soon as I'm alone again."

He laughs as he pushes me into my bedroom. I land face down on the bed but quickly turn around.

"Who said you're gonna be alone again? You're a liar and a thief. Clearly my threats didn't affect you one bit. Maybe I'll keep you close to me from now on. You can be my personal little pet." He says this so naturally I'm actually starting to believe he lacks any sort of feelings.

He starts looking through the mess on my bedside table. "Where is it? I don't have all night. It's Chris' birthday tonight and I'm not missing his party because some stupid bitch decided to turn into a spy kid."

"I don't have it!" I get up from the bed and hold onto his arm as he goes through the drawer of my desk. "Stop! Stop it!"

But he doesn't listen, and it doesn't change anything that I hold onto him. He just keeps searching, dragging me along with him. He grabs my arm and pushes me against the wall. He imprisons me with his arms and looks down into my eyes.

"I'm starting to lose patience, Angel."

"Leave. My. House," I say through gritted teeth.

He looks lazily from my eyes to my toes and back up before grabbing my jaw again. I instinctively push at his chest.

He chuckles. "You really are a little fighter, aren't you? It's cute." He grabs both my wrists in one hand and pins them above my head. "It's cute but you don't know me, Jamie. You don't know what I'm capable of. I'm a predator, do you understand that? I always get what I want, fighting only makes it more painful."

"You're not a predator, you're a psychopath," I seethe.

"Maybe I'm both," he smiles. This is so funny to him. "If you don't want to tell me where it is. I'll have to start searching thoroughly."

His free hand goes down to my waist and he untucks my polo.

"Don't. Jake, stop."

Couldn't sound less convincing if I tried.

"Feel free to tell me where the phone is anytime and I'll stop searching," he says as his hand slips under my top.

My brain turns liquid when his hand touches my skin.

Just tell him where the phone is.

And ruin the only chance I have at looking into what happened to my brother? I don't think so. I can do this. I'm bigger than his intimidating techniques. Stronger. Jake White does. Not. Scare. Me.

You keep telling yourself that.

His touch is light as a feather but his hand so firm that I don't dare move an inch. My skin is burning under him and my breath stays stuck in my throat. He skims over my waist and my belly before creeping up higher. He hooks his index finger under my bra and follows all the way to the back.

For a second, I'm scared he'll unhook it, but he slides back to the front and lets go of it. Before I know, his hand goes up and his knuckles graze against my hardened nipple. I think it's an accident but a second later he grazes harder on the other one and I inhale a sharp breath.

"J-Jake..."

"Ssh. Unless it's to tell me where the phone is. Keep quiet."

He tightens his grip on my wrists and gets closer as I squirm under his touch. The raw crispness of his scent is making me dizzy with pleasure. Or maybe it's his violently soft touch. I'm lost in the sensuality of it and I can't think clearly.

His hand leaves my body and emerges from under my top. A shiver runs through me at the withdrawal of his warmth, but I quickly feel it again against my leg. I wonder why my stockings are not protecting my legs anymore. Did he take them off? No, the memory of ditching them when I lay on the sofa comes back to me and goes away as quickly as it came when his hand slithers up my thigh.

"Spread those pretty legs for me, Angel."

My breath is so ragged I panic at the fact that I can't control it anymore. When I don't move, he knocks my foot with his and keeps his leg between mine, his knee against the inside of my thigh, keeping my legs spread. My panic is quickly overtaken by a thrilling pleasure again. His hand leaves a hot trail behind every inch of my skin it touches. I'm scared. Not because I want him to stop but because I don't. Because I don't want him to get any closer to the proof of my body betraying me.

He wraps his hand around my upper thigh when he gets to the top. It's so tight that I let out a strange noise. Something between a mewl and a moan. I want to clench my thighs, hide from his touch but his leg is keeping me spread out for him.

He slowly releases his tight grip on my thigh and lets his thumb trail between my legs. As soon as he touches the outside of my underwear I shiver and let out a heavy breath.

Chapter 10

He roams around and feels my underwear before letting out a low chuckle.

He knows. There is no way he didn't feel how soaked they are.

"Fuck. You're so wet for me, baby." He grazes the outside of my panties with his knuckles. Too light. Not enough. I need more.

I buck my hips, releasing a choked, begging moan, and before I can get the pressure I need, he takes his hand away. I let out a crying, frustrated whimper. His mocking laugh now sounds crystal clear to my ears. I snap my eyes open. I didn't even realize I had closed them.

"What did you think was gonna happen Angel? I told you. I'm looking for the phone. Nothing else."

I squeeze my eyes shut at his tone and the embarrassment it brings. When I open them, I look away in shame, burning heat creeping up my neck and onto my cheeks.

He finally lets go of me, turns around, and strides for my drawers. He knowingly opens my underwear drawer, puts his hand inside, and takes out the phone.

"You knew?" I ask in a short breath.

"Of course I knew. I'm always ten steps ahead. Don't you know that yet?"

I peel my back off the wall and slowly walk to him.

"If you knew then why did you just do this?!" I point my hand at the wall. I can't believe him.

"Because I do what I want. It's as simple as that." He takes a step closer to me and puts a strand of my hair behind my ear. Looking down at me with a lopsided smile. "And I knew you'd love it. You've got a soft spot for me."

"I–I don't!" I try to blurt out as honestly as possible, but my burning cheeks are saying it all.

"Ah, right, you're into Chris. It slipped my mind." He

turns back to the drawer, not even bothering to listen if I have something to say in reply. He grabs a pair of underwear from the drawer and puts it in his back pocket.

"What are you doing?!" I choke on my words, at the surreality of the situation.

"We're leaving," he finally says and grabs my hand tightly.

"Wh–what?" I try to pull back, but he tightens and keeps walking.

"Do you never listen, Angel? I told you, I'm keeping you close from now on."

"Are you insane? I'm not coming with you!" I shout at his back as he drags me along the hallway and to the front door.

"Put your shoes on," he says once we reach the door.

"Deaf much? I'm not following you anywhere, you psycho."

He shrugs. "Fine, you made your choice." He bends over until his shoulder touches my hip, puts an arm around my legs, and grabs my shoes with his other hand before straightening back up. I let out a yelp when my body leaves the floor and I fall over his shoulder.

"Jake!" Panic overtakes me and I try to kick myself off his shoulder.

"Don't make me spank you, Angel."

I freeze.

What?

He wouldn't. Right, he wouldn't?

11

JAMIE

Hotter Than Hell – Dua Lipa

After an eternity of riding in complete silence, Jake stops in front of an iron security gate. When the gate opens, he zigzags up a hill surrounded by pine trees before he finally parks in front of a huge mansion.

Chris's house is exactly how I remember it. The house is modern with a countryside personality. It is made of grey and beige stones. There is a warm yellow light leaking from the French windows and glowing in the dark porch that is big enough to host a family dinner.

Jake gets out of the car and comes around to my side. I take a deep breath and reluctantly put my shoes on as he opens the door.

"This is kidnapping, did you know?" I mumble, still trying to put some sense into him.

"Guess we're both criminals then." The smile he gives me shows that he genuinely doesn't care that I'm here against my will.

"I'm not a criminal, Jake," I sigh, still refusing to get out of the car. Maybe if I stay here long enough, he'll grow bored and drive me back.

"Last time I checked, theft was a crime."

"Look. I'm sorry, okay? What do you want?"

"We've got plenty of time for questions later. Come on," he concludes.

I reluctantly get out of the car and follow him. I expect him to walk towards the wooden double front door. Instead, he turns towards the garage in silence. We walk around the garage, through a small alley between perfectly trimmed bushes and a stoned wall from the house.

A few feet later we walk into the backyard. We walk along the paved patio and onto the thick, green grass. The pool is a huge rectangle of dark blue, reflecting the sunset. There are some lights around the yard, paving the way to the pool house. I remember when Chris and I were kids and used to pick our favorite pool toys from the mess inside the pool house. I'm confused, why does he want to go there?

When we get to the door, Jake puts me in front of him and opens the door from behind me. His arm brushes against the side of my face and, while my brain's first reaction should be to jerk away, my body takes it all in. The warmth, the sandalwood scent. I still feel sticky between my legs from earlier and his closeness brings it all back. I shiver as he turns the handle and pushes it forward.

My eyes widen when the door opens, Chris is sitting down on a sofa perpendicular to the doorway. Rose is next to him munching on popcorn while he looks for something to watch on TV.

They both look up when Jake gives me a light push that makes me step inside. This pool house had never looked like this before. Chris's parents must have renovated it for the twins.

"Well if that isn't our little thief," Rose says playfully. "Here to give me back my phone?"

I don't reply but I relax when Chris gets up and observes both Jake and me for a few seconds, frowning at us. His eyes go from me to Jake and back to me before he walks to us. That's it, he's going to tell him something. He's going to threaten Jake for bringing me here against my will, in his low, deep voice. Jake is going to complain but eventually, he won't have a choice. Chris is going to step in, he's not going to let this stupid situation go on any longer.

He stops in front of us but addresses himself to Jake. "I'll be in the house if you're looking for me."

I can feel my heart racing as Chris leaves without another glance my way.

"Chris–" I call out but within seconds he slams the door behind him.

Rose laughs as she gets up from the sofa. "I think you've lost all your allies, Goody."

She picks up a red leather jacket and puts it on before coming to a stop right in front of me, but she doesn't look at me either. She's talking to Jake, right above my head. I am sandwiched between the two. Neither of them pays attention to me while they go on with their conversation. She holds out her hand to him.

"No," Jake simply says.

"Jake," she warns in a low voice.

I can't see him, but I feel him shift behind me and sigh. The next second, he deposits the burner phone into Rose's hand.

"You're my hero," she smiles at him. "I'll be at Rachel's."

"Ozy, don't text him. Not until we've figured out a plan."

"Sure thing." She gives him her most innocent smile but I'm sure he doesn't buy it any more than I do.

"Are you coming back for the party?" he asks.

"Is that a real question? Have I ever missed Chris' birthday?" She doesn't wait for a response and I hear the door open and close.

I close my eyes for a second, swallowing the lump in my throat. I am now completely alone with Jake in *his* house. Chris has given up on helping me after I lied to him and Rose doesn't give a shit, especially now that she knows I'm the one who stole her phone. And to top it all off, I don't even have the phone anymore. My only weapon to get closer to Volkov. My only chance to get any answers about my brother.

"Move."

I jump in surprise at the order that comes with a hand at my lower back. I open my eyes and swallow hard before I take steps deeper inside the house. I walk to the right, behind the sofa, as he guides me to a hallway with his hand. It only takes us a few steps to reach two doors. One on the right and one on the left. There's another one in the middle, marking the end of the hallway.

I stop, not knowing where to go, and he pushes the door to the left open. I don't wait for him and go in straight away.

That is not what I expected Jake White's bedroom to look like. The walls are all completely white and the furniture light gray or white. Straight ahead, against the wall opposite to the door, there is a gray desk, big enough to have space for his homework spread out on one side and two computer screens on the other.

There's a wall perpendicular to the right side of the doorway so I turn to the left. His bed is against the left wall. It's an old black metal bed with bars at the bottom and at the head. It looks like it barely holds together but, mixed with the modern furniture, the contrast gives an edgy look to the room. He's got a door that, I'm assuming, leads to a closet on the left side of his bed and a white nightstand on the other side with an antique brass lamp on it.

All the walls have black and white pictures on them. Some of him and his friends, some of him playing lacrosse, in action. Some of them are beautiful pictures of nature and landscapes.

"You want to observe all day or are you gonna get in?"

Without even thinking I keep stepping inside until I'm in the middle of the room.

"Did you take these pictures? They're beautiful."

"Luke did," he replies as he looks at his phone. He's typing something and focusing on the screen.

I don't know what to say. I don't know what to do. What we shared earlier is gone. Uncomfortable tension has replaced sexual tension and I'm dying for him to touch me the way he did at my house. Not that I would admit it to him.

Jake walks around me, his gaze still on his phone, and goes to the closet. He opens the door, grabs a towel, a T-shirt, and turns around.

"Shower," he orders calmly, throwing the towel and shirt at me.

I catch them in a reflex, but my thoughts don't follow my body.

"W– what?" I stutter, completely lost. My brain can't help going to dark places, wondering why he wants my body clean.

"You've spent the whole day at school. You should shower before the party," he replies, obviously.

"What party?" As soon as I've asked, it comes back to me. Chris' birthday. How can I keep forgetting he's turning eighteen today? "I'm not going to that. I haven't been to

Chris' birthday parties in years. In fact, since you started attending."

He throws his phone on the bed and finally looks at me with a saccharine smile.

"I find it funny you stopped being friends with Chris since I moved to Stoneview. Are you that scared of me?"

I haven't particularly stopped seeing Chris because the twins showed up, we slowly drifted apart when his group of friends became more and more elitist. But I can't ignore that I always thought something was off with them, especially Jake. Clearly, I was right.

"Aren't you the one who said you didn't want to see me at a party again? I'm just following your advice," I ignore his question.

He lets out a low chuckle. It comes out from deep in his chest and forces goosebumps to break all over my skin.

"Look. I'm going to give you one last chance to do things willingly before I make you do them."

I can feel his anger rising and I take a step back when he takes one toward me.

"You don't scare me," I reply. I wish my body would follow my mind and didn't force me to take another step back. I wish my voice backed up my words instead of shaking from fear.

Jake shrugs in a 'as you wish' way and I can see the smile tugging at his lips. He takes another step toward me and grabs both my shoulders, forcing me to back up until I hit the chair at his desk.

"You're gonna want to sit down for this," he says. I frown but resist when he pushes my shoulders down. "Fine. Suit yourself."

He turns around, walks a few steps as if thinking if what he's about to do is worth it. When he turns back around, his right elbow is in his left palm by his chest and he's holding his chin in his right hand. I watch him, the back of my knees against the chair.

"Quick question." He pauses to make sure he has my attention. Once he is sure he has it all, he starts again. "The coffee shop you and your mom work at, do you know who owns it?"

I am completely lost.

When he sees my hesitation, he insists. "Do you?"

"Uh, yeah, the Bakers. Why?"

He smiles. "Yup. That's Luke's family, you know that, right?"

"I do." My brows are so close together at this point they could be touching. Where is he going with this?

He walks so close to me that I try to take a step back to try and look up at his eyes. Of course, I can't because of the chair right behind me so I just tilt my head up.

"Tell me, Angel, how much did you and your mom steal from them?"

This time, my brows shoot up, probably all the way to my hairline, and I feel my eyes go so wide, cold air stings my pupils. I freeze.

"W–what did you–" I swallow the rock stuck in my throat and almost choke on it. "What did you say?"

His smirk has turned ice cold. He's bluffing. How could he possibly know?

"I don't know what you're talking about," I say with a throat drier than a desert. I feel like I've swallowed a box of crackers. Like I haven't drank in days. Like someone forced a bucket of sand down my throat.

"Shit. You can barely keep it together when I ask you about it. Imagine when the cops will interrogate you about all the missing money."

"You're making things up now?" I spit in an attempt to throw him off. But he's got me. He's got me and the smirk on his face proves that he knows it.

"When I look into someone, I do it properly. And you and your mom have been sloppy." *Sloppy?* "Do you remember what I said when I caught you spying on me in the parking lot, Angel?"

Yes. Everything. Every single word. It was the first time he showed his true self. The first time I got a glimpse of the brute.

Memories of that afternoon come back in flashes.

'If you talk to anyone about what you've just seen, I'm going to turn your life into your own personal living hell.'

I shake my head trying to push them back, but I can feel myself starting to shake.

'You won't be able to go to work, school, or a party without having me on your back ruining your life. Hell, I'll even terrorize you in your own house if I have to.'

"Do you?" he insists.

I nod my trembling head slowly. Tears are building and putting pressure on the back of my eyes. I force myself to fight them back.

My head falls forward as I give up looking up at him.

And then, it hits me.

That dreadful feeling of being backed into a wall. No way out. No safe word. No one to come for help.

I fall back on the chair and my back hits the hard desk. My spine protests but I don't move and don't make a noise.

"You didn't want to play by the rules and now I'm afraid I'm going to have to stay true to my word."

"Jake–"

He cuts me off by grabbing my jaw in his right hand and forcing my head back. I'm forced to meet his gaze and I'm hit with full force by the eyes of the real Jake. The eyes resembling the deepest marina of the ocean. The darkest one, hiding the cruelest monsters. A horrible shiver makes my spine tremble, and his smirk widens on his lips.

"I want to make myself perfectly clear. I know what you and your mom did and if you put your nose in my shit again, not only your mom will end up in jail, but you can kiss goodbye to lacrosse, a scholarship, to Stoneview Prep, to everything you've worked so hard for."

My hands are holding the chair so tight my knuckles feel like they're going to break.

I try to jerk my head away from his grip in a pathetic attempt to hide the tears that have started falling onto my cheeks. Jake's hand tightens around my jaw. He squats in front of me, leveling his head with mine.

"Look at me, baby. From now on, you're going to listen to everything I say. Here, at school, at your house. I want your attention, your commitment, your fucking everything. If I tell you to jump, I want to hear you ask how high, if I order something, you follow without question. I want you so fucking obedient that I'll get bored of you by the end of the month. I control your life from now on. I. Fucking. Own. You"

As he talks, I feel like I'm disconnecting from my body and floating above the scene. I don't think I've had an enemy before. I've had arguments with girls. I've gained and lost friends over time. I've never been particularly liked at school, but I've also never really cared. The other students have always left me alone. I was ignored but never hated.

This. This is different. As I watch the scene unfold, I feel deeply sorry for this girl trying to hold back sobs while Jake unleashes the kind of hellish hate that will only leave one of them standing.

Jake lets go and stands back up. Looking down at the poor girl crying on the chair.

"Was that clear enough for you?"

I reluctantly snap back into my body and shut my eyes, trying to force the flow of tears to stop but it only squeezes more out of me.

I've never had an enemy before. Never had someone who's made it a point to ruin my life. Someone whose sole purpose was to bring me down. But with Jake standing before me now, I know this is about to end. I've found my enemy. Because that's what Jake is now, isn't it? He decided he wanted to ruin me and he's not going to stop until it's done.

I don't have the strength to keep looking at him and my gaze falls. I give a slow, short nod. Anything. Anything for him to keep that secret to himself. If the Bakers learn what mom and I did...I don't even want to think about it. I don't know how he found out but it's too late to lie about it now.

I can feel his hand on the top of my head, stroking my hair.

"Good. Survival instinct, Angel. Now go shower," he concludes in a satisfied voice. He seems to have relaxed now.

Of course he has. He's made up a whole new game, with a whole new set of rules, and it's barely started but he knows he's already won.

12

JAKE

Passion and Pain Taste the Same When I'm Weak – Tove Lo

Control. Control. Control.

How far do I need to take it before I'm satisfied? How far until my unhealthy need is satiated?

When I went to Jamie's house, I thought I'd give her a good scare and take the phone back. Then she lied to me. Tried to hide that she stole from us. So, I decided to play with her a little before leaving. But the way she reacted, how hot she got for me, panting like a bitch in need, it stirred something in me. It woke up the beast I'd managed to keep down since moving to Stoneview.

Jamie Williams doesn't go down without a fight and I can't stand not having control over her. She stole, lied, and went directly against everything I threatened her with. She left me with no choice. She poked the devil inside me until I broke and now, I've gone too far to come back. Now I *need* to control her. And right now, the only thing bringing me satisfaction is the fear in her eyes when she realizes I've got her cornered and she's left with no choice but to play my game by my rules.

"Door to the left," I say as she opens my bedroom door.

She gets out without a glance back and I let myself fall on the bed, looking at the ceiling.

Shit!

As soon as she's out of sight I'm hit with what I've just done. I've let the worst of me take over. It hadn't happened in years. Almost three years to be precise. Three years of pure control over the darkest parts of myself. And it took Jamie all of two weeks to fuck it all up.

Last Friday, I started to lose it then. Because I threatened her, and she didn't give a shit. I like it when everything goes my way. I can't live any other way anymore. But fuck knows that deep down I enjoy it the most when there's something to tame. The reward feels a hundred times better.

That's what I used to love about Camila. She used to be feisty, she used to fight me on my shit. But she quickly gave in. She fell in love with me, she gave up by fear of losing me. Now she likes to be controlled, especially by me.

As if summoned by my thoughts of her, my phone beeps next to me to a text from Camila.

> Cam: Can I come early?

"Shit," I mutter in a sigh.

I grab my phone and reply a quick excuse to keep her away from here as long as possible. My mind is focused on Jamie, I can't even begin to think of Camila. All my thoughts are turned to the girl in the shower.

I have to restrain myself from bursting into that bathroom and drag her naked body back to my bed. My cock tightens imagining the water trickling down her shoulders, the drops rolling down her breasts, and dribbling from her tight buds. My hand slides to my dick and I hold it through my jeans when there's a knock on the door.

"Fuck," I let out. *This fucking girl.*

I jump off the bed, snap the door open, grab Jamie's wrist, and drag her inside in a harsh pull. I slam the door closed without releasing her wrist. She drops the clothes she was holding.

"You don't have to knock, idiot," I say as I push her on the bed.

She lets out a small yelp as her back hits the mattress, but it doesn't stop me from going after her. Her knees are bent on the edge of the bed and her legs dangling, her foot unable to reach the floor. I'm still holding one of her wrists and pin it above her head before I drop on top of her. I put my other hand beside her shoulder, staying well above her and slide one knee between her legs.

My t-shirt looks ten times too big on her and it reaches mid-thigh. I spread her legs a little further apart with my knee and her free hand tries to keep the t-shirt down.

"Don't," she whispers in a weak attempt to stop me.

Jamie fucking Williams, I need to have her. To control her. To break her.

I shake my head trying to calm down the devil in me.

I put my free hand on her jaw, running my thumb on her bottom lip.

"Are you naked under this?"

I can see her struggling to swallow as she blushes. "I don't–I don't have any clean underw–"

"Mm, I know that." I can feel my voice getting lower and raspier. My cock is so hard in my pants the button might pop open soon.

I press my thumb hard against her lips and she goes to protest but as soon as her mouth parts open, I push it inside.

"Suck."

Her pleading eyes are making me harder if that is even possible.

"Don't make me repeat myself," I growl.

I can see her hesitating; one hand is stuck in my fist and she's not sure what to do with the other: keep her pussy hidden from me or try to pull my hand away from her mouth.

I push my thumb slightly further in her mouth and she instantly starts sucking.

"Not like that. Wrap your lips around it," I order. She executes straight away. "Fuck," I let out in a raspy breath. It's so warm and wet, I could come right now.

I lower myself, my arm struggling to hold my body weight under the pleasure.

She tries to say my name, but it comes out muffled. She squirms under me when my chest meets her hard nipples through the shirt. I bring my knee higher, and higher until I come in contact with the hotness between her legs.

She's soaking. I can feel it through my pants. I want to listen to the evil in me and take her right here, right now. Luke is right, I love them tiny and breakable.

You're taking this too far.

That's the controlled voice of reason.

My head falls in the crook of her neck as I battle with the angel and demon on each of my shoulders.

Her tongue swipes around my thumb, her hips buck, her core grinding on my knee and I fucking lose it. I let the demon win without an ounce of hesitation.

I take my thumb out of her mouth to bring my hand

down between her legs and as I push her hand away from the hem of the shirt her trembling voice reaches my ears.

"P–please, Jake, stop..."

Yes, keep her begging, the demon says.

But when I snap my eyes back up to hers, I jerk away and back up in a split second. Those begging, scared eyes. What do they see in me?

As soon as I'm up she scrambles higher on the bed. When her back hits the headboard she brings her knees to her chest, wrapping the shirt all the way over her ankles.

"Fuck, Jamie..." I say through gritted teeth. Why am I mad at her right now? Because she was scared I was going to take it too far?

You were going to take it too far.

I run a hand through my hair as she watches me pace around the room.

"Just...just get off the bed."

She hurries off the bed and I reach in my back pocket.

"And put some fucking underwear on." I throw the black panties I grabbed from her place and she catches them. "I'll get you some clothes," I conclude as I leave the room.

Jamie

I'm still panting when Jake leaves the room. I'm speechless at what just happened. I can't believe I've let him do this. I can't believe how much I was enjoying it. I was lost in utter bliss. In a dimension between here and ecstasy. I wanted more, I wanted him. To touch me, to explore my body like a map to a pirate's treasure. But the rational voice inside me asked him to stop.

I almost slapped myself when the words came out. I didn't want him to realize how bad I needed him to continue, to stop teasing and give me what I craved. But Jake goes about with questionable seducing techniques and I don't think I could let myself give in to his bullying, no matter how good it feels.

At least I know he stops if I ask him too. Although the look on his face when he pulled away was like he was fighting something deep within himself. Like he wanted to hurt me but stopped himself when he got close to his goal.

I quickly get back to reality and put my underwear on. Once I've slipped into my clean panties he grabbed from my house, I pick up the bra I was wearing today from my pile of clothes on the floor. I put the bra on without taking his shirt completely off. The last thing I want is him to come back in while I'm trying to put my B-cup back on.

I pick up the towel I dropped earlier from the floor and hang it on the back of his desk chair. I slowly walk to the closet door and open it. There's a mirror on the other side of the door and I check myself.

I look exactly the same, but I feel different. I feel desperate. All I want is Jake's touch on me again. On the outside, I look like I can control myself but deep down I feel like I'd do anything to go back to the ecstatic state I get in when he touches me.

I frown at myself in the mirror. I look like an eight-year-old in his shirt. It's way too big for me. The seam of the shoulder is on my arm and the bottom of the shirt is low on my thighs.

I let out a frustrated sigh as I close the closet door. I look down at the shirt and bring it to my nose. It smells like him, his dark wooden scent. Like I'm lost in a deep forest but still surrounded by the warmth of citrus tickling my nostrils.

The bedroom door opens, and I jump in surprise,

releasing the bit of the shirt I brought up to my nose. He walks towards me and hands me a skirt and a black t-shirt.

"Here, you can wear this. It's Rose's."

I can't help the laugh that escapes my lips. "You want me to wear Rose's clothes? Have you seen her, and have you seen me?"

"You're both skinny," he shrugs. Is he that unobservant? Did he never notice his sister is about twice my height?

I give a second look at the skirt and top. It's a small black denim skirt and a simple tee.

"Whatever," I mumble. I go to leave for the bathroom, but he holds me back by the shoulder.

"Where are you going?"

Was he even there when he asked me to get changed? "I'm going...to put these on?" I hesitate.

He lets out a short chuckle and I feel like I missed the joke. "Who said you should get changed in the bathroom?"

I open my mouth to say something, but I can't find the words.

"I've probably seen more girls in underwear in my life than you have, Angel. You're not that impressive." He goes to his desk and sits on the chair.

I pretend his words don't hurt as I slide the skirt on. How can he be so hot and cold? One second he wants to make my life hell, the next he wants to fuck me, and the following he tells me I'm not special. As Emily said, I don't know if he wants to kill me or fuck me. I decide to keep his khaki tee on and tuck it in the denim skirt.

"There."

He looks up from his computer and turns to me, raising an eyebrow as soon as he notices I kept his top on. He gets up and walks to me slowly, like a predator closing on his prey, and according to the smug smile on his face, he knows this prey isn't going anywhere.

He stops barely one step before bumping into me. He's so close that I have to tilt my head up to watch him as he looks down at me. He puts a hand on my hip and holds me tight. I can already feel the flush growing on my chest for the third time tonight and I silently wonder if there will ever be a time when my body doesn't respond this way to his.

"Why did you take the phone, Angel?"

I didn't expect this, and I try to take a step back to think but he easily stops me by putting his other hand on my other hip. His hands are so big on my narrow body, he easily cages me in and brings me back to him.

"Why?" he repeats.

All sorts of thoughts are going through my mind but none of them seem like a plausible lie. One that he would believe and that would be good enough for him to let me go.

He lets out a frustrated chuckle and his smug smile turns into a smirk that makes me uneasy. I squirm under his hold and he tightens.

"Stop it, you're gonna get bruised."

"I don't know what to tell you."

"The truth." He untucks my shirt slowly and raises it.

"What are you doing?" I ask in a panic.

He doesn't reply and a few seconds later the tee is over my head. "I never said you could wear this, baby. Do you want Camila to cut my balls off or something?"

He throws it on the bed behind us and when his gaze comes back to me, I'm too deep into thinking about him and Camila to realize I'm standing in my bra in front of him. What if she learns what we've done?

We *didn't do anything. He jumped me and I'm doing my best to survive this evening.*

Chapter 12

A heaviness grows in my stomach at the situation. Is this what it's like to be just another girl he cheats on Camila with? In the end, no matter what, he'll always run back to the beautiful Camila Diaz.

"What's this?"

I jump at his voice and the touch on my shoulder. His finger is hooked under my left bra strap and he's looking right at my scar. It's a fairly big scar, especially for a shoulder the size of mine.

The bullet entered just above my pectoral and lodged in my clavicle. It stayed there for hours before someone found me. They had to go so deep to get the bullet out that I have a long horizontal line running across my front deltoid. It's ugly, my skin burns all the time because of the psychological trauma and lacrosse gets painful if I play too hard since my clavicle was shattered by the bullet. Mainly, it's a constant reminder of the night I lost the two most important men in my life. When I woke up, my dad was dead, and my brother had disappeared.

Jake runs his fingers along the scar, and I wince. It doesn't hurt, it's all in my head but I can't help it.

I must have paled because he takes a step back and observes me with a frown.

"Tell me," he demands like it's just that easy. The distance between him and human feelings is unfathomable.

I shake my head in negation, but he comes back on me too quickly for me to react. He grabs the back of my neck, his fingers pulling my hair.

"Fuck, do you think because I stopped when you asked me, you get to say no to me?"

My heart picks up in fear. "I–I–"

"Did you already forget what I said earlier? I'm more than happy to remind you that I've got shit on you, Goody."

"No, I know, I know," I panic, putting a hand on his chest to try to keep him away.

"Then start talking."

"Please, Jake, I can't. Not this." My begging voice sounds annoying even to me.

He lets me go harshly and takes a step back, an animalistic growl coming out of his mouth. Is this just how it works when he doesn't get what he wants? Violence and threats? His phone rings on the bed, and he lets out another annoyed grunt.

"Don't move," he whispers as he walks around me to go grab his phone.

"Chris, bro, this better be important because I'm busy," he says in a friendly voice.

What is it with me? Why is it that every time he turns to me, he's a demon and every time he addresses himself to someone else, he turns back to the chill Jake.

"Shit," he says in a rush, "I'll take care of it." He hangs up at the same time as someone knocks violently on the front door.

"Ugh, sonofabitch," he mutters to himself. He heads for the door. Before opening it, he turns to me.

"You. Don't move an inch. I want you in this exact position when I come back. Got it?"

I quickly nod my head as he walks out of the room.

But of course, there is no way I'm going to stay still for this bastard. So, I hurry up and quietly follow him. If he thinks he can use shit against me, then why can't I do the same?

I make sure he's not in the hallway anymore when I get out of the room. He's pushed closed the door leading from the hall to the main area but it's still ajar and I can hear multiple voices coming from the living room.

Chapter 12

I pad towards the door, the light in the hallway is off and the only illumination comes from the small gap. When I finally reach the end of the hall and look through the gap, I can see Jake talking to two guys at the door. It's Roy and Carlo. Camila's brothers.

Two gang members that used to work for Volkov.

And now for Samuel.

"...not picking up her phone. Any idea how long I've been waiting? This ain't no game *huérfano*," Roy complains.

"Appreciate the nickname, as always boys," Jake replies. I can't see his face, but I can imagine the smug smile on it.

"Where is she?" Carlo asks. "Can't pick up without her."

Is he talking about going to Volkov's strip club?

Jake shrugs. "It's not really her specialty. She's more about the using than the dealing now."

Carlo, the oldest and biggest of the two brothers, takes a step forward but Jake doesn't look intimidated. He doesn't step back and casually pulls his hands out of his pockets to cross his arms over his chest, showing off his broad shoulders and bulging biceps. Jake is taller than both of them, but Carlo looks like 200 pounds of pure muscle.

"We need a girl. Unless you're feeling like dressing up, better tell me where your cute sister is."

Jake lets out a short breath, halfway between a chuckle and an unimpressed sigh. "If you need a girl that bad, take your own sister. She looks great in a stripper outfit. You can take my word for it."

My jaw falls at Jake's nerve. Carlo takes another step, ready to punch Jake in the face but Roy holds him back and pulls him back their way.

"Drop it, Carlo. We can let Sam deal with the *pendejo*."

I can almost hear Jake's smile when he replies to them. "Perfect. You do that. Great talk guys. Come back anytime."

As soon as they've slammed the door behind them, Jake takes his phone out of his pocket. He taps it a few times and puts it to his ear.

After a few seconds, he runs his hand through his hair in frustration.

"Ozy, pick up your fucking phone," he growls in the phone before hanging up.

I guess Rose decided to ignore the texts from Samuel. In that case, she also decided to ignore his threat of going to the police. I run back to the room before Jake can realize I was spying but I can't stop wondering what he's done that's bad enough for Samuel to use as blackmail.

Where is Jake's limit? Does he know when he crosses a line or is it never enough for him?

13

JAMIE

Are U Gonna Tell Her – Tove Lo, MC Zaac

The party is raging by the time Rose and Rachel walk into the huge kitchen where Jake is making himself a drink. I'm standing a few feet away from him, the only person sitting down on one of their highchairs, and hoping, for the nth time tonight, he will leave me alone and soon let me go home. But when he turns to me and downs his I-don't-know-how-many drink of the night I know there's no way in hell he'll be sober enough to drive me back. I don't have my bike and his house is not a walking distance from mine.

Jake is talking with Chris, they're both slowly walking toward me when Chris spots Rose and Rachel.

"Here she is," Chris mutters. He's been drinking tonight, and I can see he's not being his usual calm self.

He's been flirting with tons of girls that came to wish him a happy birthday. Every time one leaves, Jake tries to convince him she's good enough for a 'sexcapade' and every time, Chris says he shouldn't.

"You," Jake growls as he changes trajectories and heads for his twin.

Chris is still coming my way as Jake scolding Rose turns into background noise. Chris' eyes are locked on mine and his smile is more predatory than I've ever seen. I feel like I could watch him forever, but Jake's deep voice takes priority.

"...20 fucking times," I hear by the kitchen entrance.

"You need to fucking chill, dude. I told you where I was," Rose is clearly no more sober than him.

"Next time the Diaz brothers show up here I'll smash your stupid phone in your head. Glue it to your face. Maybe then you'll learn how to pick up."

At Jake's violent words, I turn my face to look at the trio. Rachel is looking at Jake with eyes as wide as saucers. Rose is clenching her jaw as if stopping herself from retaliating. She turns to Rachel, says something in her ear, and kisses her forehead. Rachel nods and leaves.

Rose turns back to Jake. "A word," she manages through clenched teeth.

Jake shakes his head annoyed but follows his sister out of the kitchen. When I face forward again Chris is right in front of me, making me jump in surprise.

Why does he look annoyed at me?

"Do you know when was the last time I saw Jake acting like this?" he asks.

"Like what?" I reply, fidgeting on the highchair. Why does it suddenly feel so uncomfortable? I get off the chair and stand up to continue the conversation.

"Constantly angry. Threatening his own twin. Bullying a random girl."

I shift on my feet when he mentions bullying. Is this what it is? Is this how it starts?

"He's not bu–"

Chapter 13

"Why did you lie to me, Jamie?" He cuts me off, not caring one bit about what I have to say.

"Chris, I–I'm sorry."

"Whatever you're doing, that makes him like this. Stop it. Before it's too late."

"Before it's too late? How bad can it get?" I ask, incredulous.

Chris doesn't reply. He just takes another sip of his drink.

"Please tell him to leave me alone," I say in an almost inaudible voice.

He shakes his head, and his gaze hardens. I try to take him all in but it's impossible. Chris is too much for me to handle. His gaze is too bright, and despite how angry he is at me right now, his warmth is drowning me in delicious heat.

"I gave you a chance to let me help you out of this." The muscles on his neck tighten at the same time as his grip on his beer bottle. "You didn't want my help. You chose to lie to me instead."

His words break my heart. I had no idea he thought so highly of our friendship, or whatever was left of it, and I ruined it all. I crushed it under my boot for my own personal reasons.

I'm about to protest or at least try another round of apologies, but Camila approaches Chris and grabs his arm. "Come on birthday boy, we're gonna do a round of Do or Drink!" she exclaims excitedly.

As soon as Chris has left my field of view, I feel two strong hands on my shoulders. I don't need to turn around to know Jake is back in the kitchen.

"We're gonna play a little game, Angel," he whispers in my ear. I can't help my body trembling at his mouth so close to me. My mind automatically drifts back to our position on his bed earlier.

He comes in front of me, puts his cup down, and pours another drink in a new cup.

"Here," he hands it to me. "You're gonna need it."

I reluctantly take the drink and he puts a hand at the back of my neck, guiding me around and out of the kitchen. I let him, still wondering at what point am I going to be able to stop this? At what point is he going to get bored?

The music is much louder in the hallway. We cross a good chunk of the house until we make our way down twisted wooden stairs leading to a basement. It's a space with bean bags spread everywhere, big enough to host a few friends in a quieter, more private area of the house.

A giant flat screen hangs on the wall and too many consoles to count rest under it. The lights are dimmed, the mood intimate.

When Jake and I get downstairs, Chris, Camila, Rachel, Beth, and Jason are already sitting on bean bags spread around a round marble coffee table that probably costs more than the quarterly rent for my house. I spot a couple making out on a bean bag in the corner of the room. According to the light blond hair, I'd say it's Luke, but he's on top of a girl and this part of the room is way too dark to make out who the other person is.

Camila's eyes dart to Jake's hand on my neck and I feel so uneasy I twist to try and push him away. He tightens his grip and gives me a look so dark it freezes me on the spot. Does he not see she's right here? Does he not understand that this is wrong on so many levels even if she *wasn't* here?

When he starts walking again, I'm forced to follow until Camila scoots over, inviting Jake to sit between her and Rachel. He stops a few steps away from the table. I can sense him hesitate for a beat and I don't know what to do with myself.

Thankfully someone else is walking downstairs and what seems like a split second later, a hand lays on the small of my back. Before I have time to look, I hear Rose's raspy voice. She's speaking low enough that only Jake and I can hear her.

"Any explanation as to why you're dressing your new toy with my shit, Jake? Are we back in kindergarten?"

Jake lets out a low chuckle and his grip lessens, allowing me to let out the breath I didn't know I was holding. My brain is screaming at me to run away as quickly as I can while simultaneously sending images of my mom being arrested for stealing from the coffee shop's till.

"I don't know, are you going to steal my toy?" Jake asks.

She laughs before pulling her hand away and putting it in the pocket of her chinos. "Nah, you can keep that one."

"Then no, we're not back to kindergarten."

"Glad to hear. F. Y. I, that's your girlfriend over there. Might want to keep your hands to yourself, I don't want no murder tonight even though she'd be well in her right to kill you." She doesn't wait for a reply and goes to sit between Camila and Rachel. She smiles at Camila's frown.

"What? You didn't keep that seat for me?" she asks innocently as she puts an arm around Rachel's shoulders.

Camila makes space again and Jake walks over still holding me. He sits on Camila's left and pushes me down to his left so I'm sitting between him and Rose.

When Camila gives him a dangerous look followed by a head gesture toward me, he smiles back at her. "What? I can't sit next to my sister for this game. Would be awkward."

I still have no idea what game they're talking about, but

Camila seems stuck and she can't say anything but mutter a 'right'.

Everything Jake and Rose do always looks planned even if they never have to talk to each other about it.

Chris is sitting right across from me and I do my best to avoid his stares. I put my cup on the table next to Jake's and wait while Beth shuffles a pack of big black cards with the words 'Do or Drink' written in white on the back.

Jake takes his phone out and leans toward my side to whisper in my ear, "Do you want to see how I make Chris do what I want? It's fun, you'll see."

I frown in confusion as I turn my face to him but understand when I see the text he's typed.

> Jake: I'll go easy on her if you come sit next to her.

When I look up from the phone Chris and Jake are in a staring contest. Jake has a smug smile on his face and Chris's jaw is tightening by the second, muscles ticking below his ears.

"What are you playing at?" I whisper angrily at him. "Haven't you done enough tonight?"

"What? Aren't you in love with him or something?"

"I'm not–"

"Whatever, he makes you wet, Angel, and so do I. I want you between him and I. So, you keep your pretty mouth shut and let me do what I want."

Rage is boiling inside me and I put my hands on the table to push myself up. I can't do this. I can't do everything Jake says. I never could, it's just not in my nature to bend to someone else's will. I don't understand how Camila can stay with him. Maybe she likes it, but I don't. I can't. I start pushing myself up but a hand on my shoulder pushes me

Chapter 13

back down and when I look up, Chris is sitting down next to me, forcing me to stay down with him.

"Come on, Angel, you were doing so good tonight." Jake puts his hand on my other shoulder and I've never felt so trapped in my life.

Chris doesn't say anything, but I can sense him silently fuming beside me.

"Nooo, man, that's weird," Rose exclaims, a cigarette in her mouth, as she realizes Chris has just sat down between her and I.

"I got you," another voice comes to my ears.

I look up at Luke sitting between Rose and Chris.

"Hmph," Rose keeps her complaint going.

"Oh my God! 'Me!'" It turns out, the girl Luke was making out with on the bean bags is no other than Emily. My eyes widen as she hugs me from the back. "I'm so fucking glad you're here."

She's drunk. So damn drunk. At least being here means I can keep an eye on her tonight. She sinks between Chris and Luke and everyone looks ready to start playing.

"No cheating," Beth says as she pushes the deck of cards at the center of the table. "No quitting."

I look around the table. Beth is on Camila's right and Jason on the right of Beth. Then the circle goes back to Rachel, Rose, Luke, Emily, Chris and me.

"What's the game?" I ask Chris as quietly as possible.

"Pretty simple. You do what's on the card or you drink," he replies as if I was the dumbest person on the planet.

Right, so kind of truth or dare but instead of truth, you drink. How hard can it be?

"Who wants to start?" Beth asks.

"Here," Jason says. "I'll start."

He picks a card from the game and reads it out loud.

"Call your ex and tell them that you want to get back together. Do this or take two shots."

Jason's eyes flip to Rose for a split second before putting the card in front of him. She ignores him royally and pulls Rachel closer to her. Jason licks his plumped lips as if he is thinking long and hard about it. In the low light, his skin looks darker than usual. He looks around the table with his chocolate eyes and grabs something from under the table before slamming a bottle of tequila on the marble.

"Yeah, fuck this. I ain't calling the bitch." He adds shot glasses beside the bottle and pours two shots. "This game's gonna fuck me up tonight."

I don't miss Rose's lopsided smile when he calls his ex a bitch. Jason takes the two shots and turns to Rachel. This group is so incestuous it's ridiculous. "Your turn."

If this game is about calling exes, then I definitely will end up drunk since I have no ex to call.

Rachel picks a card from the deck. "Oh that's...no. Let the whole group pinch your nipples. Do this or take two shots."

Everyone starts laughing but I can't help a gasp. What the hell is this game?!

Rose starts pouring two shots for Rachel that she takes without hesitation.

"You can play again when there's only the two of you," Luke says in a laugh. "Feel free to invite me."

Rose gives him a shove before picking up a card. "Reveal to everyone every single drug you've done or drink twice."

Jake turns to her in a split second. "Fuck no. We don't have all night. Take two, Ozy."

She laughs and takes two shots.

At this rate, we're all going to be on the floor in the next round. Especially knowing all these guys have been drinking and taking whatever earlier in the night.

Luke picks another card and less than a minute later he's downing two shots. Emily looks in her element, she's drunk, probably high on something, and has clearly played this game before. Personally, my stomach tightens the closer it gets to my turn.

"Give the person to your right a back massage for at least 30 seconds while whispering sexually in their ear, or drink four sips." Emily laughs at the card before turning to Chris. "Someone has to start the game, Chris."

She's about to put her hands on his shoulders when Luke grabs them. "Whoa whoa, wait. Four sips are nothing, no need to get handsy." He grabs her drink and puts it to her lips.

Emily giggles and lets him pour some in her mouth.

Chris grabs a card as well. He doesn't even read it out loud and just takes a shot of tequila.

"Tell us!" Camila insists when she sees him put the card down.

He simply smiles and shakes his head, putting the card on the table, facing down. No one protests again as if Chris's decisions are incontestable.

Everyone turns to me and I have to take a deep breath before drawing a card. The colors must drain from my face because I spot Camila's and Beth's sneers straight away. I have to scratch my throat before speaking out loud.

"Let...um...let one person in the group slap you as hard as they can on the ass or finish your drink."

There's a quick giggle around the table, probably at my flushed face.

"I'm happy to oblige, Goody. You certainly deserve it," Jake says loud enough for everyone to hear. My throat is too dry to reply to him, but I don't miss Camila's confused scowl at her boyfriend.

Boyfriend. The word resonates in my head at the same time as all the things we did today flashback in my mind.

I quickly grab my full drink and down it, choking on most of it. I might have alcohol dripping down my chin but at least I don't have to face any of their stares or get slapped on the ass. By the time I put down my cup, Jake has picked up a card. Chris grabs my empty cup straight away and pours I-don't-know-what up to the rim. I cough for a few seconds trying not to throw up what I just ingested. I didn't realize how strong this drink was.

"Guess which player has had anal sex. If you get it right, they drink three times. If you get it wrong, you drink three times," Jake says with a lopsided smile. Everyone but me laughs as he turns to Camila. "Should I pour a little more in your cup, baby?" he smiles at her and I don't understand why I'm the only one who finds this game so out of line.

Am I that boring?

Camila shoves Jake in the shoulder playfully as she takes sips of her drink. She laughs when she picks up her card. "Remove your pants and sit in your underwear until your next turn or finish your drink."

"Can't drink twice in a row," Beth says quickly.

Camila gives her friend a cheeky smile. "I know that."

She proceeds to take her tight jeans off in front of everyone. I can't help but notice Jake licking his lower lips as she shimmies out of her pants, and I can't help the spike of jealousy either.

Why am I this way?

Her tight stomach, her curves, her skin tone. She's perfect in every way. She looks like a woman, sensual and experienced. I feel like a child next to her. Jake would never leave her for me.

"Enjoy guys, it's only for one round," Camila giggles as she sits back down.

A few rounds later, everyone is more drunk and starting to follow the actions on the cards. Everyone except me.

I got curious when Luke admitted his and Rose's first time was together, and they fist bumped about it. I was ready to leave when Beth let Jason 'spank her for 30 seconds while repeating 'harder daddy harder.' I don't want to do any of these actions with people that aren't my friends but if I keep drinking, I might pass out before the end of the game.

Rose picks up another card after Rachel had to dance topless on the table for twenty seconds.

"Confess which players' dad is the hottest or drink three times," Rose says. "Huh." She taps her index finger on her lips, pretending to be thinking. "Well, it sure ain't mine."

Everyone laughs at her dark humor, but she doesn't let it last long before admitting, "Jas your dad is hot. We all know it." Everyone agrees.

Chris picks up a card again and I know he's drunk when a predatory smile appears on his lips as he reads his card. "Pick someone in the group to unzip their pants with your teeth. Both of you must do this or take two shots.

My heart sinks in my stomach when he turns to me, lust shining in his golden eyes.

"Be good, Angel. For me." Jake's whisper is hot in my ear and my head feels fuzzy with all I've been drinking. Or maybe I feel fuzzy because of Jake's voice and Chris' stare.

The whole table is cheering when I get up and Chris goes on his knees. He grabs both my hips with his strong hands and my heart stammers in my chest. He pinches the skirt's zipper with his teeth and slowly drags it down. It only lasts a few seconds but it's an eternity in my head.

"Your turn," he smiles as he gets up. He smells of alcohol and something sweet I can't place.

I swallow the lump in my throat and get on my knees. I feel everyone's eyes on me, especially Jake's, and I want to get up and run away just as much as I want to keep going. An equal balance between going back to my boring life or finally letting adrenaline fill my body and wake a pleasurable and dangerous side of life.

I bare my teeth, looking right into Chris' eyes and drag the zipper down, keeping eye contact with him. I sense something shifting below his jeans but don't even think about it. Again, it only lasts about five seconds but it's all my body needs to melt and for pleasure to pool between my legs.

Everyone claps as I sit back in my space, pulling my zipper up. Chris keeps his eyes on me as he sits back down, and I know I must be the color of the cranberry juice bottle on the table.

"I think we're gonna have to find a new nickname for you. Something like, 'not-so-goody'," Luke says in a mocking voice. Emily gives him a shove as everyone starts laughing.

"Your turn," Jake says with a lopsided grin.

I pick a card and my heart drops. I try to put it down on the table, but Jake grabs it and reads it out to everyone.

"Blindfold yourself and have someone spin you around. Walk until you bump into a person or object and make out with it/them or finish your drink."

He marks a pause before putting the card down. I extend my arm to grab my drink, but Jake snatches it before I can.

"It's called do or *drink*, Jake. You can't decide for me," I complain, exasperated at his behavior.

"We're past that point of the game, Goody. We *do* now," he throws back at me in a mellow voice.

I frown at him and look around the table. Everyone seems to agree with him.

"Fine," I say through gritted teeth.

I stand up and try to look confident but it's hard when I'm seconds away from having my first kiss with I don't know who or what.

Jake grabs a scarf that's been left in a corner of the room. He comes back to me, turns me around so my back is facing him, and puts the scarf over my eyes, tying it behind. It pulls at my hair when he tightens it a second time, but I don't say anything. Emily has a whole collection of perfume and I recognize her English garden perfume on the scarf.

"Everyone spread out!" I distinguish Camila's voice. "Don't spin her too hard, baby. It would be a shame if she ends up making out with the floor." I don't miss the sarcasm in her voice. I do my best to ignore it and focus on not falling face first.

"I'll do my best to catch you," Jake slips in my ear before spinning me around.

One.

Two.

Three.

Four times.

I almost lose balance when he lets go. He steps away so quickly that I have no idea in which direction he went. I put my hands out, my head is spinning with a mix of the alcohol buzz, the spins, and the reverberations of Jake's whispers in my ear.

I take a few steps forward but change directions when I don't bump into anything.

"Not this way, you're not my type," I hear Beth's mean girl voice.

I change directions again and three steps later bump into a body. I want to run my hand all over it to make out who it is exactly, but the need to cut this short takes over.

I run both my hands along the arms. They're strong and bulgy. I reach wide shoulders, a solid neck, and finally place my hands on either side of a face. The physique and lack of long hair confirm that I'm about to have my first kiss with a boy and the consequent height difference tells me it's not Luke. It could be Chris or Jason.

Or Jake.

My heart is beating too fast for my ribcage to handle. An arm slides around my waist helping me up on my toes and, before I know it, I'm kissing soft lips. The kiss is gentle, and I start to feel more comfortable until the tip of his tongue forces my lips apart. I let him in and part for more, lost in a tornado of feelings. His tongue intertwined with mine, I completely forget that I'm much less experienced than him. I don't think if I'm turning the right way around, he's completely taken over and I let him. Blush burning my cheeks, stomach full of butterflies, my hands slide from his cheeks all the way to his chest.

When we part, I have to catch my breath. I take a few steps back before uncovering my eyes. When I open them, there's no one in front of me.

I snap around. Camila and Beth are giggling at me. Jason, Chris and Jake are right next to each other smiling at me and Luke and Emily have disappeared. I turn my head to the side, where Rachel and Rose have laid down on multiple

Chapter 13

bean bags, then back to look at the three boys not far from me.

"You looked like a fish trying to make out with air, Goody," Camila mocks.

"You're allowed to breathe through your nose, you know that, right?" Beth adds.

I frown at them, mad at them but especially myself for not knowing what to retort.

Camila takes Jake's hand and whispers something in his ear. A satisfied smile appears on his face. His gaze snaps to me for a brief second, like he's hesitating. He whispers something back to Camila and she leaves, walking proudly like she owns everything and everyone around here. Really, she does. She's got Jake and whoever has Jake White rules our small world that is Stoneview.

I observe the boys, trying to focus on them only. Do any of them look out of breath? Flushed? I'm looking for anything but there's nothing. I'm lost.

Who did I just share my first kiss with?

14

JAMIE

Señorita – Kurt Hugo Schneider, Madilyn Bailey

"Don't you think you've pushed this far enough," I fume. "I'm not going to wait for you while you go have sex with Camila. Enough is enough Jake."

Only Jake and I are left in the basement, and my legs are itching to leave this house.

Jake laughs at what I just said and I'm ready to punch him.

If only I was sure he wouldn't hit me back. I'm sure he's not above hitting a girl. He would do anything to show his superiority.

"I'm not going to fuck her," he keeps on laughing. "I'm just walking her back to her car."

"She can't drive. She's drunk!"

Why am I worried about her?!

His laugh accentuates and I'm seconds away from kicking him in the balls.

"Camila doesn't *drive* on these nights, baby. She's got a driver. You wait here, I'll be quick."

Chapter 14

"Will you stop calling me baby–"

I don't even bother finishing my sentence because he's already running up the stairs. I should go. I should go and not care what he'll do. Walk home. It doesn't matter if it takes me all night, I just want to be away from him. But the thought of what could happen if I stay is like an itch begging to be scratched. A promise of dirty pleasures.

After a few minutes trying to make a decision, I head for the stairs. To hell what Jake thinks. He has no proof of what I've done. As I reach the bottom of the stairs, I see a figure walking down.

Chris.

"What are you still doing here?" he asks in a tired voice. "Everyone's left."

"I was just leaving. Happy Birthday," I say as I move out of the way to let him go down the stairs.

He murmurs a thank you, clearly not in the mood for whatever reason.

I take my first step up just to see Jake appearing at the top of the stairs. Messy hair, shirt wrongly buttoned. He *did* go and have sex while he left me here. Anger rises in me like a powerful tsunami.

"Going somewhere?" he asks as he lifts an eyebrow at me.

"Yes. Home."

I keep going up the stairs, ready to push him out of the way.

"There's no one to drive you home. You're drunk. Or at least buzzed. It's not safe for you to leave on your own at this time." He takes each step down looking straight at me.

"If you're so concerned, feel free to call me a cab. So much for not having sex, by the way." Why did I say that? I don't care. I shouldn't care and most of all I shouldn't show him that I care.

He smiles at me but there's no kindness in it, only his predatory grin. We finally reach each other mid-stairs.

"I didn't fuck Camila. Now go back down," he orders.

"No." I almost stamp my foot, but I decide to simply cross my arms over my chest.

I'm slightly lightheaded from all the drinks but I don't feel *drunk*. I've drank enough to feel brave but not too much that I can't control my body anymore.

"No?"

"You heard me. Get out of my way." I insist.

He takes another step down and I try to move to the left, but the staircase is too narrow, and he just grabs my upper arm, carrying me along with him as he walks down the stairs. I have to move backward and almost fall twice.

"You really are the worst human being on the damn pla–" I cut short when I realize that Chris is still down here. How could I forget?

"Are you for real, Jake?" Chris scolds.

"Who did you think I was talking about?" Jake asks, sincerely confused.

What the hell are they on about now? Jake brings me in front of him and he lets go of my arm. Chris comes to stand in front of his friend, and I'm sandwiched between them, facing Chris.

"Anyone but her," he answers deadpan.

"Guess again?" Jake says innocently.

"I don't know, man." Chris runs a hand through his hair. He's still drunk, his eyes sparkling gold even in the dimmed lighting.

"You're thinking too much," Jake claims. "You're eighteen now, time to enjoy life."

Jake spins me around, bends slightly to bring his face to my eye level. "You're gonna be a good girl for me, aren't you?"

"What?" I ask, completely incredulous at the whole situation.

Before I can ask any further, two hands come from behind. One holding my waist, the other grabbing my jaw. I inhale a sharp breath that gets blocked in my throat.

Jake takes a step back, happy with his work, and observing as Chris starts kissing my neck.

"What are you do–"

"You too, Goody. Less thinking, more enjoying."

When Chris' tongue runs up my neck, I let out a sigh of pleasure. In a few seconds, all my thoughts seem to melt into a pool of pleasure between my legs. Chris' hand around my waist drops to my thigh and he grabs it tight.

"Chris," I sigh, needing to feel more of him.

Am I dreaming? Is this some kind of alcohol-induced hallucination?

He brings his hand back up and under my shirt, then under my bra, and grabs one of my breasts. My body stills as it finally catches up to the situation.

"Just trust me," Chris whispers in my ear. "I would never hurt you."

My brain tries to work something to reply but my body seems satisfied with a few words. My back still to him, I arch into his hand and feel his erection on the small of my back. My eyes feel heavy when he starts massaging my nipple between his thumb and index. A small moan escapes my mouth and Chris' lips graze at my jaw.

"Fuck. You're loving this, Angel."

My eyes jerk open at Jake's voice. He's sitting on the marble coffee table, watching Chris and me, his jeans strained by his erection. I come back to reality when he gets up and takes a few steps towards us.

"Please don't mind me. You're welcome for finally landing you in the arms of your all-time crush. *And* for your first kiss with him."

My eyes widen at the revelation but when Chris' fingers grab my other breast and his lips fall on mine, my body seems to not care about Jake's statement or the fact that he's watching us. It doesn't even care a little bit.

Chris pulls my head closer to his and takes further hold of my lips. I let his tongue slip through and recognize the softness and sweet taste from earlier.

"I'm sick of seeing this skirt," Jake says in an annoyed voice. As if it's stopping him from joining the fun.

Following orders, Chris slides his hand down my belly, unbuttons the skirt, and pushes it over my hips until it falls on its own to the floor.

"Step out, Angel," Jake commands.

I step out of the skirt, my brain not controlling my body anymore. It only follows Jake's orders from now on. My whole body is on fire and I can't control my moans. Especially not when I feel two hands spreading my legs apart. It takes me a second to realize it's not Chris' hands. My eyes snap open mid-kiss and Chris pulls away, settling behind me again. I turn to Jake, in front of me.

How many times did the school hear of rumors of Jake and Chris sharing girls? I never thought they were true even if I've heard dozens of them. And now here I am, barely an hour after my first kiss, sandwiched between the two men and letting them run their hands all over me. Worst, *enjoying it*. Enjoying to the point that I can't tell either of them to stop. To the point that I can barely refrain the moans forcing themselves through my lips.

Chapter 14

"Wider." Jake's breath is right in my ear and Chris is nibbling at my shoulder.

I spread my legs wider, my breath coming out in pants. But when I feel Jake's hand between my legs, I can't help my hand from grabbing his, trying to stop him.

"Wait," I sigh.

He presses his palm against my hot core and grabs my wrist with his other hand. "You're soaking wet, baby. Trust me with this."

The hand holding my wrist forces it behind me and I feel Chris take over behind my back.

Chris grabs my other wrist and holds both of them on the small of my back. It's not too tight that I couldn't get away if I *really* wanted to but it's enough to stop me from grabbing Jake's hand again.

As Chris grabs my jaw with his other hand, forcing me to crane my neck and kiss him again, I feel Jake pushing my panties to the side. I can't control my breathing as Chris deepens his kiss, making me beg for air.

"So. Fucking. Wet," Jake whispers as he rubs my clit with his palm. The hotness boiling inside me is making me sweat down my back. I buck my hips forward, dying for more pressure.

Chris stops kissing me and grabs my breasts one after the other again, pinching slightly and pulling at my nipples.

"Oh God," I moan as Jake grazes my entrance with his fingertips.

The mix of his hand so close to my core and Chris' hands on my body is bringing me so close to the edge I want to dive right in but they both keep teasing me. Bringing me close to exploding and quickly retiring.

"More," I whimper in frustration.

I can see Jake's satisfied smile through my half-closed lids. "More?" he asks for confirmation.

I nod my head.

"Are you gonna listen to me from now on?" As he says that his hand stops moving, and Chris' quickly follows.

I buck my hips and arch my back, looking for more. "I will," I mewl, desperate for their touch again.

He slowly starts moving again. One of his fingertips presses at my entrance and I almost fall from the pleasure. I would have if Chris wasn't holding me, my legs have turned to jelly.

"You gonna be good for me?"

I try to free my wrists from Chris' grip. I want to push Jake's hand deeper. But Chris doesn't let go. He tightens his grip instead.

"I–I will…Jake," I sigh.

His thumb starts playing with my tight bundle of nerves again in the lightest touch and I want to cry from frustration. "More," I growl in a voice I don't recognize.

He chuckles and bites my earlobe. "Beg."

My heart skips a beat at his last word, my eyes snapping open. He can't be serious. But when I feel his hand starting to retreat, my brain doesn't even get a say in the decision. The words just flow out of my mouth.

"No. Please, please don't stop."

My lower belly tightens at his smug smile and it makes me feel all the shame my brain didn't get to make me feel. Heat rushes through my cheeks in embarrassment but as soon as his finger slips deep inside me, it all becomes irrelevant. I'm suddenly drowned in pleasure, butterflies battling in my stomach.

"Ahh…." The loud moan resonates against the ceiling.

Chris works at my breasts again and Jake slides in

another finger, stretching me. The addition of the second one stings slightly but as soon as his thumb works my nub again it all turns into overwhelming pleasure.

It doesn't take long for my eyes to roll to the back of my head. Jake sucks at my neck roughly. I feel his teeth on my skin and my head lands on Chris' chest. Chris' thumb slides from my jaw to my lips and I don't hesitate to part them for him. He slips his thumb in my mouth and I roll my tongue around it, desperately trying to please him the way they're both doing to me.

"Fuck," I hear Chris whisper behind me.

"You know what, Goody," Jake says in my ear. I can barely hear him; I'm riding his hand following his movement of pumping in and out of me.

My whole body is ready to explode, I just need the flicker of a flame to set it all on fire. "I think you're gonna come for me," he continues, his hot breath on my cheek. "You want that?"

I nod my head yes, incapable of talking with Chris' thumb in my mouth.

"Wait," he says, and I can hear the satisfaction in his voice. I'm so close I want to scream and cry for him to just finish me. "Hold," he orders.

"Please," I try to say but it comes out mumbled. I suck harder on Chris's thumb as if it's going to change anything.

"Fine. You can come now," he smiles.

He works me harder, unleashing on my clit and as soon as his fingers curl in me, they seem to flick a button. Everything explodes inside me, needles are prickling at my skin, the butterflies enter a trance in my lower belly, and I feel my pussy clench around his fingers.

My heart explodes, it runs up my lungs all the way to my throat, and without even realizing, I let out a loud, high moan, barely muffled by Chris's thumb in my mouth. He slides it out of my mouth and relaxes behind me.

My knees buckle as I come down from my waves of pleasure, spasms still working my body, and Chris catches my waist with both arms.

Jake pulls out his hand and takes a step back, looking at me with amusement and contentment on his face. His expression is shouting at me that I lost all right to go against him anymore.

How can I be so weak? How can I just let him make me feel so...good?

Chris pulls me backward until I can feel him take a step to the side and lower me on one of the bean bags. It's a fake fur bean bag and it's soft and comfortable, making me feel even more on a cloud than I already do.

The fog in my vision slowly dissipates and I realize the state that I'm in; in my one and only lacey panties that Jake purposely picked from my drawer. My top pulled up right under my chest and under said top, I can feel my bra has slid above my boobs. I'm wet and sticky between my legs. Not only in my underwear, I can also feel it on my thighs. Jake and Chris can probably see it. The hair at the back of my head feels like a mess from leaning my head on Chris' chest.

Chris steps away as Jake comes closer. The latter caresses my cheek and smiles at me, satisfied. "Did you like that?"

I nod, incapable of using my voice at this time.

"Are you thankful that we made you come?"

I nod again, my pussy clenching at the reminder.

"You gonna show us how thankful you are now, aren't you, Angel?"

My eyes widen in shock. Is he really expecting my inexperienced ass to take the lead? My eyes feel heavy and my whole body feels like I've been stepped on by a herd of elephants.

Chris' face shifts and he turns from a man filled with lust to emanating cold. Or regret? "Dude, I'm out."

"What?" Jake answers puzzled.

"I told you I didn't want to do this anymore."

Chris turns around but I'm not following anymore. My eyes are too heavy to open, and I can only hear their voices, barely processing what's going on. I let myself fall backward on the bean bag.

"I thought you meant short term," Jake defends himself.

"No, I mean I don't want to fuck other girls anymore. I told you I wasn't..." Chris sighs and his voice lowers, but I still hear him. Even in my sleepy, tipsy, post-orgasm state I can still hear his next statement. "I told you I wasn't interested in Jamie."

"Then why did you stay?"

Chris chuckles sarcastically. "I'm only human. She's hot but I'm done fucking around."

There's a pause and I try to fight sleep, but it slowly overcomes me.

"Oh shit, you met someone. Why didn't you say so? I'm sorry..."

Jake's deep voice is the last thing I hear.

15

JAMIE

Colors – Halsey

I startle awake at the sound of a door slamming. Daylight is coming through the window making me realize I've got a pounding headache and I keep my eyes firmly closed. There are voices coming from outside my room. Loud and clear. Too loud.

"I can't fucking believe you! How could you do this to *me*, Rose? Any of your other sluts I don't care, but *me*?!"

Rose? Who's talking?

"I didn't do any–"

"Don't. Don't lie to me. You owe me at least that."

There's a pause and I open my eyes halfway. The light is *way* too bright.

"The cheer coach?! The fucking cheer coach?!"

"It's only a text." I recognize Rose's collected tone.

"Only a text? Are you actually kidding me? He's an adult Rose! Sending flirty texts to a seventeen-year-old! He's a pedophile and you're even more fucked up than I thought! You knew our deal. We're done."

Chapter 15

Wait. Is that Rachel? And Rose? In my house? Why is the window to my left? My window is to my right when I'm lying in bed.

Last night suddenly hits me like a running train. Jake. The drinking. The game. My first kiss. Jake and Chris. My first orgasm. I can feel myself blush at the pleasure and being so exposed to them. I have a tingling sensation between my legs, remembering Jake's fingers inside me. His lips on my neck. I remember falling asleep. I have a glimpse of Jake carrying me.

Jake.

I'm in his room. I open my eyes, properly this time, and I'm hit with the confirmation that I'm currently in his bedroom and now embarrassingly aware of his chest against my back, one arm around my waist, the other under my head.

Shit.

The voices in the hallway come back. Rachel is still shouting at Rose while she feeds her excuses calmly until her voice finally rises.

"Fuck no! Rach don't even think about it."

"Oh, fuck. You!"

I hear another door slam and their voices fading away. Then another one and I assume they've left the house.

I move slightly, trying to slowly get away from Jake but he stirs and tightens his hold on me.

"Don't mind them, happens every weekend. Go back to sleep," he says in a sleepy voice.

I try to fight the headache but there's no point. I don't know the time and I could definitely use more sleep.

I relax as much as I can. Jake's scent and his warm skin against mine keep forcing my muscles into relaxation. Eventually, I fade back into the darkness.

When I wake up again, I'm alone in bed. My headache is gone but I'm so thirsty I could drink an ocean. I slowly get out of bed only wearing one of Jake's giant t-shirts. No bra. No panties. Did he take them off? Did he...do anything else?

My body shudders at the thought but this one definitely isn't a good one. There's a line not to cross. Would he cross it? What is off-limits to him?

I don't know where Jake is. I know Rose left earlier with Rachel so I'm assuming it's fine to go to the kitchen. I look for my clothes but can't find any and the thirst pushes me to just go like this. No one but Jake is here anyway.

I pad down the hall and as I'm about to push the half-closed door open, I hear different voices coming from the living area. No one has noticed me yet and I just stand here, observing the strange scene.

Jake and Luke are facing my way, standing in front of Rose. They are blocking her from getting to Chris, their eyes on her. Chris is in front of the sofa, his back to me, talking to someone I can't quite see yet.

Jake is wearing black, wire-thin glasses that make him look so much more approachable than usual.

Rose is watching everyone, her back to me. She's the closest to me but Jake and Luke are so focused on not letting her get away from them that they haven't noticed me standing in the doorway behind her, half-hidden by the door. Everyone is wearing clothes except Jake, who's topless, only wearing jeans he seems to have put on in a hurry.

I can't help but linger on his body. He looks like the child of a Greek god and a top model. His defined abs are stopping my eyes from looking anywhere else. He's got a V that disappears into his jeans and I think I'm starting to understand why Camila finds it difficult, or should I say impossible, to leave him.

Chapter 15

Chris takes a step to the side and I can finally see he's talking to Samuel. What the hell is this guy doing here?

They both look like they're about to jump each other. I've never seen Chris so bestial. I don't know what the conversation was like before I arrived, but they seem to be at the breaking point.

"Let me make this clearer. I see you around this house or around her again, you'll be able to count on one hand the number of teeth you've got left when I'm done with you. Is that easier to get for you?"

I can't believe I'm hearing these words come out of Chris' mouth. I've never seen him so angry in my life.

"Chris–" Rose tries to interject but Jake shoves her back. She scowls at Jake and Luke, both determined to not let her get to the other side of the room. "You two are fucking traitors," she says through gritted teeth.

I look back at Samuel. He's just about as tall and big as Chris but he looks more dangerous. It might have to do with the fact that he's covered with tattoos, up to the neck and some on the side of his head where his hair is shaved. It might be because everything about him is darker, his hair, his look, his eyes. It might be because I know he's part of a gang and Chris has always been this peaceful figure to me.

Samuel simply smiles back at Chris. "You think I give a shit about being threatened by a teenager born with a silver spoon in his mouth?"

I can't help but think that, just like in films, the mean guy is British. His accent is making everything he says much darker and as if his real motive is to destroy the world.

"These two, belong to my world. You know it, I know it. I'm the only *real* family they have. They might think they want to stay with you now, but they'll come around eventually. Especially this one." He smiles smugly, gives a head gesture towards Rose and I can almost hear her rolling her eyes.

"Shut the fuck up," she spits at him. "You don't know me!"

Samuel chuckles. "I don't know you? I fucking made you. Be grateful, love. We–"

He doesn't get to finish his sentence because Chris shoves him so hard in the chest, Samuel stumbles backward and hits the TV, sending it crashing to the floor. He regains balance quickly and is about to get back at him when Rose takes a step forward. Luke holds her arm, but her behavior has changed drastically. She's almost fighting her friends to get to Chris and Samuel. She gets past Luke. In a split-second Jake grabs her by the waist, holding her firmly.

"You're really looking for shit today, aren't you?" her twin says as he lifts her, so her feet don't reach the ground anymore, his arms bulging under her weight.

Samuel has a killing look on his face. He's about to strike back and I'm not sure why she would want to get between the two.

"Don't! Sam, please, don't." Her voice is nothing like her usual confident tone. She's almost pleading with Samuel. She wriggles in Jake's arms. "Fuck. Let go." Her frustration and panic are overwhelming and I'm not sure if I should intervene or not.

I'm perplexed at the dynamic this group has behind closed doors. I always thought Rose was just 'part of the boys' and did whatever the fuck she wanted. I never thought Jake was an overprotective brother or Chris to get involved in her business. Looking at this now, they all look so controlling over her.

Samuel freezes just before hitting Chris but the look in

his eyes doesn't leave much to the imagination what he was planning to do. He hesitates and glances at Rose.

"Just leave," she insists in a small voice.

Samuel steps away from Chris, although the latter doesn't seem scared of him in the slightest. They're just two beasts ready to jump at each other's throat and Rose is the only thing keeping them from doing so.

"You keep hiding behind your rich friends Jake, mate. Don't come begging when they throw you away." He walks toward the door and turns one last time. "And you," he says pointing at Rose. "I warned you what would happen if you didn't listen." He leaves and slams the door behind him.

"Wait–" Rose wriggles more in Jake's arm. "Jake, put me the fuck down"

Jake finally lets go and she steps away from him, her gaze so dark she might as well annihilate him right this second.

"Fuck you," she hisses at him, "and you too," she continues pointing her tattooed arm to Luke.

Chris walks around the sofa toward the rest of the group as Rose keeps telling everyone a piece of her mind.

"I swear to fucking God, Chris, if he goes to the cops, you're never seeing me again," she spits at him.

"Ozy, you need to chill. You can't differentiate us trying to help from us attacking you. What's your problem?" Jake retorts annoyed.

She spins to her brother and points at him with an angry finger.

"My problem is you're not my dad! None of you. You need to let me deal with him however *I* want. Not how you guys think is best!"

"You don't get rid of problems, you enhance them. It's

your thing," Chris interjects. "If we weren't here to fix your shit half the time, you'd probably be dead right now."

"Ugh," she throws her head back in frustration, "please, just *please* for once have a little bit of faith in me. Sam is dangerous! You can't just go around threatening him."

"What are you doing here?" Chris suddenly asks.

It takes me a few seconds to realize he's talking to me. They all turn around to face me and I suddenly am way too aware of being naked under Jake's shirt.

Rose raises an eyebrow under her wire-thin, gold glasses. They're big, round, almost geeky and it contrasts so much with her personality and looks that it makes her look like a model dressed up as a schoolgirl.

"I...uh..." are the only sounds I manage out of my mouth.

My gaze meets Jake's and his eyes turn dark as he understands I was spying on them.

"Go to the room," he orders coldly.

I don't reply and simply take a step back. The need to be far enough to not feel his anger is too strong to fight back.

"And y'all think I'm the one who should be supervised," Rose throws at them.

"Fuck off," Jake's voice now sounds closer to me and I hurry back to the room.

I close the door behind me, but it's angrily re-opened right away. Jake storms in the room without a word. He goes to his closet, grabs my uniform from yesterday that I was looking for, and throws it at me.

"Get dressed. I'm taking you home."

I've been wanting to hear these words since arriving here yesterday. I wanted to hear them when we were at the party, I wanted anything but having to follow him around his house like a lost puppy while he was partying with his friends. I wanted to get away when we started that stupid game, I was ready to walk home on my own at night when he walked Camila to her car. Now he's finally saying it, finally letting me go.

Then why do I feel this horrible pinch in my heart?

It's one thing to want to go, it's another to be kicked out. Did he get what he wanted? He wanted to have his fun with me and Chris and now he's throwing me away so he can go back to Camila?

Why do I care? Why does it hurt?

I quickly put my clothes on. When he turns around to put a tee on, I'm struck by a single tattoo between his shoulder blades. It's the exact same one Rose has on her arm – among the tons of other ones covering her forearm – and that I saw on Samuel's neck. That X with the crown on top, the W at the bottom, 19 on the left, and 33 on the right. Jake puts his shoes on and grabs his keys. He's boiling with rage and I don't want to take the risk to break the silence.

By the time we're driving, I'm surprised his teeth haven't shattered to pieces. His jaw is clenching so hard he could probably grind a rock into sand. When he turns onto my street, I finally dare say something.

"What's your deal with Sam?" I ask, perfectly knowing it's not a good idea.

Still, curiosity is eating at me. The way Jake gets around him, and now Chris, he's more than just a ghost from his past.

Jake sighs and his shoulders slump. He suddenly looks fragile, exhausted from the argument, from the thoughts running in his head and making him grind his teeth.

He starts massaging his temples as if his head is hurting. "Why do you want to know?"

"It affects you, badly. I thought you might want to talk

about it instead of letting it build up and attempting to break every single one of your teeth."

He looks at me in surprise and suddenly stops grinding. He takes a deep breath and releases it in a loud huff, but he doesn't say anything for what seems like a long minute where we both sit in complete silence.

"There's bad, there's dangerous, and then there's Sam," he finally says.

"What does he have on you? He threatened Rose to go to the police, about something her brother did." I inhale a shaky breath. "What did you do, Jake?"

He pauses, looking outside as if the trees hold all the answers.

"Don't play detective with me, Angel. You're not anywhere near having all the evidence you need."

"I'm not playing detective," I argue. "I'm just trying to understand."

"Why are you so obsessed with my past anyway?" he scoffs. "Fangirling doesn't look good on you."

"Because your past made you the way you are! It's the reason you're so...so..."

"Heartless? Sociopathic? Cruel? Go on, choose one."

My mouth goes slack at his cold words. He's saying them with such conviction and ice in his voice that there is no doubt he truly means them.

"Why are you trying to find me an excuse, Jamie? Maybe it's just the way I am. Maybe I even *like* it."

The smile he gives me freezes my blood.

Jake White is filled with evil and darkness, and he puts a glossy golden-boy cover on top of it all. He's not just unempathetic, he's manipulative and that's the worst part. He is deeply damaged, exactly like Chris had warned me.

Everything he's done to me before now was just a little

game for him. Something to keep his mind occupied. I don't doubt he's capable of going to lengths I wouldn't think possible just to play with me. His heart is darker than the deepest pits of hell.

My brain reminds me of how I woke up this morning and rings the emergency bell. Fear claws onto my insides. I was naked under his shirt; would he have done anything to me while I was passed out?

As he parks in front of my house, I turn to him one last time. "Did you do anything to me?" I ask as cold as possible.

"Yes." He didn't even think for a second. No regret, no remorse.

My heart drops in my stomach as he turns to me with a grin on his flawless face.

"I fingerfucked your virgin pussy senseless until you begged me to make you come. You were there."

Said pussy clenches at his words. Why does he make me feel this way? I gulp and keep my thoughts on my initial question.

"I–I meant after."

"After?" he asks clueless. Whether he's pretending or genuine I don't know yet.

"I woke up naked with only your shirt on, Jake. I want to know what happened," I say in a steel voice. I want to know. I want the truth.

He starts laughing and hits the steering wheel with the palm of his hand like it's the funniest joke he's ever heard. He looks at me again and calms down.

"Oh shit, you're serious." He pauses for a heartbeat. "Nothing, Goody. What do you think of me? I'm not like that."

"I think you're evil. That's what I think." I reply coldly.

He softly grabs my face, both hands on my cheeks as he

brings his face closer to mine. His lips are so close, hovering over mine. His breath smells of mint with a hint of weed and tobacco. I didn't see him put cologne on this morning, but it seems his natural scent is the one I'm addicted to; wooden and dominant.

For a second I truly believe he's going to kiss me, my thighs tense and I close my eyes, butterflies growing in my stomach. I open my eyes when I feel his hands leaving my face, one of them sliding from my cheek to my throat.

In a split second, his eyes go from the Mediterranean Sea to a storm in the middle of the coldest ocean. Before I can grasp how truly I've angered him, his hand tightens around my throat making me jump but helpless.

"Jake–" I try to say but my words get stuck in my tight airways.

"I *am* evil, Jamie. So much more than your naive mind can envision. I've done things you couldn't even fucking imagine. But I didn't rape you if that's what you want to know. I can snap my fingers and have a dozen girls on their knees ready to suck my cock. Cam at the front of the line. You ain't special, neither is your cunt so get over yourself."

I claw at his hand, but he doesn't shift. My ears are ringing from the strength he's using. I know I'm pleading with my eyes, my throat too tight to talk, but he doesn't care in the slightest.

He tightens his grip for effect before letting me go. I gasp and cough, trying to get air in my lungs while he sits back in his seat as if nothing happened.

"Wh–what are those things you've done?" I ask in a small voice, massaging the skin where his fingers were.

Out of everything he said, this is what my brain stays stuck on. Call it curiosity or call it suicidal, I want to know.

Chapter 15

Maybe because I care, maybe because he's another mystery I'm desperate to solve.

"I don't owe you explanations."

He really thinks he's above everything and everyone, doesn't he? His behavior is riling me up. I never asked to be the girl who awkwardly gets kicked out of the house the morning after. Nor the one he decides to bully because I was in the wrong place at the wrong time.

"So I can't ask questions? It's all fine to kidnap me from my house. It's all fine to keep me around all evening and it's all fine to...to..." I can't go further without heat spreading on my cheeks and reaching my ears.

Why am I like this? He just tried to strangle you!

Jake's self-satisfied smile spreads on his face. Is this really the only thing that takes him out of his bad mood? My embarrassment?

"Keep going," he insists.

"Screw you, Jake. You had no right to do any of what you did yesterday."

"Your wet pussy thought otherwise. So did your begging."

I can feel the anger and frustration I've built up since yesterday about to explode. Does he need to be this raw? He talks like a convict that hasn't seen a woman in a decade. There's no point trying to converse with him.

"You got what you wanted. Just stay away from me," I conclude as I open the door.

I can't help slamming it behind me.

For a second I hope he's going to get out and grab me. Be his forceful self and tell me that I don't get to walk away. Follow me inside, say he didn't get what he wanted, that he'll always want more. I'm torn between his violence and the way he was hugging me this morning. Surely that meant something.

But nothing happens. The next sound I hear is not the door opening as he runs after me. It's the sound of the car turning around as he leaves me. Because Jake is not one to run after someone when he's done wrong. He doesn't care. He's no prince, no hero and he certainly doesn't care about the effect he has on me.

I get in my house feeling more ashamed than ever. I hate him. I hate him with all my heart. Deeper than I ever hated anyone.

I go straight for a shower. I need to get him off myself. Him, Chris, this whole group is fifty shades of fucked up, incestuous and respectless, and I don't want anything to do with them anymore. Ever.

When I'm out of the shower I check the time on the oven in the kitchen. 12:34.

Jake White has already ruined my evening, my night, and half of my day. I'm not giving him another thought. I grab my phone that had been left on the counter and check it. My mom must be worried to death. As soon as my eyes land on the screen something hits me hard.

Nathan.

I have a date with him today. Scratch that. I had a date with him an hour ago.

I check the few texts he's sent me since yesterday, my heart beating a hundred miles an hour.

> Nathan: I hope you like brunches. Any plans for tonight?

He sent another one late last night asking if we were still on for today. And of course, today.

> Nathan: Everything alright? Let me know if you need to be picked up today.

> Nathan: I just hope nothing bad happened

The last one was half an hour ago. I can't believe this slipped my mind. Not only does my hate for Jake deepen further but I also hate myself. I tap on his name in a hurry and call.

Shit, who calls anymore?

What's wrong with me? I'm about to hang up when my thoughts are cut off.

"Jamie? Is everything alright?"

"Oh, Nathan. Hi. I'm so sorry I–" Haven't thought this through. "I... had an emergency last night and I left my phone here. I only came back now."

"I hope you're okay?"

I don't know. Am I? The boy I hate the most in the world kept me at his house against my will but also gave me a mind-blowing orgasm with the help of his best friend. It was good enough to make me forget about my first date ever, with a very decent guy as well.

"I am. I am. Honestly, I feel horrible for letting you down."

"No hard feelings. We can make plans for another time."

"Or now if you're free." The words slip out before I can catch them. What the hell am I doing?

He pauses for a few seconds as if thinking about it.

"Sure. What do you want to do? You have to sort it out now that you left me hanging," he replies in a playful tone.

"I'll text you my address," I simply say because apparently I have developed some sort of courage I had no idea I had.

He chuckles into the phone. *"You're a keen little one, aren't you? Are you on your own?"*

"Of course I am. Just come whenever," I conclude. "See you."

I hang up before I can chicken out and stare at the phone.

What did I just do?

"No! How?! I thought I'd have to let you win to make you happy. Turns out you're just too good at this game." Nathan's playful voice is filling me with undeserved happiness.

We've been playing video games for two hours and I don't ever want this to stop. The way his eyes squint in focus behind his thick glasses, the way he smiles when he gets in front of me on our racing game and how his shoulders slump and he pulls at his blond bun when I get back in front. All of the little things about him make my heart swell with love and warmth.

"I used to play with my brother. Every single day. It's the first game we got and pretty much stuck to it," I admit.

"Shit, you've got a brother?" He straightens up and gives me a lopsided smile. "Should I expect a talk about not breaking your heart?" he jokes.

I enjoy how light-hearted he is. I like that everything else that worries me just seems to disappear when he's around. He makes me feel safe and appreciated and for some reason I don't even mind telling him about my family.

"No," I chuckle sadly. "He, um, at the risk of ruining the mood he went missing a few years ago."

His eyes widen at my revelation and he puts his

controller down straight away. He fully turns to me on the sofa, his face showing nothing but empathy.

"I'm so sorry. Is this a topic you want me to avoid?"

I shrug. I usually would want to avoid it. How do you explain to someone that your dad died, and your brother disappeared? That even three years later, your mom can't get herself to have a funeral and that deep in your heart you know he's still alive. I don't want to *not* talk about it with him, but I won't jump on the explanation. However, I've never felt in a more trustful environment than with him.

"That's up to you. It's not a pretty story," I simply reply.

It's not my right to impose my dramatic story onto him. He seems to think about it for a few seconds, as if he is truly weighing if he wants to know that part of me or not. People are usually desperate to know. They love the gossip; they love being in the know. More than that, it's some sort of dirty pleasure in knowing atypical stories.

"What happened?" he asks after a few seconds of reflection.

"They were shot. By gang members. My dad was the Sheriff here in Stoneview. As far as I know, he tried to take them down. They didn't appreciate it. I was there when it happened."

"You were?"

I pull down the sleeve of my shirt over my left shoulder and show him my scar. His mouth falls slack as soon as his eyes land on the bit of thick skin.

"I know, it's ugly. Aaron, my brother, he tried to shield me from the bullet. It went straight through him and lodged into my shoulder. He literally took a bullet for me." My throat tightens as I finish my sentence. "When the ambulance showed up, they thought I was dead. I woke up in the hospital. Dad didn't survive. I asked about my brother, but they said there were only me and my dad at the scene when they arrived."

He slowly raises his hand and grazes his thumb over my scar. I don't flinch. For the first time in years, it doesn't hurt, it doesn't burn. He's soothing me with his gentle touch. He tenderly grabs my shoulder in his hand.

"It's not ugly Jamie, it shows you're a survivor. It shows you've been through the worst and still came back stronger. You're a warrior," he smiles.

I can't help but smile back. As we were talking, we slid closer to each other on the sofa. I now have one leg bent on the sofa, fully turned to him, and the other dangling over the edge.

"You really know how to find just the right words, don't you?" I question with a smile.

He shrugs. "It's easy to find the right words when I'm facing someone like you. And I know what it's like to wear ugly scars."

My mouth falls. "Really?"

He lifts his shirt up to his chest and... holy Mary mother of God. He is *ripped*. Every single one of his abs is defined without him looking big like Chris does. He is completely covered in tattoos all the way to his chest. It stops perfectly at the neck of his top and I wouldn't know they were there if he wasn't purposely showing them with short sleeves or open buttons. He must be covered with hundreds of them.

There are a few scars over his stomach and, as I look up, I see a round, thick patch of skin just below his chest, around his solar plexus. It's bigger than the other scars and darker than his golden, tanned skin. It's surrounded by a beautiful black rose, the thorns making it look like they've cut into him and some drops of bright red blood leaking from one of the thorns. It's elegantly done and powerful. This man is pure art.

"What happened," I whisper as I run my fingers above the scars. I didn't ask, I don't even care what he thinks of me right now. I feel compelled by him. We're sharing stories, what we've been through, and I've never felt closer to someone.

His voice is darker when he replies, "Abusive father."

I look up from his body and back into his eyes. We share a long, comfortable silence.

Kiss me.

He slowly leans towards me, grabs the back of my head, and plants his lips on mine.

Did I say this out loud? Or are we just on the same page that badly?

I part my lips when I feel his tongue and let him take control. He's the perfect balance between passionate and loving. Controlling and gentle.

I push toward him as he lays back and I end up on top of him, straddling him, my legs on either side of his waist. I lean in, grabbing his face with both my hands as he grabs my waist with his.

After a few seconds of fiery passion, he pulls his head away slightly and I breathe in, not realizing I was suffocating with devotion.

"We...we should slow down," he says out of breath.

My eyes open wide and I question him with a look.

"Don't get me wrong, I'd want nothing more than to keep going but I don't want to do this like...*this*. You've just opened yourself to me. We have all the time in the world to get to know each other."

I'm suddenly very aware of the bulge under me and sit back down next to him as he straightens up. I eye down at his crotch and he quickly grabs a pillow, placing it on his lap.

"Does this prove I'm interested? I just want to take things slow," he chuckles, and I can't help but laugh.

"Point proven."

"Wanna watch a movie?" he asks. "Let's watch a film."

I grab the remote, adjust the pillow on his lap, and lay down on it. "How do you feel about reality TV?"

He laughs at me and pats my head. "Whatever you want, 'Me."

My heart jumps at his use of my nickname. It feels so natural coming from him. Everything we do feels natural. Like it was just meant to be. I simply smile and put Hulu on.

After an episode of 'Keeping Up' in complete silence, I twist and turn so I'm facing up and he looks down at me.

I know he reads my face when he says, "Why do I feel like I'm not gonna like what you're about to say?"

I can't help a small laugh. He's right. "Maybe I'm the one who's not going to like the answer," I reply.

"Only one way to find out," he quips as he runs his hand through my hair. I want to do the same. Undo his tight bun and run my hand through his sandy blond hair.

"How old are you?" I ask.

He sighs and takes his hand out of my hair. "Twenty-one," he grimaces.

I don't say anything for a few seconds. Taking it in. Four years. "I'm turning eighteen on the first of January," I reply. "Three and a half months."

He chuckles but he's lost his humor slightly. "If you feel uncomfortable with this, I understand," he says. "God knows I do."

I don't reply and turn back to the episode currently playing. I adjust the pillow and make myself more comfortable.

Eventually, I grab his hand and put it back in my hair. "My parents were ten years apart. Mom was his second wife."

"Whoa. Ten years."

"I know right? I'm doing so much better than them."

I can feel him relax and he starts running his hand through my hair again. "I like the way you think," he concludes as we both get back into our series.

That night, I fall asleep on a cloud of happiness but can't shake the uneasy feeling in my stomach. Is it wrong to have been with Jake and then Nathan in the same 24 hours? Not even mentioning that I also kissed Chris. For a good part of the night I question everything. What kind of girl am I becoming? When I finally fall asleep, new thoughts come to me. So what if I enjoyed myself with three guys on the same weekend? No one judges Rose for doing it, no one judges Jake or Luke. Jake and Chris have slept with countless girls. Why should I judge myself for finally enjoying sexuality and making my body feel good?

16

JAMIE

Daddy Issues – The Neighborhood

It took Jake exactly four weeks before he got on my case again. How naive of me to think that he would actually leave me alone. I was so sure he got what he wanted out of me that I was stupidly living my best life. Nathan and I have been spending all of our free time together. I usually spend one evening a week at Emily's, three nights on my own and the whole weekend with Nathan. If we're not together, we're constantly texting, finding any excuse to send pictures and memes to each other. He even comes to Church with me on Sundays and I'm sure my mom would appreciate it. We still haven't gone past making out and every day I'm more appreciative of taking things slow with him. We're truly getting to know each other.

He hasn't heard from his family since he left his house when he was eighteen and, while he won't get too much into it, I understand the loneliness. I think we were both extremely lonely when we met, and we luckily found each other. He's become a pillar for me since mom left for

Tennessee and I can't begin to describe the consuming feeling of love when I'm with him.

He still lives in his apartment in Silver Falls, and I promised I would help him settle in his new house in Stoneview over the weekend. Only, it's Thursday and the text I just received from Jake is not announcing anything good.

> Jake: I'm a bit sick of seeing these pants. Wear your skirt and show those pretty legs of yours.

My stomach twists at his demand. I'm not even sure if it's out of anxiety or because my body is remembering what happened the last time I wore a skirt around him. The temperatures have started to drop, I stopped wearing the school skirt and decided to switch it for the pants. I'm aware I could wear stockings but I'm so much more comfortable in pants and I have no one to try and impress at Stoneview Prep.

Because I'm dating someone four years my senior.

Dating? I'm not sure. We haven't had that kind of talk yet and I'm not sure how to initiate it.

Jake has been completely ignoring me in the past weeks. In fact, his whole group has. Chris hasn't been addressing me with a single word since what happened at the party – which is probably a good thing because I don't think I'll ever see him as the embodiment of kindness and respect ever again. No one has mentioned the fact that I was there when Samuel showed up at their house and saw that they can be so hostile to each other behind closed doors.

The twins have gone back to being their arrogant selves. The image everyone has of them as two gods among humans, contrasts dramatically with the two mere mortals that were arguing at their house with their glasses and messy hair. The way Jake avoided talking to Samuel, the way Rose's voice faltered when she begged him to leave.

Everything they present to the rest of the world is pure show. From the contact lenses in their eyes to the way they carry themselves. Jake is darker than he lets out and Rose is weaker than she pretends.

In the last few weeks, they've passed me in the hallways without as much as a glance. They've eaten a table away from me and kept to themselves. Even sitting next to Jake in English didn't earn me a single word. At no point did I think he would have noticed what I was wearing.

The only thing keeping me remotely close to the group is the fact that Emily has been regularly hooking up with Luke. She is actually looking like she's falling for him and who am I to get in the way of that? Luke is probably the nicest of all of them. He's the goofiest and the most open and, while he's got a player's reputation, she's no stupid girl. She knows what she's doing.

I decide to ignore Jake's text because fuck him. When I show up to school the next morning, I'm wearing another pair of pants, the navy-blue ones. Emily takes extra time to perfect her make-up before we head out of the car and toward our school. Not far, Luke gets out of his car and soon enough he is heading towards us with Rose and Jake.

"I'll catch you in first period," I say, eager to get away before they reach us.

I'm about to escape but Emily puts her hand on my arm. "Wait, how do I look? Does it look like I put too much effort?"

"What? Since when do you care if you've put too much effort in your looks?"

She frowns, not quite understanding my reaction and I

try to run away again but the three of them have already stopped right in front of us.

Fuck. My. Life.

"Morning, gorgeous," Luke beams as he grabs Emily by the waist and brings her closer to him.

He looks tall compared to Emily, which is funny because Jake and Rose make him look tiny. She lets out a giggle and they start making out.

"Dude, get a room," Rose complains straight away as she pulls a cigarette out of the pack, and I can't say I disagree.

I avoid looking at Jake at all costs and keep my eyes on my best friend.

"See you in English, Em," I say as I leave even though I know she can't hear me. She's in Luke's world now and God knows she won't come back down until the end of the day.

I walk away without glancing back. I want to support Emily dating new people but how am I meant to hang out with her if her circle of friends becomes the same as Jake's? This is simply not compatible. Of course, she knows nothing of the game Jake has been playing but she knows I don't appreciate him. How can she just leave me behind?

I angrily push the door to the girls' bathroom and check every stall before I let out an angry growl. I'm so lonely and the only person I want to be with right now is Nathan. Only, Nathan is somewhere in Silver Falls and I'm probably the least of his worries.

I look through my backpack to find my lip balm, but I think it got lost somewhere between my books and all the shit that's accumulated with time. I keep one knee up to maintain the backpack high enough to dig deep. I finally pull it out, balancing books in my other hand and trying to keep my bag open enough to pull the lip balm out, my knee still in the air. The door suddenly bursts open and I jump in surprise, dropping my books, the lip balm, and half of what remains in my bag on the floor. As I put my leg down, I slip on one of my books and end up ass first on the floor.

I shake my head trying to process what just happened. I look up and catch Jake locking the door. He turns to me and I can read the anger on his face.

"This is the girls' bathroom." I attempt to sound like I don't fear what's about to happen but my voice quavers.

He snorts as if saying 'like I care' and steps toward me in huge strides. I get up in a hurry but before I can ground myself, he's got a hold on my jaw and pushes me until my back hits the wall. I bring my hands up to his arm, but he doesn't budge.

"I've been trying to get you out of my head for weeks, Angel, and yet my thoughts keep going back to you. I think I'm really going to have to fuck you out of my system, making you come didn't work."

My eyes widen at his words but my whole body tenses in anticipating pleasure. I don't have time to reply as his mouth crushes mine. The taste of mint and tobacco invades my tongue as he forces past my lips. I moan in his mouth when his other hand grabs my ass to pull me higher. On my tiptoes, I'm out of breath, my lungs are about to explode but I still never want this to end.

When he breaks away from me, I gasp to get air in my burning chest. "Jake, you have a girlfriend," I protest.

"Don't act all innocent now, it didn't bother you at Chris' party."

He pins me harder against the wall and starts kissing my jaw, my neck. He nibbles at my earlobe and I melt under his touch. He starts unbuttoning the top of my shirt.

"Admit it, you can't resist me, Angel."

"I– " I have to take a huge gulp of air when his lips caress the top of my breasts. I can't admit that I can't resist him. He knows it already anyway. So I settle on something else.

"We're at school," I sigh in pleasure when one of his hands starts massaging my breast through my bra.

He chuckles at the way I try to avoid the topic and stops touching me altogether. I'm a panting, wet mess. He looks at me with a superior smile on his face and brings two fingers under my chin to tilt my head up.

"Fine. I'll stop then."

I writhe under his stare and shiver at the lack of his warmth against my skin. He notices straight away and digs his gaze in mine. I try to hold it, but I can't. I break our staring contest as my gaze focuses on his right shoulder.

"Why don't you want to let go, Angel? You could do it, just for me," he whispers in a gravelly voice and I can feel the lust in his voice.

He lets go of my chin and takes a step back.

"Don't try to act all understanding now, Jake. There's no point. Not after what happened in the forest, not after breaking into my house or holding me at yours against my will."

"Against your will," he chuckles. "Please."

Anger boils in my chest and my breathing accelerates. "Y-you blackmailed me with something you have no proof of!"

"I have proof, trust me. I'm trying to be nice here. I'm giving you a chance to stop fighting tooth and nail when you're clearly attracted to me. You're trying to avoid something that is inevitable."

"It's not inevitable," I insist. Really, who does he think he is?

"Oh, Angel," he mocks. "I'll have taken your virginity before your mom even comes back from Tennessee."

I scoff and fold my arms over my chest, trying to hide the embarrassment and hoping my cheeks are not as blushed as my belly feels tight.

"Even *I* don't know when she's coming back. It could be tomorrow."

"Really? Maybe we should hurry up and get rid of it right this minute then," he smiles.

I feel my nostrils flare-up at his cockiness. "In your dreams," I spit.

"We do so much more in my dreams, Angel."

"Really? Do you have something more cliché or are you done? Do you really pick up girls with these lines?"

"I don't need to pick up girls. Unlike you, so desperate for punishment, they always do what I say."

"I highly doubt that." I try to shoulder past him, but he grabs my upper arm.

"Why didn't you do as I asked, Angel?"

I frown, unsure what he means but decide to reply something I'm at least sure will be clear. "Because you can't *make* me do anything, Jake."

I only have time to see the flash of the monster, everything happens too fast. He turns me around and bends me over the sinks. I barely have time to unfold my arms to catch myself so that my head doesn't hit the stone. I try to get back straight, but he pushes me back down with a firm palm between my shoulder blades.

"What are you–"

He cuts me off when he kicks my legs apart.

"Jake–"

"Shut up. You think I can't make you do anything, baby? Think again. Think real fucking hard."

I'm fighting to get back up but before I can go anywhere, he's cupping me between my legs with a harsh and strong hand. I let out a desperate whimper. The effect he has on me is undeniable. Like a match lighting my body on fire. Even through the thickness of my pants and underwear he makes me feel amazing.

A weight lifts off my shoulders and I suddenly feel high on Jake. High on his touch, his scent, his voice. I let out a moan when he starts rubbing me through my pants. Everything picks up exactly where he left me a minute ago.

"What did my text say yesterday?" he asks in an authoritative voice. He pushes harder when I don't answer.

"To wear a skirt," I whimper.

"Are you wearing a skirt, Angel?"

"N–no."

He enters a painfully slow rhythm. "So, I get too busy to deal with you for a few weeks and you think you can take a fucking break?" he mocks.

I'm lost, how can he go from the butterfly kisses on my neck to *this?*

"Do I need to remind you why you don't want your little secret out?"

He stops circling between my legs and I cry out, "No!"

I don't even know if I said no to answer his question or because I'm desperate for him to keep going.

"I know you're a good girl deep down. I don't know what braveness got into you but it needs to stop now."

He pops open the button of my pants, unzips them and slides his hand behind the elastic band of my cotton panties settling his fingers between my folds.

"Oh, Angel, look at you. You get so wet when I control your body."

I try to bite my bottom lip, but I let out another uncontrollable sigh when one of his fingers slips inside me and he presses his palm against my clit.

"Jake..." I mewl.

My body is a traitor. It responds to Jake like he knows the exact passwords and combinations to unlock my darkest desires, the ones I'm not even aware of.

When he inserts another finger and presses his palm harder, I'm close to exploding. It's at the tip of my fingers or...*his* fingers.

"Look up, baby. I want you to see yourself when I make you come."

His words twist in my stomach and sink to my lower belly, making me wetter than I already am. I look up and catch a glimpse of my blushed face before looking at him. He's looking down on me with his self-satisfied grin, proud that he can play with me however he sees fit.

"I'm so close," I manage in a whisper, my eyes rolling to the back of my head.

He rips his hand away and out of my pants, and I let out a strangled moan. "What the–"

He suddenly grabs my hair and pulls my head back to talk right in my ear. I wince at the pull, but it eases when I follow the movement. I'm still trembling from the pleasure but it's fading away and, like an addict, I need more. I need more now and only Jake can give it to me.

"Good girls get orgasms, Angel, bad girls get punished."

He brings his fingers to my mouth. "So be good and lick them clean."

I don't hesitate one second and part my lips for him. He pushes his two fingers in my mouth, and I do my best to please him. Because right now I would do *anything* for him to give me the drug I crave the most: him.

He lets out a satisfied growl when my tongue rolls around his fingers. I can taste myself on him and it's driving me insane with lust.

Chapter 16

"I bet you taste fucking delicious," he whispers in my ear.

There's a sudden knock on the door, hard and impatient. It makes me jump and I fall back down from my high, straight into reality.

Shit.

How long have they been waiting outside?

Jake slowly takes his fingers out in a loud pop as if not a care in the world. He casually puts his hands back in his pockets and walks to the door.

I hurry to button my pants back up, my hands trembling in shame. He turns one last time as he unlocks the door.

"Make sure you're wearing a skirt next time I see you."

"Jake? What are you doing here?" I recognize the voice straight away.

He leaves without looking back or replying to the person outside, and the next second I hear a gasp as I see Beth walk in. She takes in my state for a few seconds and I'm sure it's not a beautiful sight.

I take a quick glance at the mirror, my face is pink, my hair messy and I realize I've buttoned my pants but haven't zipped them up.

"You *fucking* slut. Wait until Cam hears about this. Your life is over, bitch." She turns around in a hurry.

"No, Beth wait!"

I try to quickly re-do my pants correctly but by the time I'm walking through the bathroom door, Beth has disappeared around a corner.

Fuck. Fuck. Fuck. How could I let him do this to me?! The first image that comes to my head is Nathan. I'm so weak to Jake, I disgust myself.

For the first time in my life, I skip school. I have always been a straight-A student. I've always seen school as a place where I feel relaxed. I like learning, I like solving problems I don't initially understand, and my dream has always been to get into an Ivy League. But today...I can't face Jake in English and I can't face Camila knowing that Beth has told her what she saw. There is no questioning what happened in this bathroom and Beth is going to be more than willing to ruin my life. Rightly so.

So I head home. Or I plan to head home but as soon as I leave school, I hop on a rare bus from Stoneview to Silver Falls.

I'm on the bus, questioning whether this is how Jake goes about every time he finds a girl to cheat on Camila with, when I receive a text from Emily asking me where I am. I get where she's coming from, it's unlike me to not show up to class. I don't reply and when it's followed by a text from Jake asking me where I've gone, I simply turn my phone off.

I follow my feet as they lead me to Nathan's apartment. I shouldn't go there after what has just happened with Jake. This is possibly the last place where I should be, but I can't help it, he's the only one who can make me feel better, safe, *loved*.

I punch in his building code that he had given me a couple of weeks ago, and head to the top floor. He's got a gorgeous penthouse with a view of the falls and I make a mental note to ask him what he does for a living because I always forget to. He usually keeps me busy with other things.

When I knock on his front door no one opens. I wait a little and try again. My heart picks up as reality hits me. What if he doesn't want to see me right now? What if he finds me clingy for showing up unannounced?

What if he's in there with someone else?

We're not actually together, he might as well be making breakfast to last night's hookup as I'm waiting here.

Or maybe he's just not home. Either way it's just another sign I shouldn't be here.

I turn around ready to leave when his smooth voice reaches my ears. "'Me?"

I switch back around with a shy smile on my face. "Hey."

"What are you doing here?" he asks, trying to refrain from a yawn.

I can't help noticing he's only wearing boxers, his tattoos and chiseled body on complete display for me to enjoy. There's dark regret growing in the pit of my stomach as I remember what I let Jake do in the school's bathroom.

"I...uh..."

"Shouldn't you be at school?"

I can't help a laugh. "Alright, dad."

His brows shoot up at my statement and I freeze on the spot. That's just awkward. That's just daddy issues 101.

I lost my dad, can I really be blamed for having daddy issues?

"Sorry. That just came out. I just don't feel like being at school."

"That doesn't sound like you," he says, brows furrowing. "Everything okay?" He's keeping the door behind him barely open and I can't see inside at all.

"Can I come in?" Maybe I shouldn't ask that. I have a feeling I'm not going to like the answer.

"Now's not the best time, 'Me."

A sting of jealousy hits me right in the chest and it's probably karma for earlier. Still. It hurts. How did I get so attached so quickly?

He must read what I'm thinking because he hurries to reply. "Oh, shit, no. Not what you think! I have a friend in the spare room. We got stupidly drunk yesterday; he's still sleeping."

"Oh," I simply reply.

"You know what," he opens the door fully, "just come in. I'll put something on, and we can go somewhere for breakfast."

"It's fine, we can see each other another time," I exclaim putting my hands in front of me.

The last thing I'd want to do is impose. That's the worst I could do to my potential future boyfriend.

Really? I'd say the worst you could do to him is make out with another guy before running to him.

I slightly cringe at the thought.

He grabs my wrist and pulls me inside with him. "Don't be ridiculous."

I follow him in until we enter his open-plan kitchen. Everything at his place is sleek. A mix of white and gray that fit perfectly together, completed with some light wooden furniture that gives the whole place a Scandinavian vibe. I sit on a stool by the huge white marble kitchen island and admire his ass as he crosses the room, past the huge L shaped sofa that can probably host twenty people, and down the hall.

I put an elbow on the counter and my head in my hand while I wait for him. For some strange reason, I suddenly feel lighter knowing that he's happy to spend time with me.

A minute into my deep thoughts, a phone pings on the counter. I look down and notice an unfamiliar phone next to Nathan's. It must be his friend's. Curious, I move my head to read the message. Wrong? Yes. Do I care? Nope. Feeding my curiosity is my favorite pastime. Why do I even want to become a surgeon? I should be a detective.

Chapter 16

> Baby girl: Cool. Don't pick me up. I'll come over.

Nathan walks back dressed in dark denim jeans and a tight white tee. I think he sees me ogling because he gives me a lopsided smirk.

"Anything I can help you with?" he asks self-satisfied as he ties his hair in his usual tight bun.

He grabs a gray sweater on the back of the sofa and heads towards me.

"I could do with a kiss I guess," I shrug.

He laughs and hurries to grab me in his arms. He captures my lips in a tender kiss and I reluctantly let him go when he takes a step back.

"Should we go?"

"Yup," I say as I jump off the stool. "Hey, your friend's 'baby girl' is probably coming over tonight. So I think you should be staying with me." I say in my most playful voice.

"'Me,'" he stops walking, "how do you know that?" he asks, perfectly knowing how.

"Might have seen a text," I mumble quietly.

He shoots me a disapproving look but can't hold it too long. "Don't look at people's phones." He grabs my arm and pulls me closer to him. "You're a little sneaky vixen, aren't you? Your curiosity will get you in trouble one day."

He turns me around after giving me another kiss, so I'm facing the direction of the doorway, and gives me a small slap on the ass. "Let's go before I show you real trouble."

We both start walking as he puts his sweater on. His head pops out and I watch as his tattooed fingers bring back the hood that got stuck on his head. God, this man is beautiful.

Nathan takes me for brunch at a fancy place by the falls,

a short walk from his. He orders us fruit, eggs, pancakes, and bacon with maple syrup. To complete it all we get unlimited coffee and freshly squeezed orange juice.

I love watching him take the lead. I feel tingly everywhere when he takes care of me and I want to take care of him back. I want to make him feel good, *everywhere.* I want to show him how much I care but I know he's hesitant because of the age difference. He doesn't want to pressure me, and he doesn't even know I'm a virgin.

My only sexual experience ever has been Jake. Yes, he gave me a mind-blowing orgasm, but I want to know what it's like to give and take in a loving relationship. I want Nathan to be my first because I know he'll worship me and my body. He makes me feel complete to the point that I miss him simply when I'm looking away.

It's *that* bad.

"Everything alright?" he asks while chewing on a mouthful of pancake. "You're staring at me."

I blush before replying, "Sorry." I dip my bacon in syrup. I'm such a sucker for a great brunch.

"What's wrong? What brought you here on a Monday morning? You wouldn't skip school for no reason."

I swallow my food slowly and avoid his gaze.

"'Me, come on."

I take a deep breath. I can't talk to him about Jake. It's impossible. But I can ask him the other thing on my mind.

"Are you..." I start. How can I put this? "Are you seeing anyone else?"

His brows furrow at the question as if he's completely lost as to why I would even ask.

"Would it bother you if I was?"

One hundred percent yes but I can't be a hypocrite, not to him.

Chapter 16

239

My throat suddenly feels tight and I have flashbacks to the bathroom. How, how, *how* could I let this happen?

"It would," I admit. He's about to say something but I'm obligated to cut him off. "But I want to tell you something." He stays completely silent, so I carry on. "I–I kissed someone from my school. Well, more like I let him kiss me. I–God I'm sorry, maybe I shouldn't say it, but I also feel like I have to if I want things with us to keep going."

He stays quiet, chewing on another mouthful of pancake. He takes his time and he appears calm but there's a storm brewing in his eyes.

There's no disappointment on his face, just his jaw tightening and releasing as he chews, just his fingers gripping his cutlery harder than necessary. When he finally swallows and talks, his voice is its usual smooth, but I can't help noticing his knuckles turning white from the grip on his knife and fork.

"You said he kissed you, was it consensual?"

I frown in confusion. Is that what really matters to him? If I was forced? He's a good person and that makes me feel even more remorseful. I still reply, "I didn't try to stop him so that makes me just as guilty."

He thinks for another minute and my stomach turns into knots.

"I haven't seen anyone else since I've met you," he admits. "And, I'm not gonna lie, I thought we were pretty exclusive. I don't go to Church every Sunday with girls I don't care about."

I have to avoid his gaze at the shame. He's been so perfect to me and I went and ruined it all with Jake. Someone for whom I'm just another name on his list.

"I'm so sorry," I murmur.

"You're a beautiful girl, Jamie. The more you're out in

this world the more guys are gonna hit on you." I'm about to tell him that he's wrong, that no one ever has been interested in me, but he keeps going. "And next time, I want you to tell them that you're mine, and I don't share."

A zip of electricity courses through my body making my thighs clench. How did he turn from so sweet to so sexy in a split second?

"My bad for not mentioning it before. No need to get all worked up but now you know I'm not seeing anyone else and from now on, neither are you." His voice is just as suave as usual when he asserts his order, and it renders me speechless.

I have to pick up my jaw off the floor and pause for a heartbeat before asking the question I might regret. "So, if you're not seeing anyone else and I'm not seeing anyone else. What are we?"

He calmly puts his fork and knife back on the table and wipes his mouth with his napkin. He pulls his long sleeves up to his elbows. I notice he does this when he gets uncomfortable or anxious. Like he's preparing for a fight but there's no one to fight and no real danger. I admire his tattooed forearms but do my best to focus back on the conversation.

He looks deep in my eyes and I want to dive in his marine ones. He takes a deep breath before talking and I understand this is not easy for him.

"Look, I like you. I like you a lot, 'Me. I want you to know what you're getting yourself into before we start doing this," he gestures at the table and the restaurant around us, "more and more. We're not the same age. You still go to high school. People are gonna talk, your mom won't agree, my friends will disapprove. Of course I want to be with you in public but it's not gonna be easy. I want you to be sure you want to do this. This ain't some stupid high school romance. I'm past that."

I can't start to describe the warmth that overtakes me as he talks. I suddenly feel adrenaline rushing through my body as I understand we both want the same thing. This is it; this is where I'm tracing a line. I'm choosing Nathan over Jake and whatever he makes me feel.

"I don't care what anyone is going to say. And we both know my mom can't really talk." I grab his hand in mine. "I want this, Nathan, I promise."

"Come over here," he says, his voice not leaving me much of a choice.

I happily get up from my chair and walk to him, still holding his hand. He pulls me on his lap and captures my lips in a passionate kiss.

I'm overtaken by lust and love as I grab his face. He pulls away slightly, holding my waist.

"I want you. Now," he says in a heated growl. His voice is filled with desire and I melt under it.

"We're in public," I manage to say between two kisses.

"Fine. Let's get out of here."

We both get up and he throws some cash on the table before pulling me out of the restaurant. We power walk to his place and ten minutes later we burst through his door while making out. He grabs the back of my legs, pulling me up and wrapping them around his waist. He carries me to the sofa and puts me down.

"Your friend. Where is he?"

"Let me check."

He heads toward the hallway and I take my phone out of my pocket, turn it back on and check the time. 12:12. Officially my favorite time.

Nathan comes back to the living room with a smile on his face.

"Gone."

"Perfect," I reply in a smile.

He leans over me on the sofa, holding himself on the back of it. We go back to making out and it quickly heats up as we take each other's tops off.

He pulls my pants down and I suddenly feel overexposed. He straightens up, goes on his knees in front of the sofa. He grabs me behind my knees and pulls my legs, so my ass comes to the edge of the sofa. I barely have time to get over his gesture before he comes back up.

He hovers over me before taking my lips with his and I let him. Our tongues intertwine and dance with each other, making it the second man I make out with today. Only this time, it was on my own accord. It was with the person I truly wanted to kiss.

As if I didn't want to do anything with Jake. Jake is the most addictive drug I've ever tasted.

Stop thinking about him, I order to myself.

Nathan's kiss brings me back to the moment and I truly feel the need to go further. I undo his pants and help him out of them. His erection is straining his boxers and I push them down too.

Holy. Fuck.

I don't have much to compare him with, but I've seen dick-pics that guys have sent to Emily before.

This is never going to fit.

"You okay?"

I jump at his voice and look up from his huge erection to his face. I'm on my knees on the sofa and he's standing up in front of me. I suddenly feel like the tiniest creature on the planet facing a giant.

Chapter 16

His hair broke free from the bun and they're hanging to the side of his face, reaching his chin. I take a second to admire him, his hard jaw covered in a blond stubble, his deep blue eyes, his messy hair. I feel completely compelled by him. I nod but little does he know I have no experience to rely on. I guess it's about time to confess.

I fall back on my heels and take a deep breath. "Nathan, I have to tell you something," I say, trying to sound as confident as possible.

"Mmhm?" he replies, distracted by my boobs as he strokes his length.

"I think I should let you know that, uh, I've never really had sex before."

He freezes on the spot, his eyes snapping to mine and he suddenly lets go of himself.

"Wait, what?"

"I–I wasn't sure I should tell you but looking at *this*," I say pointing at his dick.

"You're a virgin and you weren't gonna tell me?" His voice drops a shade darker and he looks down at me frowning, clearly unimpressed at my statement.

"I don't know, I haven't really thought this through. Does it change anything for you?"

He opens his mouth multiple times trying to say something, but nothing comes out.

"Please say something."

"No–Yes...I don't know!"

"I want to do this with you," I say as I grab his hands and pull him towards me. "I trust you. I want this. Please don't do this to me, don't walk away."

He raises his hands and cups my face on both sides before dropping a kiss on my forehead.

"I'm not walking away. But you can't do it just to do it.

Our age difference is hard enough on my conscience to add the fact that you're a virgin. We should only do this if you're ready."

My heart skips a beat and I finally relax.

Oh, I am so ready for this.

"I'm ready. I promise you, I'm ready."

Just as we start kissing again my phone rings. I ignore it once, twice and the third time he pulls away.

"Just take it."

I grab my phone on the table and my eyes widen at the name on the screen. Mom. I pick up in a hurry, worried something might have happened but the voice on the other side is not too happy to hear me.

"*Jamie. Alexa. Williams! Where the hell are you? I just received a call from school saying you didn't show up to classes today.*"

My stomach twists in terror and embarrassment.

"Mom, I can explain."

"*I thought I could trust you, Jamie. Skipping class? How can you do this to me? I'm coming back right away.*"

"No! Gosh, mom no! I was feeling so ill this morning and I tried to go to school but once I got there, I felt even worse, so I just headed back home. I didn't want to text you and get you all worried, I thought I'd just wait and see if it passed. Please don't be mad."

Her voice changes drastically from angry to worried and I feel awful for lying to her.

"*What's wrong sweetie? Is it the nightmares? You know Doctor Swift is always a phone call away.*"

Ha. As if we could afford a Stoneview therapist now that dad's work wouldn't pay for it anymore.

I gulp and look at Nathan to check if he's heard but he isn't looking at me. He's putting his clothes back on instead.

"No, no that's fine. I've had a horrible stomach ache. But I'm starting to feel better. Promise."

After a few minutes of reassuring her, she finally lets me go, promising she'll stay in Tennessee as long as her sister needs her.

I turn to Nathan as soon as I've hung up and he gives me a small smile before handing me back my clothes.

"You should go home, 'Me. I don't want you skipping school and lying to your mom for me. It's not like you."

I knew the conversation with my mom would put him off. It makes us both aware of the fact that he's twenty-one and I'm still a high school student. I nod as I grab my clothes and quickly put them back on.

Once we're both dressed, he takes me in a tight hug. "I really like you, Jamie. We don't need to rush anything."

His words put a balm over my heart. "I know. I really like you too."

"Do you need a ride back?"

"I can take the bus."

"To Stoneview? Fuck that," he chuckles. He grabs the keys on the counter and head-gestures to the door. "Let's go, beautiful."

17

JAMIE

Bad Things — *Machine Gun Kelly & Camila Cabello*

I'm standing in front of my mirror on Monday morning, scrolling through the texts Jake sent me on Friday.

I thought I'd spend the weekend with Nathan, but he told me his friends were helping with the move and I understood he didn't want me there. So instead of spending my weekend with him, I spent it worrying that he didn't want his friends to know about me and that he got freaked out after my Friday revelation.

I also spent it reading and re-reading Jake's texts he sent when my phone was off on Friday and worrying about what I should do to get him to leave me alone. Not only because I'm scared of what he could say to Luke's family but also because I need to stay away from him if I want my relationship with Nathan to work.

My head drops back to my phone as I re-read his texts for the hundredth time, biting the inside of my cheek.

Jake: Where are you?

Chapter 17

> Jake: I swear you better be back by lunch.
>
> Jake: You and I need to have a chat.
>
> Jake: You're just digging yourself a deeper hole Angel. You're not gonna enjoy Monday.

I take a deep breath and look at myself one last time. Do I really think wearing a skirt will keep me out of trouble? No. Do I hope it will at least tame his anger? Absolutely. Hope is all I have.

While I'm on my phone, I check my shifts for this week. Mom has been unable to send me money and if I want a dress for the Halloween ball next Friday, I'm going to have to pay for it myself.

I started working at the café again but have been feeling uneasy knowing that Jake discovered my embarrassing secret. I haven't taken anything from the register again, obviously, but my time there has been rather awkward.

Emily's honk outside brings me out of my thoughts and I grab my backpack before hurrying to the door.

I freeze as soon as I step out. In the passenger seat of Emily's car is Luke Baker. I shake my head to check I'm not dreaming but no, he's sitting right in *my* seat. Emily must see me stop because she hops out of her car and runs toward me.

"Hey, I hope you don't mind, Luke's car broke down on his way to school and he asked me to pick them up. It was on my way to yours," she explains.

"Them?"

"Yeah, he drives the twins, right?"

Of course he does. Luke often drives the twins because we get extra credits for carpooling and Chris goes early in the morning to use the school gym.

I suddenly feel a cold sweat all over my body.

"Right..."

I was so focused on Luke that I didn't notice Jake and Rose sitting at the back of her car. What did I do to deserve this? Surely, I must have killed one of America's sweethearts in my previous life to be punished this way.

I open the back door and I'm met with Jake and Rose staring at me. Rose is sitting on the far left and Jake in the middle. Jake's eyes dip down to my skirt and back to my face. He greets me with a satisfied smirk and I instantly know this is not going to be a good day.

Emily starts the car and party music follows. I'm in a mood for anything but a party right now. This is a funeral. Mine to be precise.

"Party at mine next Friday. After the Halloween Ball. Babe, you should come for pre-game too," Luke says. "You know...just you and me."

I roll my eyes and turn to the window. I've got nothing against Luke but the situation I'm in right now is because he and my best friend have decided to start something serious. Couldn't they stick to a one-night stand?

"Guys, who are you taking to the ball?" Emily asks as she looks at the three of us through her mirror.

Rose huffs before replying. "Ciara."

"What?" Luke asks in shock. "Since when are you and Ciara a thing?"

"We're not," she replies, annoyed. "But my initial date thinks I cheated on her with the cheer coach in case you don't remember. So, we're going...as friends."

"Coach Swift?" Emily laughs. "He's gay!"

I would know that. His partner used to be my therapist.

"I know that," Rose replies, rolling her eyes. "Only Rachel doesn't seem to believe it. Or the fact that I would never flirt with some random old dude. Hey Emily, do you want to go with me to the ball?" she says with a lopsided smile on her face.

Emily's face blushes straight away and Luke turns in his seat, pointing his forefinger at Rose. "Fuck. Off."

Rose and Jake explode laughing. "When did you become so jealous?" Jake asks.

"Since Rose wants to put her dirty paws on my girl."

They all laugh but I keep silent, looking out the window with my chin in my hand and my elbow resting on the door. I'm really not in the mood for jokes.

"My paws ain't dirty," Rose jests. "They've definitely seen more pussies than yours though," she mumbles, making everyone's laughs double.

When the laughter dies down slightly Emily starts on the initial topic again. "'Me, you should go with Chris. I heard of that kiss…"

I straighten up and widen my eyes at her in the mirror. What is *wrong* with her? Why would she bring this up?

Because she has no idea what truly happened that night.

"Goody can't go with Chris. She's going with me." Jake's voice turns the car silent as he puts his hand on my thigh.

"Are you two hiding something from us?" Emily giggles.

She would love it if we were both dating guys from this group. Except she doesn't know what Jake is really like.

"Dude, you broke up with Camila like two days ago. Do you want Jamie to lose her head?" Rose chuckles in her raspy voice.

My eyes widen without me being able to control my reaction. Jake broke up with Camila? When? On Friday? This weekend? Before or after the bathroom incident?

As if reading my thoughts, Emily lets out a shocked, "Whaaaat? When did you break up with her?" she asks.

"Friday," he shrugs.

"But she's always the one who breaks up with you," she keeps going.

Emily has this power of making friends with anyone. She was never close to Jake but is capable of talking to him as if they've known each other since elementary school.

"She is. I guess it's for good this time. I'm done with her."

I cut their conversation short when I interject. "Sorry but you're going to have to find someone else. I'm not going with you." I take his hand from my thigh and push it away.

He turns to me, his brows rising in surprise that I dared to push him away. His facial expression quickly turns from surprise to evil as if telling me I will regret the gesture. I don't care though, I hold his dark gaze with mine because I can't do this to Nathan.

No matter how much my body is calling for Jake.

Rose's mocking laugh cuts our stare down. "I hope you didn't delete Cam's number."

It makes the two at the front laugh again, but Jake's eyes don't leave me and his mouth turns into a tight smile.

Surprisingly Jake doesn't get back at me for the car scene. At least not in English. It's not until lunchtime that he decides to strike back.

I stayed late to discuss my missed class with my calculus teacher. When I finally get out of the class, the halls are practically empty. Everyone must be at the cafeteria.

I'm walking past the computer room when I feel a hand grab my arm and pull me into the classroom. It's so fast that I don't even have time to scream.

Jake pushes me deeper inside the room and closes the

door behind himself. I feel relieved when I realize it has no lock on it.

"Jake!" I try to regain balance before facing him but he's already walking to a computer. "What are you doing?" I ask as I follow him with my gaze but take a step back toward the door.

"Don't even think about it. Not if you don't want the mark of my hand on your cute ass." He doesn't even raise his eyes from the computer.

I freeze at his words. "You wouldn't dare," I hiss at him.

He lifts his head up and gives me an evil grin. "Please, try me. Nothing would make me happier."

I try to swallow but my throat suddenly feels too tight. "What do you want? If it's about the car ride–"

"You should take a seat."

I pick the closest seat to me, but he tuts me. "Nah, front row. Face the screen."

I huff as I slowly get up and walk to the front of the room. There's a huge screen for teachers to show what they're doing on their computer.

I sit down anxiously, having no idea what he's got in mind and not enjoying the fact that he's now a few rows behind me and I can't see him anymore. The projector is on but there's nothing being projected yet.

"See Angel, a few months ago, Luke's parents told me they thought money was missing from their registers."

At those words, my heart picks up and I can feel cold sweats rolling down my back.

"They know I'm incredible at computer shit, so they asked me to build them a software to track down their money. The one they were using was old and full of bugs. I started with that. Everything looked fine, so they asked me to dig deeper."

I try to take a breath, but my chest is too constricted.

"So, I got Ozy on it 'cause I had no idea what they wanted from me. And I swear...that fucking genius. She can't code for shit, but she always comes up with great ideas. She said if someone was taking cash without registering the orders, no one could trace the money. She told me to build something that would track supplies, orders, and money. And boom, magic. What do I see? That you've been sloppy *and* greedy. You can't take that much cash and expect not to get caught. It can't take *that* many supplies for such few orders. Easy math, Goody. Last March was the worst. I'd say you and your mom took about two-hundred dollars."

The screen lights up and he opens a few documents followed by a software which I've never heard of. He shows his calculations and the monthly sums equal almost exactly what I took from the Bakers.

"Isn't March when we have to pay for the East Coast lacrosse tournament? Sadly, there's no one but you and your mom who work there that *truly* need the money. We do live in Stoneview. There's also no one as smart as you, that could take cash without anyone realizing."

I turn my head away in shame and get up in a hurry. "Stop. I get it," I say turning toward him. "I get it."

He looks at me with a winning look on his face. Proud that he's a computer genius and I'm a thief

"Does it match?" he asks.

"You know it does," I reply with a dry throat. "Please turn it off before someone sees this."

"I will. In a second."

"Please Jake, someone could come in at any moment, just turn it off and we can talk."

I stand in front of the projector, hoping it hides some of what's on the screen.

"I don't want to talk, Angel. I want to remind you why you shouldn't play games with me."

"I'm not! Please, I'm not. Just turn it off."

"I haven't told anything to the Bakers. I told them everything was fine because I believed your theft was justified. That was before you started putting your nose in my business. Now, I'm happy to go back to them with the truth."

He's talking like he's a million miles away from feeling anything and that's when he scares me the most.

Panic is completely taking over me and I squirm under his gaze, shifting from one foot to another. "Please, Jake..."

"You know you only do what I want you to, right?"

My stomach twists at his words but I don't want to drag this out. I just want him to take it down. My whole damn life depends on it.

"I know..."

"If I asked you to undress right in front of this projector, would you?"

My breath stops in my throat. "Please...don't do this to me."

I run a hand on my forehead as I can feel cold sweat forming.

He gets up and walks towards me until we're only three rows apart. "Be honest with me and I'll turn it off."

"What do you want? I promise I'll be honest." I reply instantly.

"Did you enjoy your night at mine?" he asks.

It takes me a second to understand what he means. "Yes, I did," I say in complete honesty.

"Do you regret it? Any of it?" He digs his ocean blue eyes in mine, and I have no choice but to tell him the truth, no matter how ashamed I am of it.

"No."

A small smile tugs at his lips. "Do you like me, Angel?"

"I despise you," I snarl.

"Well, that sounds very much like the truth. Too bad your body completely disagrees with you."

I know that, you bastard.

"What do you want from me, Jake?" I sigh. "Do you really know any girl who would stay stoic to your advances? Has it happened to you before? I might react to what you do but I don't want it and I'm not asking for it. The further away you are from me, the better."

He chuckles at my statement and I can feel the heat coming to my cheeks. A mix of anger and shame. "I like your honesty, Angel."

"Please take this thing down."

He comes closer and this time we're only separated by a desk and chair. His deep scent is overtaking my nostrils and bringing back with it all the memories of the times he's been close to me. My insides clench at the flashbacks.

"I broke up with Camila for you."

My heart drops to my stomach. Did I just hear this right? "What are you on about now?"

"I don't know what the fuck you're doing to me, Jamie, but I can't stop thinking of you. I'm pretty sure I dreamed about you every single night this week. You've become an unhealthy obsession and I think I'm starting to get addicted to your moans." He runs a hand through his hair. "Your moans are a fucking drug, you know that?"

I take a step back; his deep voice and scent are overpowering my rational thoughts.

"And you know the best thing about all that? It's that you're addicted to me too. Your body already knows it, your mind only needs to catch up."

"You're wrong," I blurt out too quickly and too low for it to sound credible. "You're wrong," I repeat a little louder.

"Who cares what you think, really? I've got your unexciting little life in the palm of my hand, Angel. One bad move from you and the Bakers are taking your family to court. Trust me, Luke's dad doesn't joke around when it comes to business. You don't become a powerful man like him by being nice with insignificant people like you."

His words hurt. They hurt because they're true. People like the Bakers would take no pity in my case. They wouldn't care why I took the money. They wouldn't care that it's because they underpay their staff and that mom could barely afford the rent after dad's death.

He sits down at the desk in front of me and rests his hands on the table. "Who cares what you *think* when your primitive instincts respond so well to me, Angel? I got you figured out. You think too much, you want to do what's right, you don't like giving in to pleasure. I can change that."

I take another step back, not liking how my body instantly responds when his voice gets lower and darker.

"You're wrong," I try one last time, but my voice is barely a whisper anymore.

"You crave me. You ache for me to touch you again, don't you? You want my lips on your skin. You want me to make you come, to make your legs shake and beg for release."

I can't help my thighs from clenching nor the wetness between my legs. I don't know how he does it, I don't know why I'm so reactive to it but there is something in Jake I've become addicted to and all I want is for him to make me feel good the way only he knows how.

I can't respond because I'm too focused on trying to stop myself from crossing the table, straddling him, and kissing him.

"Fine," he gets up from his seat and I have to force myself not to back away one more time. "You want to pretend you don't feel shit for me? That's okay, we'll have much more fun that way."

He can probably see the confusion on my face because he walks around the table and grabs my waist.

"It's a shame you're putting us through this, Angel. I just want to get to know you, but I'm happy to torture you with pleasure. Our game can keep going. I think I'm going to rename it: How long can Jamie last until she gives in."

"We don't have a game, Jake," I fume. "Take this damn thing down."

"I'll take it down once you've taken your stockings off."

"What?" I squeak.

"You heard me. Come on. Someone could come in anytime."

I try to get my brain to start working but it's all too much. I unexpectedly feel dangerously hot. Jake's scent, Jake's presence, the light from the projector blinding me, Jake's wide shoulders, Jake's hand resting on my waist, his forefinger tapping impatiently. Jake's tongue running through his bottom lip.

Jake. Jake. *Jake.*

I feel drunk on him and too hot to keep my tights on. I just need to cool down a little bit. This is what my body is telling me, trying to convince me to take my clothes off. It's fighting my rationality because all it wants is to follow what Jake's voice is telling it to do. It wants to obey because it wants pleasure.

Jake takes a step back as I'm sure he can read the defeat in my eyes.

Without being able to stop myself, I slip out of my shoes

and my tights follow. I let them drop on the floor, next to me. He picks them up and smiles at me.

"See? Not terrible to listen to me, is it?"

I shake my head trying to keep up with reality. "Please take it down now."

"I will, because you've been such a good girl today. You deserve it."

I squirm under his gaze.

A few seconds later the projector is displaying nothing but a white screen and I let out a sigh of relief.

"You're gonna have to trust me on this one. When you listen, you get rewarded. When you don't," he chuckles, "you don't want to know. So, every day, skirts. No stockings. Right?"

I nod but don't give him more. I just want to get away from him. I hold my skirt at the hem and bend down to put my shoes back on.

"This is going to be fun," he smiles as he watches me struggle to put my shoes on and keep a shred of dignity. He heads for the door. "Oh, what's your favorite food by the way?"

I shake my head, unsure what he means.

"Well," he presses.

"Sushi, why?"

"Have a good day," he waves as he exits the class.

How naive of me to think that settling things down with Nathan would magically get Jake off my case or...make my attraction to him disappear.

18

JAMIE

Still Don't Know My Name – Labrinth

My nightmare doesn't stop at Monday's embarrassment. Jake is relentless and to say he's hot and cold would be an understatement.

On Tuesday morning, he texts me to tell me he's taking me to school. Apparently, he told Emily, who happily agreed. When did my best friend stop knowing me?

I take my bike and decide to head to school before he can come pick me up. When he walks into class to settle next to me, he's holding a cup from Starbucks.

"Vanilla latte, right?"

I nod in confusion. How does he know my favorite drink?

Emily. Who else?

Butterflies dance in my stomach at the thought of him bringing my favorite drink to class for me.

Before I can extend my hand and say thank you, he turns around and whispers to Ciara, "Hey, you drink vanilla lattes?"

Chapter 18

She blushes and nods. Did anything ever happen between these two? I thought she was gay.

"Here you go, baby," he says as he passes her the cup.

I can't help but roll my eyes at his pathetic attempt to make me jealous.

"You're ridiculous," I shoot in an annoyed whisper.

Doesn't he understand that he can't make me jealous? I chose Nathan. He doesn't know there was a choice for me to make but I made it.

He smiles at me and starts opening his notebook. "I just wanted to take you for coffee before class, there was no need to get all scared and run away from your own house."

His condescending tone makes my hand itch to slap him, but I decide ignoring him is the best thing to do.

I should have known it was a terrible idea.

I stop at my locker between English and science to pick up my textbook. I feel Jake's presence behind me before he says anything.

One hand lands on the edge of my open locker door and the other on the shut locker next to me, trapping me between my books and him.

"You smell particularly good today, Angel. Is it for me?"

I stare at my stuff in front of me. I've stuck pictures of my family all the way at the back rather than my door. I don't want to see them all the time, but I like to know they're there if I need. Right now, it's not ideal though. My eyes are stuck on a picture of Aaron and me in these same hallways during my freshman year.

I try to take a step back, but Jake doesn't budge.

"Jake," I snarl.

Anger is boiling in my chest and I feel claustrophobic, trapped between Jake and this picture.

"Move, I'm not joking around," I seethe.

"Me neither, I don't joke when it comes to you."

His hand on my waist makes me jump and I feel sick to my stomach. I can't do this, not like this. Not while the younger, happier and braver version of myself is looking straight at me, her brother healthy, alive and present. Jake's other hand slowly slides on the side of my left thigh until it's under my skirt.

"Stop. I'll scream." My voice is steel, and I feel his hand freeze on my leg.

I don't know if it's my threat, if it's because some people are still in the area or if maybe he's taken pity on me, but his hands suddenly disappear. Not long enough to allow me any respite, though. They both come to rest on my shoulders heavily and his mouth comes close to my ear.

"Follow me, we need to discuss your latest theft."

I haven't stolen anything from the coffee shop since I've started again but the threat of revealing my secret is clear. I swallow the lump in my throat and follow him.

I try to keep as much distance as possible, so people don't get the wrong idea but when he stops and I'm forced to catch up, I know he's got something in mind. He grabs my waist just as my gaze lands on Camila and Beth walking to class late. I try to push his hand away but there's nothing to do, their gazes are lethal, and I feel them on my back until they walk into their class.

"You're delusional," I scoff when he opens the door to the janitor's closet. If he really thinks I'm getting in there with him, he's got another thing coming.

"Again, you don't have to fight me every single step of the way," he smiles.

"Every single step of the way?" I exclaim. "What way?! Where the hell is this going?"

He huffs and pushes me inside, following me and

blocking the exit. It's pitch black and I look for the switch but I can't seem to find it.

"Jake, this isn't funny. I don't want to be late to class. Unlike you, if I don't meet the conditions of my scholarship, I won't go to college. No one else is going to pay for me."

"That's exciting, where will you be going?"

"UPenn, asshole."

He chuckles. What's so funny to him?

"What are you really angry at, Angel?"

"You," I growl.

"I didn't ask who, I asked what."

He can't see me, but I feel my brows furrowing in confusion. I don't know what he's talking about but I'm not going to reward him with an answer when I know he's trying to trick me into something.

"Some problems you're never going to solve, Jamie."

"What?" My brain tries to work out what his goal is, but I'm completely lost.

"I saw what you were looking at, the picture in your locker. You don't usually get that angry at me. You know, because you got a thing for me. But today, you saw that picture and you're shutting me out. I don't think I'm the one who made you angry."

My heart drops in my stomach, heavier than rocks. I have to take a step back, but I hit shelves straight away. I'm suffocating in here, it's too dark, too small, a second ago it smelled of bleach but now all I can smell is Jake. This is why he froze; he didn't push me because he saw what I was looking at.

Jake doesn't reach out for me, he stays where he is, his voice lacking emotions. "You can try to get to Volkov. You can try to do it through Sam, or you can walk into his bars and sex houses, talk to his sellers. You can put your life at risk all you want; some questions might never be answered. Some mysteries are never solved, no matter how much you investigate, no matter where your morbid curiosity takes you."

"I–you," I stutter, but the words don't come out.

How does he know? He knows about my brother, he knows about Volkov. He knows everything. Who told him? It's not impossible to find in old news articles but he traced my whole plan, understood entirely what I was trying to do.

"He's gone. It's not your job to look for him," he concludes.

The tears building up in my eyes are begging to be let out. I let anger overpower me instead.

"You don't know what you're talking about," I argue. "You weren't even here. You have no idea what happened, you didn't know him!"

If I was the one missing, Aaron would have given every single second of his days looking for me. The police dropped the case after six months, and that was them doing us a favor because of dad.

'He's not a minor anymore, Mrs. Williams, we'll never know if he left of his own free will or not' I remember the new sheriff saying. If they're not going to look for him, who will? The last people who saw him alive were Volkov's men. The man with the huge scar on his face, more precisely.

"I know when something is a lost cause. And this is eating you up from the inside."

How did this turn from his sketchy flirting technique to telling me my brother's case is a desperate cause?

Because he saw the picture, idiot, he just told you.

"Let me out." I have to force the words out of my throat. It's too tight to sound convincing and my voice resembles a mewl. So, I accompany them with a big push. "Let me out!"

The light suddenly turns on and I have to put my arm in front of my eyes to not be blinded. Jake's hands land on either side of my face and he pushes me hard against the shelves.

"Stop wasting your time and energy on things that make you miserable. Stop trying to be a P.I. for yourself. Some people are never found, Jamie. Trust me, I know that. It's been three years; your brother is dead. And if not, he simply doesn't want to be found."

The sob that wrecks through me cuts my airways. I want to slide to the ground, but Jake is holding me up. He's forcing me to face reality in the mirror of his eyes and I don't know if I want to kill him or kiss him for taking such a huge weight off my shoulders.

I can't count the number of times Emily has begged me to let this go, but how could I? Coming from him, it hits differently. He doesn't beat around the bush, he doesn't know how to treat others' feelings carefully. The cold hard truth is hard to swallow but makes me feel freer than ever.

Aaron. Isn't. Coming. Back.

And I think I truly needed to hear it.

On Thursday, Jake texts me asking to join him for lunch. Scratch that, Jake texts *ordering* me to join him for lunch. Since Emily is with the group of assholes, I ignore them and join some friends who are putting together the yearbook.

They're not my friends per se but everything they do has to run through me or Cole, the other student body president. Cole doesn't get involved though, he's only on the committee because of his popularity, so responsibilities fall back on me. Good, it keeps me busy and it gives me an excuse to eat with this group.

"Who is going to take the pictures when lacrosse season starts?" Mila asks.

She's a little thing with curly red hair and big brown eyes but she can get annoying real quick. She's the one putting everything in order for the book and editing it.

"Taylor M. took them last year but obviously he's gone now."

I can barely focus on my lunch because every time I look up, Jake's eyes are right on me. He's got a smirk on his face, as if he knows exactly why I'm eating at this table and knows how futile it is. He won't reveal my secret just for this, he loves playing with me too much. But I can tell he's got something in store and it's stopping me from swallowing any of my food.

"Jamie W.?" Mila insists.

My eyes snap back to her and Landon, both sitting in front of me. Why does she *have* to call everyone by their first name and the initial of their last name? It can be so irritating.

Landon gives me a shy smile. He could be attractive if he tended to his teenage growing beard and got a haircut occasionally. His eyes are a piercing green and I always feel like they can read my thoughts. He adjusts his Armani glasses resting on his nose as they both wait for my answer.

"Uh…" I hesitate. "I'm sure we've got plenty of other photographers. Have you asked Kaylee?"

"Kaylee R.?" she asks for confirmation. God, Mila it's not like there are a hundred Kaylee's in our school.

"Yes," I answer, barely refraining the 'duh' from passing my lips.

"She said no. She said it means she can't be on the cheer team and she doesn't want to give that up."

I refrain myself from rolling my eyes and glance at Jake's table again. He's finally stopped staring. I look at all of them, eating and laughing together. Chris is trying to get Rose to finish her fries – it's a weird move but she is skinny and it wouldn't hurt her to eat – but Luke gets in their way and grabs her plate. Hold on, this gives me an idea.

"What about Luke?" I suggest. I remember the pictures in Jake's room, he said Luke took them and they were beautiful.

"Luke?"

"Yes, Luke…B.," I say so she understands.

She explodes laughing, earning us the looks of many people in the cafeteria and I just want the ground to swallow me.

"Oh God, Jamie W., I think you've lost it a little bit since you and Jake W. do stuff. Luke B. doesn't take pictures, silly!"

I almost choke on her words as Landon elbows her in the ribs.

"What did you say?" I rasp.

"Oh…no nothing sorry," she quickly replies.

"She didn't mean to offend you, Jamie," Landon pacifies as he puts his hand on my free one resting on the table.

It confuses me because he's not really a touchy-feely person and I don't exactly like his skin on mine. It's nothing compared to J–I mean Nathan's. It's nothing compared to my boyfriend's.

"Mila," I press. I don't know what to do about Landon's hand. It would be so cruel to just pull it away but it's not okay for him to make me uncomfortable either.

"She just said Luke doesn't take pictures," Landon smiles

and there's a slight movement of his thumb as if to calm me, except it makes me even more fidgety.

"No, I mean the other thing. About Jake." Her face falls at my strong voice but I don't let her reply anyway. "Jake and I don't do things–*anything*. Who told you that?"

"I–I don't know, I just overheard it, I guess. You know how it is…rumors." She shrugs both her shoulders and I want to stick my fork in her face. What a bitch.

"Nothing happened between us. Ever," I defend.

It's a lie but it's also none of these guys' business.

"You promise?" Landon asks as he caresses the back of my hand with his thumb again.

This is bothering me so much. Much more than it should. Why does he need to know so bad if something happened between Jake and me? And why is he touching my hand?

I despise when men think unwanted touch is okay. And I despise that us girls feel rude when all we want is not to be touched. It might be innocent, but it doesn't *feel* innocent and I hate myself a little for not being brave enough to just pull away and for being scared to look bad-mannered.

"I–yes!"

"Right…" Mila trails her eyes behind me, and I don't miss the smile twitching at her lips.

I jump in surprise when a hand grabs the back of my neck. I recognize Jake's touch because my skin doesn't want to crawl off my body like it does with Landon's.

Aren't you the one who just ranted about unwanted touch from men?

That's exactly the problem. Jake's touch is not unwanted. It never is.

"Baby, tell me what's the name of that friend of yours," he sits down next to me, his hand still wrapped around the back of my neck. "You know that nerdy one with glasses that thinks he can touch you, when we both perfectly know I would break his fingers if he ever dared?"

Landon's hand flies away from mine in record time but I keep my eyes on my plate. I can't bear looking at them after I just fought that Jake and I weren't a thing.

He has to make me a liar by showing up with the sole intention to piss on his territory. I hate Jake's technique, but I can't help feeling grateful for finally being able to bring my hand back to my side. It feels clammy and, while I don't want anything to happen to Landon, I couldn't bear it anymore.

"So?" Jake insists, tightening his grip.

"L–Landon," I reply reluctantly. My eyes are so fixed on my plate I can memorize it by heart.

"Right," he exclaims, snapping his fingers as if finally remembering the name we all know he didn't know in the first place. "You should tell him, next time I find his hand on yours, I'm gonna be forced to rearrange his dentition."

I shiver at the thought of Jake punching Landon's face until all his teeth fall out. I glance at Landon who now looks paler than the china on his platter.

"Are you telling him, or should I?" Jake urges.

God, he really can't let this go. He doesn't have the capacity to understand people's emotions and it's like he can't see that Landon is seconds away from pissing his pants right now. Regret is plastered on his face, but Jake can't read that. He keeps going because he'll only stop when it's enough for *him* and him only.

"Jake–" I try to intervene, to say there's no need to terrorize Landon, but he doesn't let me talk.

"Apologize for making her uncomfortable," Jake orders.

"I–I'm sorry if I made you uncomfortable," Landon quavers.

Mila is looking at her plate to avoid looking at the situation unfolding in front of her and I can't blame her. This is embarrassing, for everyone but Jake.

"I didn't say *if* I said *for*, if you couldn't see you were making her uncomfortable you need a new pair of glasses."

"I–I'm sorry for making you uncomfortable, Jamie," he blurts out.

His eyes lock on mine and I can't stand his pleading look. He's screaming 'please make him stop' and I try to respond with a silent 'if I could make him do anything, this wouldn't be happening'.

"It's okay," I reply instead. "Apologies accepted."

"It's not, really," Jake cuts in. "She's being too nice." He turns to me to say, "Are you not eating anymore?"

"My appetite is gone suddenly," I fume through gritted teeth.

"We can get you something later," he smiles as he gets up.

I stumble up as he brings me with him and barely have time to grab my bag.

We cross the whole cafeteria with his hand still on my neck and I feel the colors of humiliation on my cheeks.

He only lets go when we're alone in a classroom and I think I'm the one who's going to explode with anger but he beats me to it.

"What the hell is wrong with you, huh?" he demands. "Do you have to make everything so difficult? I said to come eat with me. What were you trying to do? Make me jealous?"

"I–" I try to defend myself but he's already on me, pushing me hard enough against the teacher's desk that I have to go on my toes and sit on it as my bag falls to the floor.

"Because if that was the plan, here, you got me, jealous and fuming. What are you going to do about it now?"

"I wasn't trying to make you jealous."

I push at him but it's pointless. His shoulders are too big, and his chest is rock hard, anger rippling through his body.

"I wasn't trying anything. Has it ever occurred to you that I'm just not interested? You're the one making this difficult, get the hint!"

Lies. Lies. Lies.

His hands are on my waist the next second, crushing me so hard I struggle to breathe. His forehead comes to rest on mine and his hard breathing is hot on my skin.

"Stop playing games, Jamie. Stop it." His teeth are so clenched I can barely make out the words. "You're hard to get, you've made your point. Now give in," he orders.

"Or what?" I snarl. "You're going to tell everyone I'm a thief? You're going to send my mom to jail and leave me parentless. Like you? Is that what you want? For me to be as broken as you are?"

I regret the words as soon as they slip my lips but amongst the regret there is pride hiding. Pride for finally being able to hit him as hard as he usually hits me. For finally not holding back, just like he does.

I jump when one of his hands grabs on my jaw hard enough for my teeth to rattle.

"Jake–" I squeal but his hand is pouting my lips so bad I can't get any sound out.

"You have no idea how fucking broken I am, Angel." His smile is so cold it freezes my blood.

He is pure satisfaction right now. It's like all this time he's been waiting for me to push back hard enough so he could let his real demons out. The same ones that took me to the woods that night. I recognize the darkness in his eyes.

"But believe me, you're about to find out."

His free hand goes under my skirt. He grabs at my panties. I fight him, but my strength is nothing compared to his. I push at his hand, kick my legs to try and get myself off the desk but he doesn't move one bit.

My eyes widen in horror when I hear the sound of my panties ripping. I shake my head, pressure building behind my eyes.

"No, no, no" I force out of my mouth.

"Don't worry," he mocks me. "I told you before that rape isn't my thing. I prefer you wet and willing, baby."

But I didn't say no because I was scared of sexual assault. I said no because I don't want him to feel how wet my panties are. Shamefully wet. I don't like him, God, I hate him but his touch...it does things to me.

"Oh Angel, so wet for me. Always. So. Wet."

I have to squeeze my eyes shut as my face burns with embarrassment. I open them to see him putting my panties in his back pocket. He lets go of me so hard I almost fall on the other side of the desk.

I see him bend down and when he reappears, he's holding my bag. He searches through it and when I see my house keys emerging, I jump off the desk.

"Give me that," I order, holding my hand out to him.

"You can get them at the end of the day."

"I–I can't, you have practice tonight. Please just stop this." Begging is even more humiliating, but I don't know how to get to him anymore. He switched, and I'm scared I'll never bring him back.

"Right and make sure you wait through the whole thing

or you might have to break a window to get inside your house tonight."

He leaves without glancing back. I call him one last time to try and change his mind, but he doesn't turn back. My fist hits the desk in frustration.

He is driving me insane.

I wait on the bleachers, with no underwear on, and spend an hour and a half trying to keep my skirt down in the freezing wind. The smirks Jake sends my way confirms that this was exactly the point. It's embarrassing and my cheeks are on fire, but my body is trembling with the cold.

After everyone has gone home, Jake appears from the locker room and comes back to me.

"Let's get you home," he smiles his pearly teeth at me. His hair is wet and messy from the shower.

The winning look on his face is adding to the list of shit I hate him for. He took the time to have a shower when he knew I was waiting for him in the cold with barely anything on.

I get up, shivering and my teeth clattering. Does he even realize the temperature right now?

"You're cold," he frowns, and if I didn't know he was a sociopath I might have mistaken concern in his eyes.

"No shit," I growl.

His hug comes unexpectedly and harshly. He holds my head against his chest as his arms wrap around me. A sigh of contempt escapes my lips at the warmth emanating from his body. He starts moving his hands up and down my back to warm me up and I just let him. It feels too good, too natural to stop him.

I'm not exactly sure where he's driving us but when he parks on the side of the road, I raise an eyebrow at him.

"I'll be two minutes," he says as he unbuckles his belt and jumps out of the car.

I check my phone for texts from Nathan, but I've had nothing from him today. Guilt feels heavy in my stomach for being in Jake's car. For letting him play with me today like he did.

Jake comes back in the car fifteen minutes later with a medium brown paper bag that seems full to the rim.

"Here," he breathes as he settles back behind the wheel. I grab the bag in confusion. "It's for you."

I look inside to find platters of sushi stacked up on each other.

"Sushi?" I question.

"I thought you liked sushi," he smiles.

"Jake–"

"You barely ate anything today, Angel. I can't have my pretty girl starving."

I don't say anything as he starts the car. Is that his way of saying sorry?

You're not his girl. Say it. Say it, Jamie!

I keep quiet.

When he parks in front of my house, he takes my keys from his backpack and opens his car door. I follow with the food and my own bag.

"Are you really just going to invite yourself to my house?" I scoff as he puts the keys in the door.

He opens for me and gets out of the way while still holding the door open for me.

"Sadly not. I promised Rose we'd have dinner together tonight. Otherwise I would."

He must see the confusion on my face because he raises an eyebrow. "I thought you said you liked sushi."

I almost want to laugh in his face. This guy has inexistant social skills, how did the whole school end up liking him? I bet he learned the right things to say, the facial expressions from other people and is just copying and pasting them on his face. Like a real sociopath. I shake my head and walk in.

"Thanks," I murmur.

"They're really good, I go to this place all the time. I hope you like them."

A smile tugs at my lips at how random he can be, but I try not to show it. I can't let him think that he can bully me during the day and offer me sushi for dinner as a sorry. Surely, he can understand that's not how it works? I mean, I'm still naked under my skirt.

"Bye Jake," I say as I close the door on him.

I drop the bag on the kitchen bar that separates my tiny kitchen from the rest of the living area. I look into the sushi bag, the boxes are elegant. This is not regular takeaway. This is Stoneview takeaway. I reach for the receipt all the way at the bottom. Sushi for one, 90 dollars.

"This town makes me sick," I mumble to myself.

Jake makes me feel sicker. I'm getting whiplash from our interactions and I am so mad at him right now. How can he think this is okay?

And yet, I wish he had stayed to eat with me. I wish we could have sat and got to know each other better. I wish I could understand the reasons why he doesn't get affected by basic human emotions.

I can't see Nathan over the weekend, he's out of town for work, although I'm still not one hundred percent clear on his job. Something to do with sales.

I try not to think about Jake, but his face keeps slipping back into my mind. I keep being reminded of his hard muscles and his stupid smile. I try to control my brain but two nights in a row I fall asleep touching myself to thoughts of him, of his deep voice when he ordered Landon not to touch me, of his hand holding me and his other ripping my panties away. I think of all the things Jake said to me, all the promises of pleasure.

On Sunday night I fall asleep with a new thought creeping up at the back of my mind. Despite the kindness and the love between me and Nathan, maybe he just isn't the one.

19

JAMIE

Dancing With Our Hands Tied – Taylor Swift

On Monday, I have to skip lacrosse practice for a shift at the Bakers' café. They extended the opening hours to early evenings and I got all the late shifts this week apart from Friday since it's the Halloween Ball night.

Cole Cooper asked me to go with him and since Emily is going with Luke, I gratefully accepted. We usually only hang out because we're both co-presidents of the student body. He's a handsome guy, sadly he's only a jock trying to get extra credit.

He's truly the typical high-school lacrosse player. Blond hair, pale blue eyes, big square shoulders. We never have deep conversations, but I guess he's not horrible to be around. When I told Nathan and said we were purely platonic he laughed and said I was cute, but that he wasn't worried about a high school kid stealing his girl. Apparently, I'm too 'mature' for that. I wish that was applicable when it comes to Jake.

I'm lucky tonight, we're closing in half an hour and every

customer is gone already. I'm cleaning the counter when the bell rings as a group comes in. I knew it was too good to be true. When I realize who the girls walking in are, my heart accelerates. Beth and three of her cheerleader friends are walking in followed, lastly, by Camila.

I let out a huff as the five of them sit down at a table. Last week was hard enough at school. I've turned into the girl that wears a skirt without stockings in cold weather, the one who shows her legs to attract the guys' attention. I've become the girl who shows up with Jake and leaves in his car.

Beth and Camila have taken pleasure in getting their friends to fill my lockers with dirty condoms full of God knows what and tearing my textbooks apart. I had to buy a new calculus textbook twice now, and everything I've saved for my dream dress is slowly but surely disappearing.

I don't even bother saying hello when I get to their table. "We only do take away at this time."

"I'll take a caramel latte, soy milk, zero-calorie syrup, oh, and make it foamy," Beth replies in her annoyingly nasal voice.

"You can order at the counter," I coldly retort before heading behind the counter. Strangely I feel safer behind here since all of them are about a head taller than me, except Beth.

They all get up and walk to the counter. The three extra cheerleaders push their chairs hard enough for them to fall over.

I roll my eyes at their childish acts and wait to take their orders. Beth tells me everyone's order and I know she's making them complicated on purpose. She's not destabilizing anyone though. I've worked in this café long enough to be an expert in basic bitches' drinks.

She gives me a hundred-dollar bill to pay and I look at her deadpan.

"It's $24.89, Beth."

"It's all I have," she shrugs. "You've probably never seen one of those, have you?"

I clench my jaw to stop myself from replying. This shift is almost over. Just give them their coffee and close up.

"I'll be back," I smile tightly.

I walk to the back to get more change and check the authenticity of the bill according to employees' guidelines. This machine is old and slow, and it takes ages for it to process a single bill. Without surprise it comes out a minute later with a green light, confirming that it's real. I walk back to the café floor and can't refrain from gasping.

Camila and her posse have turned everything upside down. Chairs are on the floor, the cups, straws and cup sleeves are spread out everywhere. They've thrown and crushed all the small cream packs on the floor, all the way to the front door. They even went behind the counter, spilled the milk cartons, emptied the sticky syrups on the counter and floor.

"Are you out of your minds?" I scream at them as they head for the door.

Camila is the last one to get out and she turns back to me.

"I hope Jake pays for your dates, Goody, because you won't be able to afford much when they fire you."

"What is wrong with you?!" I hurry to her but as I'm closing in on her I slip on the cream on the floor and land on my back.

The hard floor knocks the air out of my lungs, and it takes me a second to bear my surroundings again. Camila is standing high above me, her stilettos making her more impressive than she should be.

"What's wrong with me? I'm just a girl who got cheated on and dumped without respect for a two-year relationship. I'm a hurt woman. And you? You're a slut disguised as a saint. Don't think this is the end of it."

I want to reply but the shock and pain from the hard fall crush the words in my chest. I hear the front door slam and I just stay where I am. Lying in cream and cup sleeves.

I try to push back the pressure behind my eyes but it's all too much. I let the tears flood my face. It doesn't take long before it turns into full-on sobs. If Jake's harassment wasn't enough, the bullying from his ex is surely too much for me to handle. I start to feel like a stupid little girl when I suddenly feel the urge to call my mom. Maybe if she was here this wouldn't have happened? Who fucking knows?

I don't hear the door open again and all I see is a man suddenly towering over me.

"Are you okay, miss?"

"Oh my God." I jump to my feet, wincing at the back pain from the fall, and wipe my tears with the back of my hands. "I'm so sorry."

I adjust the apron on my hips. "I'm sorry about the mess. There was...there was....a...dog." I finish my sentence and don't even expect him to believe me. "What would you like," I eventually ask.

"Are you alright? Do you need help cleaning up?"

I finally take the time to look at him. He looks in his early 30s, strong build but not very tall. His skin is so pale I can see his veins bulging on his arms and around his neck. He's wearing jeans that look slightly too long for him, the extra length accumulating around his ankles, but his black shirt looks too small for his huge arms.

"I'm fine, thank you. Did you want a coffee?"

"Did someone come here and bother you?"

His lack of answers regarding what he came for – aka a drink – and his tone make me take a step back and away from him. He sounds insisting for the wrong reasons.

"Honestly, everything is fine. My colleague is at the back getting the cleaning supplies," I lie.

I have this strange instinct that tells me not to let him know I'm alone in the café.

"Alright, alright. Could I use your bathroom? I'll buy something after."

I nod, not wanting to make this longer than it should be. "First door on your left."

"Hallway over there?" He points at the hallway behind me and I nod again. Fear is starting to creep up and I just want him to leave. His black eyes are looking at me intensely and I notice when they quickly glance down to my chest.

I remark a familiar tattoo on his inner arm, on his bicep. Where did I see this before? A tattoo of the moon cycle in a line. Seven moons lined next to the other, the full moon in the middle.

As he walks around me and toward the bathroom, it hits me. It's the Wolves' tattoo. Volkov's gang. My heart drops from my chest and I'm about to turn around when I feel a movement behind me, a hand grabbing my shoulder and a blade against my throat.

"HEL–"

My scream is cut off by his sweaty hand on my mouth.

"You make one noise and you're gonna choke on your own blood. And that's a horrible death, little girl."

I freeze at his words, barely biting back a whimper.

"I'm gonna take my hand away now. You keep those pretty lips sealed, alright?"

I nod slightly, his voice and words making my stomach coil and bile rise up my throat. I'm scared, I've never been so scared in my entire life.

His hand moves away from my mouth, but the blade of his knife stays at my throat.

"There's a hundred dollars on the counter. Take it. Take the whole till," I say with a shaky voice.

I always thought I would be braver than that if the café ever got robbed. I ran this sort of scene in my head a hundred times. Now that I'm living it, I only want one thing: to make it out alive and untouched.

His blade comes closer and I feel its sting on my flesh. "I thought I just told you to keep quiet."

"I'm sorry, I'm sorry," I whisper as quietly as possible.

"Unfortunately, I'm not here for the money."

Tears break out as I hear this. I squeeze my eyes shut trying to wake up from the nightmare.

"What's your name?" he asks.

I stay quiet at his question. Why does he want to know my name? What has it got to do with anything?

"Answer."

"Ja–Jamie."

"Williams?"

I can't refrain a sob. How does he know my name? What does he want? I only nod as an answer, feeling like this is sealing my fate.

He comes around, his blade still on my neck, and faces me. He drags his knife from my throat to my collarbone and a shiver runs down my spine. He slides it to the left and hooks the knife behind the strap of my tank top and my bra.

"N–no please," I beg but he does it anyway. He pulls and cuts the straps, making my tears double.

Chapter 19

"Please..." I sob. "Please don't do this. Just leave. I won't say anything, I promise. I won't go to the police."

He chuckles and points the knife at my scar. Below, my top and bra are hanging low, exposing the top of my breast.

"Nice scar."

It's never burnt as much as it does now.

"I remember when Alek shot your dad. I was just outside, guarding the door to make sure none of you escaped." My heart stops altogether and so does my breathing. "He made a big mistake thinking he got all of you that day."

I don't say anything, I just keep eyeing the blade on my scar, my arms frozen at my side. I know I'm going to risk my life asking this, but my head is going to explode if I don't.

"My br–my brother, is he alive?"

He laughs, loud and cold and it freezes my blood. "Ah, Aaron." My heartbeat doubles, thinking my question will finally be answered. "What's the point in telling you, girl? You're going to die anyway. Do you know why you saw my face tonight?"

I know the answer, but I don't want to say it. It is well known for the Wolves to never show their faces. It is well known that they always hide their faces when they 'work'. No one knows who's actually part of the gang. It is well known that when they *do* decide to show their faces, it's because the person won't live to tell the tale.

"Because a Wolf face is the last thing you ever see," he says. Repeating their motto. "I was sent to kill you, but nothing stops me from having a little fun before, right?"

I shake my head, my whole body trembling. The blade glides down my whole body, tracing disgust across my skin, until he settles it between my shaking thighs.

His phone rings loudly, making me jump, and his attention goes to his pocket as he tries to take it out.

I take this as my chance. I push away his hand holding the knife and make a beeline for the door to the stockroom. I type the code the fastest I've ever had and barge into the room, slamming the door with all my strength.

The door locks automatically and I take steps back as I hear him hit against it on the other side. I put my hand to my throat, suddenly feeling the pain from where he was holding the knife.

"Open the door, you fucking bitch!" he shouts.

I know he won't be able to open it, but my heart is still hammering against my chest. I'm shaking at everything that just happened. I almost died. I almost...worse.

I try to gather my thoughts and look around the room. I'm safe here but there's no exiting the café this way.

"I have all fucking night but just know the longer you take to open, the more you'll suffer."

Another sob escapes my mouth and when I go to wipe my cheeks again, I realize there's blood on my hand. I touch my neck again. I'm bleeding and the panic grows thicker in my body.

It takes me a few minutes to remember that my phone is in the pocket of my apron. I grab it, try to unlock it too quickly, and watch it drop to the floor. My hands are shaking so much.

"Shit, shit, shit...shit."

I never curse out loud but tonight got the best of me.

"Please, Lord, please let it not be broken."

I do the sign of the cross before squatting. I pick up my phone and turn it around. The whole screen is crushed in a mix of colors. I can only read the top left corner anymore.

"Why," I scream in frustration. "Why me?!"

I don't know if I'm talking to the crazy guy banging on the door or God, but who cares, I've gone completely insane. This town has finally pushed the sanity out of my body.

My hope raises again when I recognize something in the top corner of my screen. The letters NA. I know the last person I called was Nathan on my way here before my shift. I must have managed to unlock it to my call log. If I manage to tap on his name, I can get him to call 911.

The banging on the door becomes harder and I know he's using something to try and break it. I don't hesitate one more second and do my best to tap exactly on the letters. I can see the screen changing and when I put it to my ear the ringtone is music to my ears.

"Pick up, pick up, pick up...."

"Hey, beautiful. Are you done with–"

"Nathan! Nathan, you have to help me. You have to call the police. I was–I was..."

Another, louder bang pulls a scream out of me.

"Me? What's wrong? Where are you?"

"I'm at the café," I sob. "Th–this guy he came in and... and... please call the police. I'm locked in the back room but he's trying to get in... Nathan, please call the police."

There's another bang and this one actually puts a dent in the door.

"The police are on their way," I shout at the door. "Leave now!"

"Jamie," Nathan's low voice suddenly grounds me. *"Don't talk to him. You talk to me. You got me? Do* not *talk to him."*

"Yes...yeah. Okay."

"Describe him to me. I'll describe him to the police if he tries to leave."

"He–he's small, dark long hair, black eyes. White. He's got a tattoo on his left bicep."

"*What tattoo?*"

"The W–" I stop myself. Nathan probably has no idea who the Wolves are. "It's the moon cycle."

There's a brief pause.

"Nathan?"

"*Do not move. I'm on my way.*"

I don't have time to reply, he's already hung up. Is he calling the police? What is going on?

I take steps back from the door, my eyes never leaving the first dent he's made. My back hits the back wall and my legs totally give up. I slide against the wall until I hit the floor, pull my legs to my chest, wrap my arms around them and drop my head on my arms.

I keep repeating to myself that the police are on their way, that this is all going to be over soon, but the banging becomes one with my heartbeat and I can't stop the tears. This guy came to finish the job Volkov started three years ago and even if I make it out alive tonight, my nightmare will be far from over.

What feels like an eternity later, the banging stops and I hear some struggling outside. I get up and get closer to the door. I hear a fight, but I have no idea what is going on exactly. Voices, grunts, struggle, it all mixes together and suddenly nothing.

A few knocks on the door make me jump but it's nothing like the banging.

"Jamie, it's me, open the door." Nathan's voice is like that of an angel.

It releases a wave of relief over my whole body and I rush to unlock the door from the inside.

As soon as I open, he rushes inside and grabs my shoulders. Our height difference is such that he has to bend down to level his face with mine.

"Are you okay? Let me see your face."

"I'm okay...I'm fine..." I cry as I say this, but they're tears of relief.

"Your neck," he says as he inspects my body and he freezes when he notices the state of my top and bra.

He takes a step back, his jaw clenches as he runs a hand through his hair.

"Fucking...motherfucker..." He pulls his sleeves up to his elbow, exposing his ripped arms and walks back out of the room.

"Nathan..." I follow after him.

Up until now, I've never seen Nathan angry. He never raised his voice at me, never let out any hint that he ever got in fights or arguments in general. He's always calm, funny, and lighthearted, especially with me. But as I follow him to the shop floor, I wonder if I got him all wrong.

Completely wrong.

The guy from earlier is practically unconscious on the floor, his face a bloody mess. One of his arms is bent behind his back in a way that is clearly broken.

"Oh my God," I gasp. "Did you do this?"

I look up at him but he's not listening. He's back on the guy, kicking him in the ribs.

"You thought you were gonna touch her? Huh? You stupid. Fucking. Bastard." Every breath he takes, he gives him another kick.

"Nathan...Nathan, stop," I say in a panic, trying to catch his arm.

He stops for a split second to turn and point at me. "Stay back, Jamie."

His voice doesn't leave me much choice and I take a few steps back.

"Nathan, you're going to kill him. Please stop," I plead as the guy on the floor grunts every time he gets a kick.

Nathan squats next to him, grabs him by the hair, and bends his head to the side so he's facing me.

"Take a good look at her, Dimitri, because if I see you or any of your puppy friends in the same zip code as her again, I'm taking the whole fucking pack down. One by one. And I won't go as easy on them as I went on you tonight."

My mouth goes slack and my mind numb at all the things I realize I don't know about my boyfriend. Starting with the simple fact that he knows my attacker's name.

He gets back up and spits on the semi-conscious body.

"Tell Volkov that Bianco says hello."

The car ride to Nathan's house is in complete silence. The shock has me mute and I'm still trying to swallow what I just saw my boyfriend do. He keeps asking if I'm okay, but I can't reply because I don't know.

My body is trembling, and a thousand questions are clouding my mind. My neck is burning, and I can feel drops of blood spread all over my throat and collarbone. It's nothing, I don't feel like I'm losing that much blood, but it gives me something to focus on.

As I'm taking a shower at Nathan's house, I know that nothing is the same anymore. I saw a side of him I'm not sure I can understand. It has put a million questions in my head. Questions I'm going to want answers to. It has put doubts in everything I see around him.

Like how does he afford this huge Stoneview mansion at twenty-one years old, living on his own? How does he dare call the Wolves a pack of puppies? How did he know the guy's name? How did he understand it was them when I told him about the tattoo? How does he even know about them?

My thoughts suddenly track to the bullet scar in his stomach. Why did I not pay more attention to this?

When I'm clean and dressed in one of Nathan's giant shirts I go down to the kitchen. He is sitting at the kitchen island, his back to me, on the phone.

"...no, just go there and clean up. He was alive when I left so he should be gone by now. Make sure you clean the whole shop. I don't want my girl getting in trouble with her job."

There's a pause while he listens to the person on the other line.

"I don't care about that right now, man. Make this your priority."

He hangs up and I wait a few seconds, watching him run his hand in his hair and mutter 'fuck', before clearing my throat to announce my presence. He turns around in surprise and his whole body and face relax when he sees me.

"'Me," he hurries to me and grabs both sides of my face in his hands, bending down to give me a kiss on my forehead. "Are you okay?"

I shrug because I'm okay but lost and confused.

His brows furrow when he looks at my neck. "It's still bleeding. Let's fix you up."

"I'm f–"

I don't have time to finish my sentence because he's already out of the room. I sit down at the kitchen island in a sigh. Why does everything always get ruined?

Home was fine, then mom had to go to Tennessee. School was fine then Jake had to ruin it. My relationship with Nathan was perfect until this whole situation came and messed it up.

How can I trust him when I've seen a whole side of him he's purposely been hiding from me for almost two months? I put my elbows on the table and my face in my palms. Someone has cursed me. There's no other justification.

I frown as a drop of blood falls on the counter. Maybe that cut was worse than I thought. The adrenaline has completely come down and my neck hurts, I'm cold and my body won't stop trembling.

Nathan comes back with a first aid kit and I twist on the stool to face him. I can see genuine concern in his eyes, so I attempt a weak smile. He spreads antiseptic on a cotton pad and applies it to my cut. A few seconds later he puts one of those big band-aids on it, but the worry hasn't left his expression.

"Nathan, I'm fine."

He sits down on a stool next to me and takes both my hands in his. His touch warms me up and stops my body from trembling. He has this reassuring power over me. No matter what I've seen earlier and no matter what he did, he makes me feel safe.

A silence falls on us, but his eyes don't leave mine. He must see the questions in mine because he sighs and runs a hand through his hair. Then he pulls his sleeves up to his elbow.

"I know I've got a lot of explaining to do," he admits.

My shoulders relax at the fact that he is already thinking of giving me the truth. Question is, can I take it?

Before he can even start explaining, I ask the question that's been burning my tongue for the last hour. "How did you know his name?" I blurt out.

"Are you sure this is where you want to start?"

Chapter 19

"Yes," I reply more determined than ever.

He takes another minute to think it over then takes a deep breath. "Three years ago, when I left home, I did a couple of jobs for a man called Mateo Bianco. His main rivals were the Wolves. I encountered a few of them when I worked for him, including Dimitri."

I try to swallow the news while staying as stoic as possible.

"Work*ed*? Do you not do this anymore?"

"No! No, of course not. I was young and stupid, and I needed money. I mainly dealt with security shit."

"Security? What were you, a bodyguard?"

"Kinda." He keeps his reply short and I know he's hiding something.

"What did you do for him, Nathan?" I insist with a cold voice.

"Look, 'Me...I–"

"Just spit it out already."

"You need to understand, when Mateo found me, I was not in a good place. I made whatever money I could in underground boxing rings. He spotted me at a fight and offered me tons of money to get rid of whoever caused him problems. At the time it just seemed like easy money to me."

My heart accelerates as I start to imagine scenarios in my head.

"You want the truth? I'm not proud of what I did. I beat people for a living. Some of them to an inch of their lives. Left them for dead. Don't ask me if I killed anyone because I don't know. To this day I still hope I haven't."

I can't help but pull my hands away from his. He looks hurt and it breaks my heart, but I need a moment to swallow the news.

"'Me... I'm sorry, please."

He leans towards me, but I get off the stool and take a few steps back.

"Please don't look at me like this. I was young and out of options. I regret every single job I took, and I left as soon as I could. I had to deal with the Wolves more than once, this is how I know them, how I knew you were in danger tonight. There would have been no point calling the police because half of the force here is on their payroll."

"You're lying to me," I reply.

"What? I'm not! I promise you this is what happened."

"Are you really going to tell me that you don't work for this guy anymore, Nathan? Look at your place, look at your car, look where you take me for dinners! I haven't seen you work once since I met you. Where does all this money come from if not from beating people for a mafioso!"

I spread my arms to show what's around us. He is drowning in money, probably more money than what you get from beating people up. I wouldn't be surprised if he does much more for him now.

"Jamie, you need to listen to me. I do *not* work for him anymore. I promise you on my life."

"Then where does all of this come from?" I hiss at him.

If yesterday someone had told me my first fight with my boyfriend would be because he's part of the mafia, I probably would have laughed in their face. Look at me now.

"Inheritance," he finally says deadpan.

"What?" I ask, incredulous.

"My dad died last year. I wasn't talking to him, but I was still in his will. I received all of this when I turned twenty-one."

My mouth goes slack at the news.

What. The. Fuck.

"I–I'm sorry about your dad."

"I don't care about my dad. I left for a good reason. But I care what you think of me. I care if you're scared of me. This is all behind me. I live a good life on money I never worked for." He shrugs. "It keeps me out of trouble."

"Oh God, I'm dating a trust fund baby."

He lets out a laugh and I relax. Yes, he has a dark past but if it wasn't for him tonight, who knows what could have happened?

"Is that a problem?" he asks as he takes a few steps towards me.

He grabs my waist in his strong arms, swings me around and lifts me on the kitchen counter. I spread my legs automatically and he settles between them before giving me a passionate kiss. Our tongues intertwine and, in a split second, all my problems disappear. My only focus is Nathan. Only Nathan because only he can make me feel this way. This safe.

He pulls away but my core is burning with a need for him. It's never burned so hard. I know my mind is fucked up, I know I've completely lost when I realize that the reason I feel more lust toward him is knowing that he's got a dark side. Like Jake.

"I'm sorry I never told you about this, 'Me. I never thought it would catch up with me so suddenly."

"You're fine," I reply. "I don't think I know anyone in this stupid town that's never had to deal with a gang. You're no special, really," I wink at him.

I see him hesitate before he keeps going. "Your scar. Was it the Wolves? I assumed it was when you said it was a gang, but I never checked."

"Yes, it was Volkov," I reply with anger in my voice. "Not him exactly but one of his men."

"What happened tonight? What did Dimitri say to you?"

I tense at his name and remember his words. "He–I think he came to…" my throat goes dry and the words refuse to come out. He came to finish the job.

"I won't let it happen," he says calmly, knowing what I was going to say. "They won't get close to you."

"I don't get it. It's been so long, why now?"

He shakes his head. "I don't know but nothing will happen to you. I promise."

He kisses me again and this time, there's no extinguishing the fire in me. I take the lead to intensify the kiss and undo his pants. I slip my hand behind the elastic band of his boxers and grab his already erect dick. The sensation makes my insides clench and I breathe in his mouth as I move my hand up and down, up and down.

We still haven't had sex but there's nothing I want more right now than having him inside me. My core is tensing and begging for him to take me. The wetness between my legs is only missing one thing: him.

But to my surprise, he grabs my hand and breaks our kiss.

"Not now, 'Me."

"What?" I squeak. "Why?"

"You've been through a lot tonight. You need to rest. *I* need to rest."

He rests his hands on my legs and I notice his knuckles are bruised and bloody. I look up and I know he can read the guilt in my eyes. In response, he smiles at me and bends down, grabbing my waist and flipping my body on his shoulder easily, fireman style.

"You're going to bed, missy," he says as he heads for the stairs.

"What the hell!"

Chapter 19

He runs a hand up and down my leg and tightens his grip around my thigh, making me clench.

"My little vixen is going to bed. Do I need to repeat myself?"

I giggle and he gives my ass a harsh spank. "Don't get yourself in trouble with me, baby."

I laugh and he throws me on his bed before caging me between his arms and keeping his body above mine.

"I love your laugh, you know that?" he says in the sexiest voice.

I hide my face in my hands. I can't handle a compliment. "Stop," I laugh.

"Never," he says as he spreads kisses everywhere on me. "I'll never stop worshipping you."

20

JAMIE

War of Hearts – Ruelle

By Friday, I'm exhausted and frustrated. After fixing my phone screen, I had to spend money on new textbooks that had been destroyed by Camila or her friends *again*. I had barely enough left for my dress for the ball. That was until the bitches decided to destroy the bike I use to go to school and I spent my last dollars on the repairs. No new dress for me I guess but I can always borrow one of mom's.

Emily doesn't drive me to school anymore because she hops in with Luke and his gang now. I guess it's a good thing because I've been spending all my nights at Nathan's. He's been reluctant to leave me alone and his house is much better than mine. Only it's also much further from school and I refuse to let him drive me there. Add waking up extra early to bike to school to the reasons of my exhaustion. And of course, the ultimate reason…Jake. Or should I say, avoiding Jake.

He tried to pick me up and drive me to school but quickly realized I wasn't staying at my house. He texted me

Chapter 20

countless times to ask me where I was staying, but I'm not giving it up. I'm not telling him about the one last thing that makes me happy in this godforsaken town.

I've been running out of classes in the evening to reach my bike and leave before he can ask me to get in his car. I've been hiding in the library to take my lunches and literally sprinting every time he calls my name. I've been asking questions and participating so much in English that the teacher's eyes are constantly on me, and as long as Mr. Ashton is watching, Jake can't do anything.

I don't know how long I thought I could keep this up but by Friday morning, Jake catches up with me.

I enter English reading a text from Cole.

> Cole: Sorry Jamie but I can't go to the ball with you. Hate to do this to you but I don't think I'll be going.

I frown as I read, head down on my phone. I walk blindly to my chair, anger boiling in me. As if the jock he is isn't going to go to the ball. He changed his mind on going with me and is feeding me a bullshit excuse.

I sit down still looking at my phone as I'm typing up a reply. As soon as my ass hits the chair, I sense something is wrong.

I look at the time on my phone and realize I'm ten minutes early. I look up and see no one else in the class. No one except Jake, sitting right next to me. My heart skips a beat and I jump up to run out of the class but he's too quick. He grabs me by the back of my neck and forces me to sit back down.

"Not so fast, Angel. You're not going to skip English again, are you?"

"Let go, Jake," I growl.

"Mm, she barks," he says in a sultry voice as he runs his tongue over his lower lip.

"What do you want?"

"You think you can avoid me all week and I'm just going to let it pass? I stopped by your house every morning; you weren't there. Where do you stay? Cause it ain't at Emily's since Luke has taken this spot."

"That's none of your business."

He chuckles sarcastically at me. "When did you grow a backbone, Goody? Are you just dying to be punished?"

I twist and turn but his grip is too hard. "Let go of me."

"I ran after you all week and you think I'm going to let go so easily? It's time to catch up. You know, just you and me."

I turn my face to him, and I can see his eyes are full of malice. He just loves this game of cat and mouse. Of course he does, he invented it.

"Please, Jake, I'm so tired of this."

"Are you?" He straightens in his chair making me straighten as well. "Does that mean you're giving in?"

"No!" I exclaim. He's pushing me to the edge, and I want to slap his smug smile off his face.

He's about to bite back when his eyes suddenly drop to my neck and his expression changes. Is that concern in his eyes?

"What happened?" he asks.

"Nothing that concerns you."

"Everything about you concerns me. Tell me what happened."

"I don't owe you any explanation. Drop it."

He looks conflicted as he frowns at me. He lets go of my neck and I understand it's because people are starting to come in.

I straighten in my chair and look at the door. Emily

comes in, holding hands with Luke and she waves at me with a big smile. I wave back but my eyes fall on Cole coming in after her. I can barely refrain a gasp when I see his face.

He sports two dark purple circles below his eyes as if he walked straight into a wall. Cottons are stuffed in his nose and I wonder if he got this during lacrosse.

Jake puts his hand on the small of my back and comes a little closer to me.

"Fine, don't tell me now if you don't want to. We'll have more time tonight."

"What?"

Mr. Ashton comes into the room and starts his class straight away. Jake takes a few minutes to reply.

"Tonight. You're coming to the ball with me."

"What? No, I'm not."

He doesn't reply and he slides his hand beneath my top instead.

"What are you doing?" I whisper at him.

"Convincing you to be my date, why? Would you prefer if I waited in the cafeteria with a sign that says, 'be my date to the Halloween ball'? It'll be my birthday at midnight, and I want to spend it with you."

"This is not funny," I hiss through gritted teeth.

"It really isn't, I'd suggest you stop this asap."

"*You* stop this asap."

"I will. As soon as you accept going to the ball with me."

I completely forgot it was the twins' birthday tomorrow. How could I? The after party at Luke's is probably the biggest event of the year. I freeze when his hand goes up, now grabbing at my bra.

"Stop. Please stop," I plead looking around to check if anyone can see.

"Will you be my date?"

"I'm going with Cole," I lie. He doesn't have to know I'm not going with him anymore.

"Aah, see I don't think you are. Especially since I nicely asked him not to take you."

My heart drops in my stomach at his statement. "Did you do this to him?" I say, glancing to the side of the room where Cole is sitting.

"I have my ways of getting what I want," he says as he hooks his fingers under the band of my bra.

"Don't–"

"Please be my date, Angel. Nothing would make me happier."

His voice is a soft whisper right now but his fingers about to undo my bra contradict it.

"If I accept, it's only to go to the ball. Nothing else."

"Of course. I know that. So, is that a yes?"

I feel his thumb about to snap the hook open. What he doesn't understand is I'm dying to say yes either way. His way of doing it only slightly helps with the guilt toward Nathan. This whole game, it went from hating him to…I can't put a name on it. I just know that, at this point, it's easier to pretend he doesn't leave me a choice than to admit I want to give into him.

I'm just that kind of horrible person.

"Yes. Fine," I comply.

He retreats his hand and a shiver runs down my spine at the withdrawal because my body is already missing its favorite drug.

"You won't regret it. Wear a white dress," he says before focusing back on his notes.

When I get home, my mood has lightened up. I might be

forced to go to the ball with Jake, but Emily spent the afternoon with me, and it felt just like before.

It brought me so much joy to catch up with her about Nathan and her about Luke that I'm pumped for the ball again. I told her everything that happened with Nathan for the past two months and she was so happy for me. It reminded me that while she's part of the cool kids, while she hangs out with the mean cheerleaders and does debutante balls, while she is truly part of Stoneview finest since childhood, her heart is made of gold.

Although she is my best friend, I couldn't get myself to tell her what happened with Jake. The embarrassment of it all is too much that I can't get myself to tell *anyone* about it. And I know he did it on purpose, he made it so bad that I wouldn't even dare ask anyone for help.

As I'm pushing my key in my front door, I see a package in front of my door. It's a big, black, velvet box with a golden ribbon and I recognize the package straight away.

It comes from His&Hers, the most expensive shop in Stoneview and that's not to be taken lightly. Stoneview might be a small town but the most luxurious brands have made sure to have a shop here. When you know the average salary of people living here, it's not surprising. His&Hers is exclusive to the top of the top. It's the kind of shop that offers champagne and strawberries, takes your black Amex on arrival, and doesn't even look at you if you can't provide one.

I pick up the package and enter the house already knowing who sent it.

I open the package as soon as I've put my other stuff down and read the card inside.

Enjoy the ball, Beautiful.
N.

I take the dress out and it unfolds as I hold it up, my eyes widening at the beauty in front of me. It's a long silk white gown and, as I lean closer, I notice it is threaded with thin gold filaments. It's a backless dress with long sleeves.

I look back in the box and of course, there are matching gold heels to wear with the gown. He thought of everything.

My stomach fills up with butterflies and I hurry to my phone to text thank you. As I send it, my phone lights up with Emily's name.

"Are you already finished?" I ask as I pick up.

"Yup, leaving Luke's now. Can I pick you up?"

"Sure, I'll take a shower at yours."

Emily refused to pre-game with Luke so she could get ready with me and everything just seems to go so well that I'm actually looking forward to this ball.

After three hours of getting ready, Emily and I are looking at each other in her bedroom mirror. She's wearing a tight light pink gown that hugs her full breasts and bum tightly and when I stare back at my B-cup, I let a sigh out.

"Trust me, I'd give anything for mine to be smaller," she says.

"Give me a bit?"

She laughs and we go back to observing ourselves. Emily's hairdresser put my long chocolate hair in a high

Chapter 20

ponytail wrapped with a golden bow, so the back of my dress is visible, or lack thereof. Two wavy strands frame my face and the gold make up makes my green eyes pop.

I feel...beautiful. I feel like Nathan knows me by heart. The dress fits perfectly, the length is not too long with the heels on and I know he had to have it tailored because of my height. Most of all, he chose a high neckline and long sleeves, knowing perfectly I wouldn't be comfortable wearing anything that shows my scar. And that means the world to me.

Emily walks behind me, and she takes a few selfies of both of us.

"Your label is out, baby girl," she says as she grabs it on the small of my back. "His and Hers," she squeaks. "How did you get that?!"

I chuckle at her shock.

"Do you know how long I've been begging my mom to get me a dress from this shop," she adds.

"Nathan got it for me."

Her mouth falls open. "Are you joking? Okay, I'm officially super jealous of this boyfriend of yours. Not only is he a hottie but he also gets you luxury dresses that fit you perfectly."

"You don't know he's a hottie. You've never seen him."

"Please," she scoffs, "I'm the social media queen. Come on. That body...the bun, the *eyes*. Phew!" She takes her phone out and brings up Nathan's Instagram page. "By the way, this is cute a.f."

She scrolls through and stops at a picture of him and me lying down on his sofa. I'm lying face down on him, looking at the camera while he's looking down at me and, boy, the way he's looking at me. We haven't talked about love at all, but his eyes...there's no mistaking it when you see it.

He's topless in the picture, with his tattoos on display, his ripped abs tensed under my body. I look so tiny this close to him that I can't help a chuckle. My eyes go down to the caption, 'Bellissima'.

"Do you follow him already?"

"I do, but he was a hard one to find. Private Insta, no profile picture. It took me all afternoon, but you know nothing escapes my stalking skills."

I can't help a laugh, it's just perfectly true.

"Can you screenshot this and send it to me please?" I ask.

"Yes, miss no social media."

I roll my eyes at her. I went off social media after Aaron's death. I couldn't stand strangers asking me about it, sending me unwelcomed messages. I never went back.

The bell to Emily's mansion rings around the house and she looks at me excited.

"Ready?" she asks.

"Uh-huh."

"Hey, 'Me, I just want to say sorry again for pushing you toward Jake. I really had no idea about Nathan."

"It's fine," I wave a hand in the air because whether she tried to set us up or not, Jake doesn't care. He just does what he wants.

"Are you sure you're okay to go with him to the ball?"

"Sure. It's just as friends," I shrug.

I'm really not that okay but what choice do I have at this point? I didn't even tell Nathan my date changed. I didn't think he cared. He trusts me, now all I need is to trust myself around Jake, and tonight is the ultimate test.

As we open the front door we're greeted by Jake and Luke in tuxedos. I barely refrain a gasp at the look of Jake in a tux. He opted for a dark blue, the color of a summer night sky that fits perfectly with his eyes. His black jet hair is slicked back back instead of his usual just-out-of-bed messy style and the gorgeous smile that spreads on his lips when he looks me up and down makes my heart melt instantly and with it my panties. He locks his gaze with mine and takes half a step forward, offering me his hand.

I don't move for what feels like ages. I'm frozen in place by his beauty.

"Stop drooling and let's go, Angel."

I shake my head and take his hand. My heart is hammering in my chest as he softly intertwines his fingers with mine.

"You're wearing white," he says to me in his low voice.

I did. Nathan chose a white dress and I only remember now that Jake had asked me to wear white.

"Right," I say. I have to keep my sentences short because my breath turns shallow when he stands too close to me.

He lets go of my hand to help me into the limo.

It's Halloween ball but it really doesn't feel like it. Every ball in Stoneview is a good occasion for everyone to show their wealth with gorgeous gowns and extravagant cars. I'm usually not part of it but tonight is different. Tonight, I'm with Jake White and that changes *everything.*

When we're all settled in, Luke opens a bottle of champagne while Emily grabs the flute glasses.

Jake moves closer and grabs my waist to bring me against him.

"Jake," I whisper angrily. The others are too focused on their conversation to follow ours. "I thought I made myself clear when I said we were going as friends."

"I can't believe you wore a white dress. I like it when you listen to me, Angel."

He tightens his grip and his breath is in my ear the next instant. "But I think I like it better when you fight me."

A shiver runs down my spine and I look around to avoid looking at him.

Chris is the furthest away from everyone, trying to call someone. In fact, he's been trying since we were outside the car. Then it hits me that Rose isn't here.

As if reading my thoughts Emily addresses herself to the boys. "Where's Rose?"

A silence falls on the car and all that can be heard is Chris muttering 'fuck' every few seconds as he massages the back of his neck.

"Hmph," Jake groans as he readjusts himself on his seat, pulling away from me. "Busy."

"Is she not coming to the ball," Emily insists, incapable of reading the room.

Luke whispers something in Emily's ear and she nods before straightening. "Champagne anyone?"

Everyone nods, including me. I most definitely will need it tonight.

21

JAKE

Barcelona – Brother Leo

October, Halloween Ball Night ...

I can't believe how *normal* my night with Jamie is. When we're not pushing and pulling at each other we can really get along. She's so much fun and I can't get enough of her laugh.

I'm pouring her another glass of punch then take it out of her hand before spilling it on the table. She promised me a dance after a drink, but I don't think I can wait.

"Oops," I say in my most innocent voice.

"Jake," she giggles, and I want to grab her face and kiss her.

I'm about to tease her some more but for the fifth time of the night, Chris pulls me out of the ballroom in a whispered 'sorry' to Jamie. We walk to the gardens in silence and once we reach a quiet space with no one around to eavesdrop he lets himself fall onto a stone bench.

"Nothing?" I ask.

"Nothing." He runs his hand behind his neck, like every time he's anxious.

"She'll resurface," I say, perfectly knowing Ozy is starting to ruin everyone's night.

"What if something happened to her?"

"Nothing happened to her. She's just an annoying little shit."

Chris sighs and looks around but doesn't say anything.

"Look. You'll have all the time you want tomorrow to ask her where she was and teach her a lesson about disappearing, which she'll ignore and disappear again. That's just how she is, Chris. The ball is tonight only and she's not showing up. It doesn't mean you shouldn't enjoy yourself. Man, it's our last Halloween ball at Stoneview Prep. Can you imagine? Please stop worrying, she'll come back by midnight. We always blow our candles out together."

I have my ideas of where Ozy is, but now is not the time to share. If I admit to Chris that she's probably with Sam, he'll want to go get her and I don't want him to get in trouble. Especially because my sister is not smart enough to keep herself out of it.

He nods but I know he's not convinced.

"Where is your date?" I ask.

"I don't have a date, you know that."

"You told me you were done with our little sexcapades because you met someone, and I don't see no one around you."

He chuckles and gets back up. "No, she's my secret. None of you get to see her."

I gasp dramatically. "You sneaky boy. Does she go here?"

He shakes his head, denying me any answer, and laughs as he heads back in.

Chapter 21

Rose is fine.

I try to convince myself that I'm allowed to enjoy my night without worrying about her. It's easier said than done. As Chris heads back inside, I grab my phone out of my inside jacket pocket and shoot her a text.

> Jake: My sweet little Ozy. If you don't tell us where you are within the hour I'm going to chase your ass around town and you don't want to know what will happen when I find you.

It only takes her about a minute to reply and I can't help but shake my head. She only reacts when she's pushed. It annoys me how similar we are.

> Ozy: I'm fine.

She accompanies her lovely text with a middle finger emoji, and I can't help but chuckle. What a bitch.

> Jake: Fine where?

> Ozy: Mind your own business. creep.

I roll my eyes and put my phone back in my pocket. Good enough, I guess. Her mysterious behavior only confirms that she's with Sam.

She doesn't get how much it breaks my heart when she stays with him. After everything he's put her through, she still runs after him like he's the ruler of her kingdom and the motherfucker thrives on it.

I try to not think about it too much and when I walk back into the ballroom my eyes find exactly what will keep my thoughts entertained.

Jamie, in her gorgeous white dress that makes her look like an angel. And it is what she is, an angel that has fallen straight from the sky. She's beautiful like one, innocent, bright and everywhere she goes the room lights up.

And what am I? The devil ready to destroy every shred of her innocence. I can't help myself; Jamie brings out the best *and* the worst in me and I'm addicted to it. I need her, her presence, her lavender perfume, her smooth skin. I want all of her to myself, to the point that I got in a fight with fucking Cole. That guy doesn't deserve a second of her attention. She's too good for him. She's too good for anyone, even me. *Especially* me. Except I don't care because I'm selfish like that.

She's dancing with Emily and the way her hips move to the rhythm makes me want to grab them and keep her tight against me. I know she's tipsy on her one glass of champagne because she's a lightweight but it's a good thing.

Jamie is part of these people that think too much before they act. And fuck does she think a lot. She doesn't realize it stops her from enjoying the smallest things in life. She doesn't like letting go, she doesn't like pleasure because she feels like she doesn't deserve it.

She likes being in control of her fun and her pleasure to make sure that she doesn't enjoy too much of it and I'm having the time of my life pushing her past that. The best part is when her mind fights it, but her body gives up. The struggle in her eyes when she's close to giving in completely and lets me take control is priceless and I can't get enough of it.

My balls tighten and my cock throbs just remembering my fingers in her dripping pussy. *Fuck,* I need her.

I take long strides toward her and put a hand on the

back of her neck. I love my hand there. She jumps in surprise.

"Come with me," I whisper in her ear. I can feel the shiver running down her neck below my touch and my body responds to hers in the same way.

She resists a second when I pull but quickly gives in. She always does. I pull her with me through the hallways and into the cafeteria where I know we'll be alone. My body is burning to touch her and the bulge in my suit pants probably shows that.

As soon as the door closes, I push her against the wall and grab her dress. The silk is just as smooth as her skin and I want my hands on her right this second.

"Jake," she hisses.

I know she's annoyed, but I can't stop myself anymore. The way my name rolls off her full lips is making me rock hard. She knows I won't push her if she puts hard limits, but she doesn't and that's what's driving me mad.

When her skirt is at her hips, I hook my thumbs under her underwear and pull them down. I grab her ankles one by one to get her out of them and pick them up, putting them in my pocket. I don't do shit with them but knowing she's naked under her dress or school skirts gives me life.

"Don't..." she sighs in pleasure.

I go on my knees and hook a leg on my shoulder. The need to taste her is overwhelming and I know I won't be able to stop myself if she doesn't stop me.

Her head hits the wall behind her when I grip her thigh tightly. Her pussy is glistening, and my heart accelerates with pride at the effect I have on her.

"Wait. Jake. Stop."

She puts a trembling hand on my shoulder and her

voice brings me back down. Shit, she's for real this time. I let go of her leg and straighten back up, towering over her.

"What is it, Goody? You never had your pussy licked before? That won't be news to my ears. Happy to introduce you to it."

Her eyes turn dark and she clenches her fists at her side. "I told you we were coming here as friends. I only accepted because you didn't leave me a choice and you chased Cole away. I've been kind enough, but this is crossing the line, Jake."

"What are you on about now? You're fucking dripping," I growl. "Stop pushing me away, Jamie. You know you want this just as much as I do."

Her little act is starting to get me seriously worked up and I can feel the monster in me crawling out of the darkness. If she keeps going, she's going to be on the front line when it comes out.

"I can't do this anymore," she says in a trembling voice.

She's probably trying to sound strong. She sounds desperate and it's making me want to take her right here, right now even more.

I crowd her against the wall, slowly losing sight of right and wrong as she brings out the beast. Even with heels on she has to crane her neck to keep looking into my eyes. Her breath on my lips tastes like peach punch and temptation.

"I'm not asking you to do anything but be good and spread your legs," I whisper above her lips.

She sucks in a breath and I know she's struggling between being good and evil and I want her on the dark side so...so bad.

She shifts to the side, but I grab her small hip with my right hand, keeping her in place. I know I'm holding her too tight, I know she's hurting by the way she just took an inward breath but I'm silently hoping to leave a mark on her skin, to bruise her just so she knows who fucking owns her.

I grab her chin with my other hand, and I feel her teeth rattling at the force.

"Y–you're hurting me," she says in a small voice.

"Am I now? Guess you shouldn't have tried to get away."

"Please, Jake. Just let me go," she pleads.

I would but what she doesn't understand is every whimper, every begging word, and every plead makes me want to hold her even tighter just to hear her beg some more. *This* is how fucked up I am.

A lot of girls have been fine with it until now, especially Camila. They loved the dominant side of me, they loved being told what to do and they loved the pleasure I gave them in exchange. But Jamie...something is still holding her back and it's driving me to the edge of insanity. What is it?

"Look at me in the eyes and tell me you don't want this. Tell me you don't want me."

She squeezes her eyes shut and struggles to swallow but I don't let go. If it's true, I want to hear her say it.

"Go on, Angel. Say it to me."

When she opens her eyes, she has a determined look in them. "Jake I–"

I don't know if it's because I'm scared of what she's going to say or because I'm an impatient bastard, but I don't let her finish. I just capture her lips with mine. I need to show her who's in charge, who controls her, who decides what happens between us.

Control. Control. Control.

Jamie brings out the worst in me. She doesn't bend to my will. She listens one minute and rebels the next. She doesn't give in and I want to take everything she doesn't want to give. Starting with this kiss. I push my tongue through her lips, forcing her to part them.

This is wrong, so wrong but I can't stop it. She reminds me of all the times I wasn't in control. All the times someone took things from me out of my own free will. Every time I suffered from being the puppet for others.

She pushes flashbacks of my fucked up childhood through my head and in exchange I feel the need to control her and prove myself that I'm not the same weak kid I used to be because, with the way she controls my heart, she's the only one that can still make me doubt that.

In one last masochist thought, I remember when she shared a kiss with Chris. I'm almost certain it was her first kiss, and I hated my best friend for taking that moment away from me. So much that I pushed him to be there when I made her come for the first time. I had to show both of them that she belonged to me.

The memory makes me tighten my grip on her, roughen my kiss. She whimpers under me but, as I expected, she finally lets go and her tongue intertwines with mine. She responds so well to my kiss it's like she was made for this only. Made to kiss me and no one else.

In a split-second everything changes, she pushes at my chest, hits my shoulder, tries to turn her head, and obviously rejects the moment. I take a step back, letting go of both her hip and jaw, and before I can understand what's happening, I feel the sting of her palm against my cheek.

The sound resonates through the cafeteria and my mouth falls open.

"You're not *listening* to me," she hisses. "I can't do this anymore, Jake. I can't be your little puppy that you call when you want to play. I'm human, I have feelings and none of them include wanting to be your toy!"

Chapter 21

I see red. I know she's talking, I know she's addressing herself to me and explaining herself but my ears are ringing with rage.

I've been hit and my brain is on high alert. I'm taken back to all the other times a hand or a fist landed on my face or my body and I. See. Red. I've been hit when I had sworn to myself that it would never happen again. I've been hit and there's only one way my beast replies to violence.

She's still talking but I can't hear her. I grab her by the throat and push her against the wall. Her head hits the wall hard and she cries out something I can't hear. She goes to hit me again, but I grab her wrist, then the other one, and lock them above her head. I know I'm holding too hard when she whimpers and twists under me.

"Stop! You're insane, stop!" she shrieks.

But I can't, because I got hit and I don't control my body anymore. She's such a fucking tiny thing, I could break her right here, right now. I could hurt her so badly she would never recover.

I bend down and graze my teeth against her jaw then go down to her neck and bite hard. She screams and it rings in my ears, electrifying my whole body with pleasure.

"Please, Jake stop," her voice falters and I look up as tears start to fall down her cheeks.

"Cry harder," I growl. "It turns me on."

Her eyes widen in fear and she wriggles harder under my hold.

"Why are you reacting like this? I'm honest with you, isn't that what you wanted? You wanted to know why I wasn't giving into you. Now you know!"

I frown at her in confusion. "What?"

"I told you the truth. I thought that's what you wanted."

"What did you say? What was the truth?"

I'm so confused. She must have said something a minute ago, but I didn't hear, I was too blinded by rage. Now she's got my attention again. "Tell me again," I order.

"I'm seeing someone, Jake. I can't do this to him, and I can't do this to you. I'm in love with him."

My cold heart drops so hard in my stomach I feel sick. That's impossible.

"That's a lie."

"It's not a lie," she says as she squirms. I know her wrists are hurting but I can't let go.

"I warned every fucker in this school that they would have to deal with me if they touched you or so much as think of dating you, Angel. So, you're lying. The question is why?"

"I'm not lying. He doesn't go to Stoneview Prep. Please let go." She pulls at her wrists, but it only makes me tighten my hold.

"You're lying."

I can't find anything else to say because it *has* to be a lie. Jamie belongs to me. She's mine.

"I'm not lying," she whimpers. "Why would I? Please... you're hurting me."

"Jake!" Camila's voice drives me out of my fury, and I look behind my shoulder.

She and Beth are standing by the kitchen. Beth is holding a huge bowl of pink punch. Of course they're here, they both offered to help tonight, pretending they wanted extra credit when everyone but Jason knows it's because Beth is fucking the calculus teacher and this works as a date for them.

Cam walks toward me when Beth stays frozen in place. The sounds of her heels on the floor and the golden Cartier bracelets she wears hitting against the other is slowly taking me out of my trance.

When she reaches me, she puts a hand on my shoulder, and I realize I'm panting with anger and hate.

"Let her go," she says in a stern voice.

It wouldn't be the first time she sees me in this kind of state. Two years. She's seen me in all kinds of states and she's not scared. If anything, I know it turns her on. The smell of Camila's strong feminine perfume grounds me. It's the opposite of Jamie's. It's dominating and imposing. Jamie's is soft and bewitching.

"Let her go, Jake," she repeats. So I slowly release Jamie's wrists.

From the corner of my eyes, I can see her rubbing them together, but I try to focus on Camila. Her golden eyes, her black thick hair, her gorgeous Latina skin. She's glowing in her pink dress and she's tall enough to almost reach my height with heels on.

"Let's go," she takes my hand, "she's not worth it. You know that."

I let Camila drag me away, my breath still too fast for me to reply. I let my feet follow her, enchanted by her beauty and her smell. I don't give Jamie a last look, I don't even turn back when I hear a splash and a loud gasp. I simply don't care. She can go back to fucking her real boyfriend for all I care. Let them have their happy ending.

I know I'm lying to myself because the hate I currently feel for Jamie for seeing someone else is burning like a wildfire in me. I have no right and I'm aware of that. I still wish I could find the bastard and make him pay for stealing what is mine.

When we reach the ballroom, I feel like I can breathe again. It's like I'm finally far enough to break the spell Jamie has on me. Camila rubs my arm lovingly and I turn to face her.

"Thank you," I say.

"Jake. You can't do this. Not here, not to her."

I run a hand through my hair that is back to being a fucking mess. "I know," I reply in a sigh.

"Not everyone is into your shit and not everyone can handle you. You need to understand that."

She looks at me with real concern and I know she cares for me. I know she always will. I also know I'll never love her the way she loves me. She loves me too much, she has deep feelings for me and me...well I have deep feelings for Jamie. They're unexplainable but they're here, making my heart hammer in my chest whenever she's too close.

I see Beth reappear in the ballroom, it seems she's left the bowl behind. A few seconds later, Jamie bursts into the room crying, her hair a wet sticky mess. No one notices her with the music and the lights low. No one ever notices Jamie.

I see her. I see her white dress soaked with pink punch, making it see-through and showing her hard nipples under it.

"Cam..." I turn back to her as Beth joins us. "Why?" I ask. "Why do you girls have to be like this."

"Because she's a little slut, Jake," Beth replies in her place and I want to drive my fist through the bitch.

Camila looks at me with a lopsided smile. "Because that's just how the game works, baby."

I don't understand how she can go from saving the girl from me to hating her. I don't get her. I never will. We're not from the same world.

I turn back to Jamie as she's about to exit the room. She slips and almost falls because of her heels, so she takes them off, going back to the small thing she is. Seeing her like this, a crying, sticky mess, holding her shoes and her dress so she doesn't step on it, I can't help it. I know I'm going to regret it, but I do it anyway.

I run after her.

When I reach the hallway leading to the way out, she's almost at the main entrance. I can see she's on the phone.

"Are you here?" she says in a small voice to the person on the other end of the line. "Okay, I'm coming out now." She sniffles as she hangs up.

"Jamie! Wait!"

She turns around and sees me running toward her. I'm struck by the look on her face. She's fucking terrified of me.

"Jamie, please, let me explain. I'm sorry."

She shakes her head no at me and gets out, but I don't stop. I follow her toward the parking lot because I know once she leaves, it'll be it. If I don't get to apologize for what I've just done it's the end of us and I'm not ready for that. Whatever 'us' is.

I need to tell her that I'm more fucked up than she could have imagined. That I had promised myself I would never let anyone hit me again in my life. That I was lost in the flashbacks of the 12-year-old me being beaten up. That the control she has over me scares me more than anything else. That I can't control my heart or my brain when she's around. I need to tell her everything I feel for her.

A flash of hope crosses my mind and I smile as I run after her.

I catch her wrist as she jogs across the parking lot. Rain is pouring but I don't care, I need to talk to the girl I love. She's crying when she turns around to face me.

"I'm sorry, Jamie," I pant. "I'm the biggest idiot on this planet."

"You hurt me, Jake. You scared me. This is more than a game, this is disturbing."

"I went too far. I lose control around you. The truth is, I'm scared of losing control because I never had any growing up. I was abused by a man that still haunts my dreams. I'm still healing. I'm still struggling but when I'm with you, everything is better. Please, Jamie. I...I fell in love with you. I don't know when it happened, I don't know how. I just know I did. And if there is even a small chance of you possibly loving me back. Please, please give in to that chance."

The smile that spreads across her lips lights up the night sky. It clears the clouds, and it brightens my heart.

"Give in?" she asks.

"Give in," I repeat, my voice barely a small plea.

The short nod of her head makes my heart explode with joy. It feels good. It's like I've never felt happiness before and she's finally offering it to me on a silver platter.

I sprint as my heart gallops in my chest. I finally reach the parking lot. I'm ready to catch her. I'm ready to turn my life around. I'm ready to –

I'm too late.

I stop dead in my tracks.

No. No. No. No. Please no.

Under the torrential rain, I see a man getting out of a black Porsche Cayenne, walking around and opening the door for her. The headlights are blinding me, but I still see her small form sliding into the car. She's not even looking my way. So that's it? That's the guy she's choosing over me? And she thinks I'm just going to accept it?

Chapter 21

I hurry toward the car as her *boyfriend* makes his way back to the other side. I can't see shit, but I don't care, I'm not giving up.

"Hey!" I bark at him.

He stops just as his hand is reaching the door and turns my way, slowly walking to me. The beast inside me roars back to life. I need to let the anger out and this guy is the perfect outlet. I put a hand in front of my eyes to try and shield my vision from the headlights and take a step toward him. His face finally comes into view and it takes me a second to understand.

My heart skips a beat before violently attempting to get out of my chest. It pounds against my ribcage, trying to destroy it on its way out. My blood freezes, my head spins.

"N-Nate?" I choke.

That's impossible. How much did I fucking drink?

"Jake," he smiles. That wicked smile only the devil himself has perfected. "How have you been, brother?"

To be continued...

GIVING AWAY

Read what happens to Jamie and Jake in *Giving Away* - out now!

He will never let her go. Not even if she chooses someone else.

Jamie

One can only escape their fate for so long.

That night at the ball, I had to make a decision. And I chose Nathan. I chose safety and love, kindness and protection. I just didn't know it would be the biggest mistake of my life.

I've been lied to, used, and deceived. I'm surrounded by monsters, but the monster I was desperate to escape is also the one I desire the most.

The problem is, can I handle his demons?

ALSO BY LOLA KING

All books unfold in the same world at different times.

This is the recommended reading order.

STONVEVIEW STORIES

Stoneview Trilogy (MF Bully):

Giving In

Giving Away

Giving Up

Rose's Duet (FFMM why-choose):

Queen Of Broken Hearts (Prequel novella)

King of My Heart

Ace of All Hearts

AFTERWORD

If you made it to the end, thank you, thank you, thank you! Thank you for taking a chance with me and entering a world I have spent days and nights creating. I truly hope you enjoyed reading this as much as I enjoyed writing it. If you have enjoyed the book, it would mean the world to me if you could leave a review, even a few words are everything to an author.

ACKNOWLEDGEMENT

I have no idea how I can ever repay all the people who have helped me make this dream come true. I'll start with saying thank you. You all obviously deserve much more than a simple 'thank you'.

Thank you to my Maman for showing me that I could put that crazy, untameable imagination on paper, make sense of it and even enjoy myself in the process. You are and will always be the (super)heroine of my story.

Thank you to my little sister, Estelle, the first person to ever hear about Stoneview and all its characters.

Thank you to my partner J. who was the first person to read this book and encourage me to go further! Thank you for loving me despite our limited QT when I write and for making sure I don't worry my little noggin too much. I love you, you are my King ♥

Thank you to Lauren, my alpha/editor/everything for this new amazing friendship, for your honesty, superhuman attention to detail and for showing me when I can do better!

Thank you to my beta readers: Gabby for giving me the courage to actually start the publishing process and for supporting me all the way. Laura for pushing me, answering all my annoying questions and introducing me to pretty much everything and everyone. And of course, Brittany, your kind words and support are the light on my dark days.

Thank you to my family Papa, Jojo, Raphou, Roro, Soso, Tito, Tita, Ate Cham, Kuya Oly…for listening to me babbling about my book without knowing the details, and accepting that I will never tell you the title…

And last but not least, thank you to every person who ever opens this book. Thank you for reading it, thank you for the time spent on this nugget of my imagination. I hope we become friends, I hope we'll go a long way together.

Let's stay in touch please! I want to talk to all of you!
    Instagram: @lolaking_author
    Facebook Readers group: Lola's Kings

Lots of Love,

Lola ♥

ABOUT THE AUTHOR

Lola King is a dark, steamy romance author who loves giving 'happy ever after's to antiheros. She writes flawed, and deeply broken characters, and focuses some of her stories around queer love. Her books are sometimes cute, sometimes angsty, but always sexy! Lola lives in London and if she isn't writing, she is most likely keeping her mind busy putting together a play or making music.

Let's keep in touch on IG @lolaking_author or on FB readers' group *Lola's Kings* !

Made in the USA
Monee, IL
02 May 2025